The Fathers and The Sons

Daniel McCoy

Racing House

ISBN 978-1-84-327924-2

The Racing House Press
20 Cambridge Drive
London SE12 8AJ, UK
www.racinghouse.co.uk

Cover illustration Caroline Mayow

Thanks to RJ and EV for help and suggestions.
It's always surprising what can come
from a few good lunches

Father Muldoon

The missile arced unerringly downrange to its target. The dull thud of hardwood on bone was followed by a sharp clatter as the blackboard duster skittered off the wall and fell to the floor. The priest leaned back and allowed himself a moment of quiet satisfaction. The old arm was as good as ever. No worries there.

"Stand up, that boy!"

The boy rose unsteadily to his feet, rubbing his head gingerly, feeling the beginnings of a bump. He stood transfixed in the glare of the priest, as a morbid silence fell upon the rest of the classroom.

"Bring your work out here."

The boy walked forward, head bowed, and placed his exercise book on the priest's desk. The priest looked down on a page blank except for the words *Labienus aedificat domus.*

"What is your name, boy?"

"Clancy, Father."

The priest adjusted his glasses and glowered down.

"Not only are you an idle boy, Clancy, you are a stupid boy as well."

Clancy stared dolefully at the page, knowing that somewhere in those three words was a horrible mistake and knowing too that he was fated to study a language that he would never understand.

"*Domus*, Clancy, *domus*. What is *domus*?"

"A house, Father."

The priest gave him a sharp clip on the ear.

"I know what it means, boy. Is it the subject of the sentence?"

Clancy hesitated. He was unsure, but the fact that the priest was asking him meant that it probably wasn't.

"No, Father."

"No, Father, he says. So what is it?"

There was only one other thing it could be.

"The object, Father."

"If it is the object Clancy, what case should it take?"

Clancy stared again at the page, the full horror of the situation beginning to dawn.

"The accusative, Father."

"And in what case have you written it?"

"The nominative, Father."

"And what have I told you?"

"Subject in the nominative, object in the accusative, Father."

"Clearly I have not told you often enough, Clancy. Go and bang your head against that wall ten times while repeating: 'subject in the nominative, object in the accusative'. Maybe that will drum things into that thick skull of yours."

Clancy trudged over to the wall and began reciting the litany, head bouncing off the wooden panelling.

"Louder, Clancy," said the priest. "There are other boys here that need to learn the same lesson."

Particulars of the priest: Above forty; five foot eight inches or thereabouts; portly; ginger-haired; ruddy complexion; wearer of wire-framed or National Health spectacles. *Apparel*: Black suit and shirt, clerical collar. *Status in Holy Orders*: priest, secular.

The rest of the class kept their heads down low to their desks, a few attempting to hide a snigger, the rest thankful that they had not been picked out. The priest looked over the rows of heads to ensure that proper attention was being paid to Latin primers and then picked up the newspaper that he had been reading.

The *Nationalist and Leinster Times* came every week, thanks to the Mammy. The Carlow edition could always be relied upon for proper news, unlike those rags that came out of Fleet Street. He turned to the court reports: "Borris man found guilty." What else would they find someone from that nest of vipers, Borris-in-Ossory? He read on:

> Joseph O'Toole, labourer, 32, of Borris-in-Ossory, Co Laois, was found guilty of malicious damage and using foul and abusive language in Carlow County Court last Tuesday, 15th March. Appearing before Mr Justice Geoghegan, prosecuting counsel Thomas Gorman said that O'Toole had met with several others, not presently before the court, in O'Rourke's bar, Tullow Street, Carlow. A quantity of strong drink having been taken, they proceeded in a rowdy manner from Tullow Street, in the direction of the Dublin Road where O'Toole was seen by witnesses administering several kicks to the horse of Messrs F Burke & Sons, Funeral Directors, then in attendance on Miss J G Larkin, recently deceased. The party then moved further down the Dublin Road where O'Toole was seen by other witnesses yelling oaths and insults through the letter box of the Convent of Poor Clares, before being arrested by Garda P J Murphy.
>
> Sentencing, Mr Justice Geoghegan said he took a most serious view of O'Toole's actions, particularly of the offence to the Poor Clares, on whose prayers and invocations, the town – and indeed the whole of Ireland – depended. He sentenced O'Toole to six months imprisonment, to be suspended on condition he leave for England immediately.

The priest nodded his satisfaction. That was justice fair and square. No nonsense was what was stood for in any court over which Mr Justice Geoghegan presided. Many a miscreant had rued the day he had come before Mr Justice Geoghegan. The

Geoghegans were as fine a family as you could find in Carlow – pillars of the community. Mr Justice Geoghegan himself was a nephew of the late Very Revd F G Geoghegan, bishop of Clonmore, whose *Meditations on Eternal Damnation* was still read in Ireland, though not, alas, widely enough.

As he was about to read another report, the classroom door swung open and another cleric entered, accompanied by a large dog. Immediately the boys rose to their feet.

Particulars of the cleric: Tall, elderly, slight stoop, but with traces of a military bearing acquired when he accompanied General Allenby into Jerusalem in 1917. *Apparel*: Full-length cassock or *soutane*. *Status in Holy Orders*: Canon of the Archdiocese of Southwark.

Particulars of the dog: Irish or Red Setter; well fed. *Apparel*: sleek coat, well combed; *Status in Holy Orders:* Tonsure, aspirations to the Sub-deaconate.

The Canon smiled genially.

"Please excuse the interruption, Father Muldoon. I don't believe I have had a chance to talk to these new boys yet."

He motioned the boys to sit down and surveyed them for several seconds.

"Now boys, as your headmaster it is my great pleasure to welcome you into our school, named after the blessed martyr, Edmund Campion. You have come here because of the trust placed in us by your parents and because by your own hard work and diligence you have passed the eleven-plus examination and therefore are worthy of a grammar school education. With the benefit of that education you will leave here and go out into the world as teachers, scientists, doctors and members of the professions. But education must not be simply about learning; it must also be about faith. Blessed Edmund Campion gave his life so that you could be educated in the one, true faith.

So you will go out into the world as Catholic teachers, scientists, doctors and members of the professions – and, we hope, a few of you as priests – secure in your faith and in the benefits of a good Catholic education. Isn't that so Father?"

"It is indeed, Canon."

"Tell me, Father, what lesson is this?"

"Latin, Canon."

The Canon nodded.

"Latin is a most important lesson, boys. Not only does it train the mind, but it is the language of the Church. Go anywhere and you will hear mass in Latin. Learn Latin and you will be able to understand anything that is said in mass anywhere in the world. All good Catholics must learn Latin. Isn't that so, Father Muldoon?"

"It is indeed, Canon."

"Now tell me, boys," said the Canon, "how many of you were at mass last Sunday?"

Every hand went up.

"Very good, and how many of you are altar boys?"

Many hands went up.

The Canon smiled.

"I am very pleased to see so many. Serving at mass can be the first step to a vocation. So if I say the words of the priest at the beginning of mass, '*Introibo ad altare dei*', which means 'I will go unto the altar of God', what do you reply?"

They responded in chorus: *"Ad deum qui laetificat iuventutem meum."*

"Very good," said the Canon. "Now who can tell me what that means?"

No hand went up.

"When you learn Latin, you will know that it means 'To God who gives joy to my youth.' You are all young and God gives you joy. Is that not so, Father Muldoon?"

"It is indeed, Canon."

The Canon looked over a sea of faces, all wondering what sort of joy it was that needed to be expressed in Latin.

"I will now leave you to your lesson, boys. Thank you, Father Muldoon."

He moved towards the door. The dog gave a look that was both supercilious and pitying, before following him out of the classroom. The priest turned to the class.

"Back to your exercises, boys. I shall be collecting your books at the end of the lesson. Any boy who has not finished will have to write one hundred lines."

Every head bowed down as they perused their primers. The priest gave a small shake of the head as he contemplated the state of education in England. The English had gone soft. It was the devil's own job to get anything into the heads of these boys, what with all the distractions they had – TV, pop music and the like. Not like in the Ireland of his day. The Christian Brothers had the right idea. The best way to teach was with a book and a strap. It was acknowledged – in Ireland at least – that the backside was the most receptive organ in the body. A lesson learned through the backside was a lesson for life, never forgotten. He knew elders back home who, though almost bereft of sense, could still conjugate perfectly the most incorrigible of irregular Latin verbs and quote verbatim from arcane parts of the catechism, all thanks to the educational practices of the Christian Brothers.

A silence had fallen on the class, the only sounds being the scratching of pens on paper. The priest fished out two letters from his pocket and began reading.

Evidence of PC Z4329 Perkins

On Friday 17th March at 10.45 pm, I was proceeding along Plough Lane, Purley, when I saw a Morris Minor, registration COY 356, being driven in an erratic manner. On stopping the car, I apprehended the driver, a clerical gentleman, who gave

> his name as Father Al O'Wishus Muldoon of Blessed Edmund Campion School, Croydon. His speech was slurred and his breath smelt of alcohol. I informed him that in my opinion he was driving under the influence of alcohol and asked him to accompany me to Croydon Police Station. He objected very strongly and made a number of remarks of a personal nature that I shall not repeat. He agreed only after I said that I would have to handcuff him. On arrival at Croydon Police Station it was found that he could not walk in a straight line or touch his nose with his finger five times in a row.

The priest eyed the summons with disdain. Hadn't the police in England better things to do than persecute a man of the cloth who was only celebrating his patron saint? Weren't there any number of murderers and robbers in England and no one catching them? It was a good job that there was still someone in this country who saw sense. A phone call to Superintendent O'Driscoll and he had been out of that police station in two shakes of a lamb's tail. Another call and that summons would be hopping into the bin. As for that jumped up bluebottle, PC Perkins, he would not be surprised if the very same PC Perkins found himself on point duty for the next six months. That would teach him to arrest respectable members of the clergy.

He turned to the second letter. It was headed "Francis Fahey, Turf Accountant".

> Dear Fr Muldoon,
>
> <u>Your Account</u>
>
> I refer to my letters of the 10th and 24th ult and 6th inst, pointing out the deficit on your account. This has now reached the total of £10 2s 6d. I would be grateful if you could take steps to settle this amount, otherwise we may not be able to take further business placed by your good self.

Yours in sport

F J Fahey M Inst T A

PS. There is still time to join our 'Under Holy Starting Orders Club', whereby one shilling in the pound of winnings on all bets for the forthcoming Derby is sent to the Foreign Missions.

The priest read the letter with a mixture of indignation and incredulity. That Frankie Fahey had a cheek! Didn't he have half the priests in the diocese on his books, and a good number of their parishioners too? Him and his Under Holy Starting Orders Club! Oh Frankie Fahey was making a mint alright. Frankie Fahey was in clover. Didn't he have a boy in Ampleforth and a girl in the convent where the Duke of Suffolk's daughters went? That would be a pretty penny in expense to anyone else, but it would be nothing to Frankie Moneybags Fahey. A shilling in the pound of winnings might be going to the Foreign Missions, but twenty shillings in the pound of all bets lost was going straight into the pocket of Mister Frankie Fahey, thank you very much. And his odds were a disgrace. Many a Protestant bookie would give you much better – and not whinge when you went a few bob into the red. And he had the gall to send the letter during Lent. Didn't Knight of Saint Columba and Catenian, Frankie Fahey, know that he, as a priest, always gave up betting for Lent, except for Cheltenham? A stiff letter reminding Frankie Fahey of his Catholic obligations would be on its way very soon.

A bell interrupted his thoughts. Every head rose in anticipation.

"Now, boys, bring your books out to me. Every boy that has not finished the exercise will write one hundred times, 'Subject in the nominative, object in the accusative' and bring it to me at the next lesson. Is that clear?"

Glum voices answered.

"When you have given me your book you may go for your break. No running in the corridor."

First days

Spectral black figures in a shadowed landscape seemed to haunt Clancy in his first days at Blessed Edmund Campion. Not at all like his primary school, where the nuns and teachers were, for the most part, kindly – all except Sister Mary Magdalene, whose response to infractions, real or imaginary, was a sharp, painful rap across the knuckles with a heavy wooden ruler.

The Campion school buildings were mostly nondescript, late Victorian and Edwardian brick, but, inside and out, there were hidden corners, unexpected rooms, gloomy quadrangles and corridors that seemed to go on longer than they should. From out of any of them a figure in black could emerge who would look down at Clancy as if he had committed some nameless wrong, simply by his very presence.

For months after he started at the school he would dream of black winged figures, like bats, swooping down and carrying him off. Clancy was used to feeling guilty. That was what being a Catholic was all about. Guilt was like a comfort blanket. God was keeping an eye on him and seeing everything he did and making him feel guilty about it. Sometimes he envied the non-Catholic boys with whom he played football in the park, who seemed utterly free from any sense of guilt, and sometimes he pitied them, because they didn't feel guilty, so God was obviously taking no notice of them, so they wouldn't get to Heaven. If he didn't feel guilty about something then he felt guilty about not feeling guilty. And, of course, he revelled in the heady, though fleeting, moment of absolution, when all guilt was expiated by confession. But it had always been guilt about something he had done, like snaffling biscuits at home or not saying his night prayers. When he went to confession he never got more than a couple of Hail Marys and Glory Bes for those things. He could live with that sort of guilt and it never stopped him doing anything he really wanted to do.

This was the first time he had been made to feel guilty without knowing why, though he assumed that he must have been guilty of something. He wondered whether other boys felt the same. Some clearly did. He could see it in their eyes, how they reflexively cringed before the priests. Others, like Worsley, just as clearly didn't.

Worsley had an older brother at the school, in the fourth year, and boasted that his brother had given him what he called the "low down" on the school. He would point out his brother, a greasy-haired, acned youth, during break, though, naturally, the brother disdained to talk to, or even acknowledge, his sibling or any other new boy. Worsley the younger was plump, freckle-faced and affected views way above his years. He had most of the class hanging on his words, as he claimed to know what some girls might do and what cigarettes were best – "Benson & Hedges or Rothmans King Size. I never touch Woodbines."

Worsley was imparting his wisdom to Clancy and two other boys, Hearne and Docherty, who had become Clancy's friends by the unspoken, almost osmotic, process common to all schoolboys. His nonchalant talk of smoking was what impressed them most. None of them were smokers. Clancy had tried it once, after pinching one of his father's Craven As, and nearly choked after the first drag. Worsley claimed to know all about the school and its priests and masters – who to "watch out for" and who could safely be ignored or even ragged. Top of the watch-out-for list was Muldoon. "He goes on the warpath every now and then. If he does, make sure you get out of his way or he'll send you to Flogger sooner than looking at you." Flogger, or Mister Flinders to his face, was another to watch out for. "You don't want to get the strap from him. He lays it on really thick."

One of the first things that struck Clancy about the twenty or more priests at the school was that they came in all shapes, sizes and demeanours. Worsley was always ready to give a running commentary on any priest or master who happened to come into view. On a very tall and thin priest who Clancy thought looked a bit like a stork as he walked. "That's Arundell. Don't go near his cricket pitch." On a young and smartly-dressed priest who always seemed to have a half smile on his face. "That's Mostyn. All the Mums like him." On a short and delicately featured priest, who gestured extravagantly on acknowledging any greeting, "That's Wendell. He's a bit you know what." Clancy didn't know what. And on a plump, bald and rather jolly-looking priest, Worsley said, "That's Brompo. Play your cards right and he might take you to the Brit Mus." Clancy didn't know what those cards might be, or what the Brit Mus was either. He began to realise that he had a lot to learn.

Well briefed he might have been, but Worsley failed to heed his own advice. Hardly two weeks after the beginning of term he was sent for an appointment with Flogger after making faces and gestures behind Father Wendell, in full view of Father Muldoon, who was watching through a nearby window. He reported back next day that Flogger did lay it on "really thick", but it didn't seem to affect his irrepressible nature.

"Do you want to hear a joke?" he asked Clancy after telling him about the strap.

Clancy did.

"Why are turds always tapered at the end?"

Clancy had never given any thought to the geometry of excrement.

"No idea. Why?"

"So your arse doesn't clap shut with a bang."

Clancy laughed and, though he didn't know it, that was the beginning of his adolescence.

Guardian Angels

Father Muldoon held up the little red book before the first-year class.

"Get out your Catechisms, boys."

He watched, with a mixture of annoyance and exasperation, as the boys scrabbled in their desks. Knowing your Catechism was the first step to being a good Catholic. Far too few Catholics in England had much idea of what was in the Catechism. Catechism teaching in English Catholic primary schools these days was a disgrace and he had found out, to his horror, that some of the boys in the class had been to Protestant primary schools. Who knew what ideas might be lurking in their heads?

Now was the time to straighten out their ideas, though not with the English Catechism. He had lost count of the many shortcomings of that milk and water document. The Irish was the one to follow. *A Catechism of Catholic Doctrine, Approved by the Archbishops and Bishops of Ireland,* with an *imprimatur* from the Most Reverend Doctor John Charles McQuaid, Archbishop of Dublin. Not for the first time, he contemplated the superiority of the Irish hierarchy over the English. Where was the English bishop that could hold a candle to Archbishop John Charles McQuaid? Archbishop McQuaid stood for very little nonsense indeed. If his like were Archbishop of Westminster there would be no more of the shilly-shallying and backsliding you see in England. Catholics in England would know that they had either to shape up or burn in Hell.

"Today," said Father Muldoon, "we will learn what the Church teaches about angels. Turn to page seventeen of the Catechism. O'Malley, will you please read out what paragraph twenty-four says."

O'Malley rose in a shambling way to his feet and adjusted his National Health glasses before reading.

24. Which are the chief creatures of God?
The chief creatures of God are angels and men.

"Now, O'Malley, will you read paragraph twenty-five."

25. What are angels?
Angels are pure spirit, created by God for his glory and his service.

"'*Angels are pure spirit, created by God for his glory and his service.*' Angels can see God in Heaven and talk to Him, like I can see and talk to you. Just like there are orders and ranks in the Church, from the Pope down to the laity, there are orders of Angels, the highest being the Seraphim and Cherubim. We will discuss these in another class. Now, who can name me an angel?" He looked around. A number of hands went up.

"Yes, Robinson."

"The Archangel Gabriel, Father."

"Correct, Robinson. And what did the Archangel Gabriel do, Robinson?"

Robinson hesitated, flustered. Other hands went up.

"Yes, Docherty?"

"He told Our Lady that she was going to have a baby, Father."

"Correct, Docherty. The Archangel Gabriel announced to the Blessed Virgin Mary that she was to become the mother of the son of God, who would come to save us from our sins. That is commemorated by the Feast of the Annunciation, a holy day of obligation, when we are all obliged to go to mass. The Archangels Gabriel, Michael and Raphael are known to all good Catholics. They are good angels, but there are bad angels too. Hearne, will you read out paragraph twenty-seven?"

> ***27. Did the angels remain faithful to God?***
> *Some of the angels remained faithful to God; others, through pride, rebelled against him.*

"'*Some of the angels remained faithful to God; others, through pride, rebelled against him.*' Make a special note of that, boys. The sin of pride was the first sin of all and it is the worst of all sins. It is known as the sin of sins. It is the sin that God hates most. A blessed saint, Saint Augustine, said, 'It was Pride that changed angels into devils.' You see what the sin of pride can do. It can even change angels, the special creatures of God, into devils. What do you think happened to those bad angels? Hearne, please read paragraphs thirty-one, two and three."

> ***31 How did God punish the angels who rebelled?***
> *God punished those angels who rebelled by condemning them to the everlasting pains of Hell*
>
> ***32. Who is the leader of the bad angels?***
> *The leader of the bad angels is called Satan or the Devil.*
>
> ***33. Do the Devil and his angels try to harm us?***
> *The Devil and his angels try to harm us chiefly by tempting us to sin.*

"Now boys, I am often asked where the Devil and all his angels are to be found. The Devil and his cohorts of bad angels, in their pride and anger at Almighty God, are to be found everywhere, whispering in your ear and tempting you to sin, so that you might join them in Hell. The Devil always starts with little sins, sins that don't seem too bad. You might be rude to your parents or friends, show jealousy of others, be quick to anger or take offence. If the Devil succeeds in tempting you to these then he will tempt you to worse and soon you could find yourself bound for the everlasting fires of Hell. The Devil will have had his way and your soul will be in torment for all eternity. It will be no use then in saying that you are sorry. There can be no escape. No amount of tears or gnashing of teeth will cause God to change his mind. If you were alone in this world, without help, then the Devil would always win and you would be lost. But you are not alone. For every bad angel there is a host of good angels. Clancy, please read paragraph thirty."

30. Has each of us a guardian angel?
Each of us has a guardian angel who prays for him, protects him from harm and helps him do good.

"'*Each of us has a guardian angel who prays for him, protects him from harm and helps him do good.*' Remember that, boys. Take it to heart. When the Devil is whispering in one ear, tempting you with all his blandishments, you can be sure that your guardian angel is whispering in the other ear, telling you to reject those blandishments. If you will only listen to him, your guardian angel will guide you on the one true path and lead you to your eternal reward in Heaven."

The class digested this news in silence. Then a hand went up.

"Yes, Mahoney?"

"Do Protestants have guardian angels, Father?"

"Yes, Mahoney. As the Catechism says, each of us has a guardian angel, though some, in rejecting the teachings of the one, true Church, do not listen to theirs. There are none so deaf as those that will not hear."

Another hand went up.

"Yes, Gillen?"

"Do Protestants have Protestant guardian angels, Father?"

The priest was taken aback by the notion.

"What does paragraph twenty-five of the Catechism say, Gillen?"

Gillen looked puzzled as he read.

"'*What are angels? Angels are pure spirit, created by God for his glory and his service*', Father."

"'Angels are created by God for his glory and his service.' What makes you think, Gillen, that good angels would be tempted by the false doctrines of Luther and his like? What do you think God would say if a guardian angel told him that he wouldn't let his charge go to mass? That angel would be packed off to Hell without so much as a by your leave."

The priest pointed to a pile of books on his desk.

"Now, perhaps we can learn what guardian angels do. Clancy and Docherty, will you give these out to the class. This book is called *Wopsy: The Adventures of a Guardian Angel*. It is written by Father Gerard Scriven, who is a White Father. Can anyone tell me what the White Fathers are known for?"

A hand shot up.

"Yes, Gallagher?"

"They are missionaries in Africa, Father."

"Indeed they are, Gallagher. We raise money for the White Fathers, so that they can convert the pagans in Africa. Many a black baby has reason to be thankful to the White Fathers for saving their soul."

The class felt a collective sense of satisfaction. Who could argue that saving the souls of black babies was not a most praiseworthy thing to do?

"What is the difference between pagans and heathens, Father?" asked Hearne.

"That is an important question, Hearne," came the response. "Heathens are followers of a false religion, like Mohammedans or Hindus. Pagans have no religion whatsoever. They believe in things like evil spirits and witch doctors. You find most of them in Africa."

"Cooking missionaries in pots," said a boy at the back in a low whisper, provoking sniggers from those near him. They didn't seem to reach Father Muldoon. "You will see, boys," he continued, "that this book is about a very small angel called Wopsy, who has been told by God to be the guardian angel of a pagan black baby, who lives in Africa, far from any church or missionary."

The book's cover had a picture of a winged angel riding on the back of a lion. Clancy opened it and began to read. Wopsy, it appeared, was not the angel's real angel name. He was called that "because even the archangels had a hard time remembering his real name, which had 14 letters". Clancy wondered why they used letters in Heaven. Did angels have to learn to read? Who would teach them? God? Maybe if he met a White Father he would ask. They probably knew more about these things than he did.

He read on. One day God said to Wopsy that he was to become a guardian angel, but, because he was small and had no experience, he would have to start by guarding a baby in Africa. "Oh, how lovely," said Wopsy. He loved black babies. All the little angels did, because they had big white eyes and beautiful shiny black skin. "May I call him Shiny?" asked Wopsy. God said he could call him anything he liked, "because he had only a horrible pagan name".

Despite being small, Clancy thought Wopsy was surprisingly feisty. "He wasn't a bit afraid of devils, for whom he had a great contempt, quite out of proportion to his size." He slid down from Heaven on a moonbeam and went in search of Shiny. He found him, sleeping under a blanket, in a hut in a village called Matongu, which was deep in the forest. Delighted, he gave him an angel kiss, "but suddenly Wopsy trembled and nearly fell over with horror, for right down in the soul of Shiny he saw nothing but darkness and he knew it was caused by Original Sin. 'Oh dear,' said Wopsy, 'I must try to change that.'"

Clancy knew that the antidote to Original Sin was baptism and he assumed that Wopsy would manage somehow for Shiny to be baptised. He was right. One day, Shiny wandered near to an open fire. Wopsy was going to hold him back, but God told him not to and so Shiny was badly burned. God then told Wopsy to go to the missionaries and use his angel wiles to convince one of them to visit Motangu. The priest, in his white robes, got on his motorbike and, just as he was passing the hut where Shiny lived, Wopsy caused it to stop. Seeing the missionary, Shiny's mother rushed out, saying, "Bwana, Bwana, come at once. My baby is burned." "Oh," said the missionary, "that's why the engine stopped." The priest put ointment on Shiny and bandaged his burns. Then Wopsy whispered in his ear and the priest took another look at Shiny. This was a sick little baby. He may die. The priest decided to baptise him in case he did die, so that his soul could go straight to Heaven. Wopsy heard the priest say the words of baptism in Latin. Wopsy looked into Shiny's soul. "How lovely it was now. Gone was all the stain of Original Sin. Shiny's soul was beautiful and clean."

Wopsy decided that Motangu needed a priest to live there. He flew off to see the bishop and whispered in his ear, trying to persuade him to send a priest. The bishop sadly shook his head. There was no money and no spare priest.

Then, as if by a miracle, two letters arrived. One contained a cheque for $1000, sent by a kind donor. The other said the mission was going to send him three new priests. The bishop, overjoyed, could now send a priest, Father George, to Motangu.

That stirred up the local devils and they decided to meet in the forest. Wopsy watched them from high in the trees. He knew that they would not see him because "devils never look up to Heaven. It gives them a headache." Important devils were there, "uglier and more horrible than the other devils. That is how you know important devils."

"The dreaded day has come at last," said an important devil. "The missionaries are starting a mission in Motangu. I called upon the poisonous snakes to bite the missionaries and the lions to maul them, but I could do nothing while their angels are protecting them."

The word "angels" made all the devils shiver, but the important devil had not finished. "We will wait till the missionaries arrive and then we will stir up the witch doctors and devil-worshippers against them."

Wopsy had heard enough. He uncovered his face and it began to shine. Fearful of the light, the devils sneaked away like rats. Wopsy chased the important devils all the way to Upper Egypt.

Father George came to Motangu and started the mission. Wopsy went to see God, who told him that he must take good care of Shiny, because God wanted Shiny to be a priest, like Father George. Wopsy must be very careful, said God, "for some day, the devils would guess this, and then there will be trouble."

Wopsy went to powerful angels to ask them about special devils who try to prevent boys from becoming priests. They warned Wopsy of all the different things these devils might try to do. They would try to make Shiny die young, which made Wopsy tremble. They might tempt him to do horrible things, like being proud and conceited. They might set the witch doctors and the sorcerers on him. But the powerful angels said he needn't worry, as God was certainly helping him to look after Shiny. So he said "Thank you, God, for the good news today about my little boy Shiny being a priest someday. I promise to watch over, guard and protect him. Thank you too, God, for sending the missionaries who will help keep Shiny's soul shiny. Good night, God."

Clancy put the book down. He had found it less than convincing. He had read better ghost stories and he didn't think God would want a black baby to be burned just so he could be baptised. Maybe there were special devils who wanted to stop boys becoming priests, but most of the devils seemed to be a wimpish lot. He preferred his devils to have a bit more backbone. What sort of devil runs away from a little angel? – and these were supposed to be ugly, important devils. That didn't make sense. It was much more likely that a little angel would run away from them. Did he have a guardian angel? He could never be sure if one was whispering in his ear telling him to be good. There were others who did – like his Mum and Dad and the priests at the school – but they tended to shout, not whisper. He doubted he would ever to be able to hear anything from his guardian angel if he only whispered. Maybe the church should encourage guardian angels to shout. What was his guardian angel called? Nothing like Wopsy, surely? It sounded like a name for a rabbit.

The bell rang for the end of the lesson

Clergy night at the Catenians

It is clergy night at the South Croydon Catenians. Dinner (mulligatawny soup, boiled bacon, potatoes and cabbage and rice pudding with tinned peaches) is finished and whiskies are being served. Father Muldoon is seated next to Superintendent O'Driscoll of the Metropolitan Police, Z-Division (Croydon)

"I expect you heard I had a little misunderstanding with one of your lads the other evening, Superintendent." Muldoon affected a chuckle.

Superintendent O'Driscoll waved his hand dismissively.

"Oh, don't you worry, Father. You'll hear no more of that. And as for that jumped up pipsqueak of a bluebottle, Perkins, six month's point duty in Croydon High Street is what he gets. That will teach him a bit of respect for men of the cloth."

The priest nodded appreciatively, then affected a little concern.

"Oh, now, Superintendent, don't be too hard on the young lad. I expect he thought he was only doing his duty. Maybe three months would be enough."

"Six months, Father; not a day less. If there's one thing I won't have in the force, it's disrespect to clergy. And not just to Catholic clergy, Father, saving your grace, but there are others that need to be shown a little respect as well."

Father Muldoon's brow furrowed a little. He nodded gravely. "Quite right, Superintendent. We're in England now. We must respect those sincere in other faiths – whatever their errors."

"I'll leave the theology to you, Father, that's your department. But take the Reverend Arbuckle, vicar of St Hilda's

Church of England, up near Thornton Heath. Now he's what I would call a real Christian gentleman."

The priest assented. "Oh the Reverend Arbuckle is a gent, no question. God must want him for something, I suppose."

The Superintendent was warming to his argument as he contemplated the panoply of denominations found in Croydon.

"That's more than I could say for a good few others though. Some of them think they only have to put a dog collar round their neck and the rest of us will doff our caps, like they were the Archbishop of Dublin himself. Look at the names they give themselves – Methodists, Baptists, Congregationalists. What sort of religion is it, Father, that calls itself 'Congregationalist'?"

Father Muldoon blinked. "Protestant, like the rest of them, Superintendent. Not for us Catholics to know the differences, I'd say."

"Oh I know that, Father, but take their Church, the one on the Brighton Road in Purley. Fine-looking building, I think you'd agree. A good few bob spent on bricks and mortar there. And what do they do? They stick a notice board outside saying 'Congregationalist.' Sure, if they didn't have a congregation, there wouldn't be any point in building the church in the first place."

The priest slapped his thigh delightedly. "'If they didn't have a congregation, there wouldn't be any point in building the church in the first place.' Oh it's easy to see you're a Scotland Yard man, Superintendent. The boys in blue are getting their money's worth when Superintendent O'Driscoll is on the case."

Father Muldoon peered down the room and frowned.

"There's someone else that's on the case I see, Superintendent, Frankie Fahey the bookie. Do you ever have anything to do with him?"

"I'm not a betting man myself, Father."

"His odds are bad enough, but Frankie Fahey is always up to something. I wouldn't be surprised if you were to feel his collar sometime soon, Superintendent. I hear he's given us the whisky tonight. He wants to look good in front of all the Catenians here. Will you look at the bottle – 'Old Caledonian'. What kind of whisky is that? I bet he got it from one of his shady friends. Why couldn't he give us Bell's or Teacher's? Oh, I see he's coming over."

"Good to see you again, Father. How have you been keeping?"

"Well enough, Frankie, and yourself?"

"In grand form, Father, thanks be to God. You might have heard that I'm starting a council of the Knights of Saint Columba for the diocese. I'm hoping some of the Catenians will join."

"That's grand, Frankie, and how's the wife?"

"In great form too, Father. Philomena is back from Walsingham. She's looking to go on another pilgrimage and has just started a novena for the Knights. That will get us off to a grand start. Oh, is that Desmond Kelly over there? I hear his firm is putting up the new shopping centre. I must have a word."

As the bookie scooted across the room, they resumed the conversation.

"Frankie Fahey will come a cropper one day, Superintendent, you mark my words. But enough of him. Do you ever go back to Roscommon now?"

"Oh I do, Father, every year. I still have a brother and two sisters there, and Mrs O'Driscoll is from Ballaghaderreen. She has family there as well. Two weeks in the county sets me up for the year catching villains in London. I wouldn't be without it."

"Oh indeed you would not. There's not a finer county, Carlow excepted, in the whole of Ireland. Very sound, that is what is always said about a Roscommon man."

"Right you are, Father, sound as a bell."

"There's not a bell cast that's as sound as a man from county Roscommon, Superintendent, if you ask my opinion. And your people, were they from there, too?"

"They were, Father. Born and bred in Roscommon, that's the O'Driscolls."

"And good Catholics too, I have no doubt."

"Oh they were indeed, Father. My mother got mass and communion every day. Stations of the Cross in Lent without fail and never missed the Angelus in her life. And she had a pile of prayer books a yard high by her bed, that she read every night."

"A saint, you can be sure. And looking down from heaven, helping you with your cases, I don't doubt. And your father, too?"

"Very good, Father, in his own way. He always stood at the back of the church on Sunday. He had to leave early at the end of mass on account of his piles. If he left with the rest of them, there would be no seats left in Murphy's bar. He'd have to stand and the piles would plague him for the rest of the week."

"Another sound man, Superintendent. The piles is a terrible affliction to be sure. Did you know Bishop Geoghegan of Clonmore, God rest his soul? A real bishop; precious few like him left, I'm sorry to say. He was a martyr to the piles, so they say. He gave a special dispensation in his diocese that men with the piles were excused prayers for the conversion of Russia, so they could be sure of getting themselves a seat in the bar after mass. Bishop Geoghegan used to swear by Clohessy's *Lubricum*. Did your father ever use that?"

"I don't believe he did, Father. What was it, exactly?"

"The sure and certain remedy for the piles, Superintendent, that's what. Made by a Cork firm, I believe. Clohessy's *Lubricum* was the stuff for the piles, all right. None of them wishy-washy, ointmenty things that you get nowadays. All from England, of course. English pile ointment is the laughing stock of the world."

"Is that so, Father?"

"It is indeed, Superintendent, a laughing stock. Mention English pile ointment in America and you bring the house down. What do you think the piles say to themselves when they catch a sight of it? 'Watch out boys. Here comes the English ointment. We'd better make ourselves scarce!' Hah! The piles is made of sterner stuff. You need something powerful strong to tackle the piles. Cork men don't stint on the ingredients, like some I could mention. Arsenic was in there, I believe – and that other stuff, the doings that makes the holy statues glow in the dark."

"Phosphorus, Father?"

"The very man, phosphorus! Arsenic and phosphorus are the men to put the fear of God into the piles. A dose or two of Clohessy's *Lubricum* and the piles is packing its bags, never to be heard from again!"

"Oh, I'd say it would be, Father. And can you still get it now?"

"You cannot, Superintendent, you cannot. And do you know why?"

"I have no idea, Father."

"Because the English had it banned, that's why."

"Did they indeed, and why was that?"

"Why do you think, Superintendent? Why do you think? The root of all evil – money. That's why."

"Money, Father?"

"Money, Superintendent. You would not believe the amount of money there is in piles in England. Say the word piles in Harley Street and you're twenty pounds the poorer before they have your trousers down. If you are a doctor of piles in England your fortune is practically made. And then along comes the Irish upstart, at three shillings and sixpence the jar, to knock the golden goose on the head."

"I'd say they wouldn't be pleased, Father."

"They were not, Superintendent. You never heard such a wailing and a caterwauling as from the English doctors. And half of them Lords and Sirs and the like. You're hardly out of medical school in England before you can grab yourself a title. Questions were asked in the House, Superintendent, very pointed questions, I can tell you, about why some Irish interloper was threatening to pack the entire English medical profession off to Carey St, without so much as a by your leave. The English government had to act."

"Oh they would have had to act all right, Father. There's no turning a blind eye to questions in the House."

"There is not, Superintendent. Questions in the House is taken very seriously in England. And so they had it banned — and not just in England either, but in the entire British Empire and Commonwealth. Wherever the map was red, there was not a jar of Clohessy's *Lubricum* to be had."

"The entire British Empire and Commonwealth, eh, Father? That's a powerful ban. But what about Ireland? Surely you could still buy it there?"

"Oh, the English were wise to that one, Superintendent. Oh, they saw that one coming a mile off. Put it on sale in Dublin and every boat from Liverpool would be packed to bursting with the punters wanting to get their hands on their jars of Clohessy's *Lubricum*. So they had to twist Dev's arm."

"Dev had his arm twisted? Who could do that, now?"

"Who do you think, Superintendent? Who but Ireland's greatest enemy since Oliver Cromwell."

"There's a few that could answer to that description, Father. Who exactly did you have in mind?"

"Why Winston Churchill, of course."

"What? Winston Churchill, the English prime minister?"

"The very same. Winston Spencer Churchill, the man that went fifteen rounds with Adolf Hitler."

"Winston Churchill himself. Are you sure, Father?"

"I am indeed, Superintendent. I had an uncle, Dan Muldoon, who was a TD in the government at the time. He told me all about it. When Dev got to hear of the ban, it put him in fighting mood. Dev had his dander up that day and no mistake. Dev was more than a match for any Winston Churchill, or any Adolf Hitler. Or any Joe Stalin, come to that."

"Oh, he was, Father."

"If them three had turned up in Dublin he would have handed them each a pasting with one hand tied behind his back."

"Oh, he would. Dev was the best ever, no question."

"He had a speech prepared, the like of which you never heard, Superintendent. 'An Irish Solution for an Irish Problem' it was entitled. He was to give it in the Dail — in Irish of course."

"Dev in Irish, eh. That was always the stuff to give the troops, Father. So did he not give it?"

"No, he did not. The English got wind of it somehow. There was consternation in Number 10 Downing Street, I can tell you, Superintendent, consternation the like of which had not been seen since William the Conqueror. Dev gets a telegram from Churchill himself. 'One word of that speech, Mr de Valera,' says the telegram, 'one word of that speech, *and you can kiss the North goodbye*.'"

"Kiss the North goodbye. That was fighting talk alright, Father. So what does he do?"

"You and I would be scratching our heads, Superintendent, wondering how the devil we get out of that one, but not Dev. Dev was too cute for the likes of Winston Spencer Churchill. Dev had Winston Spencer Churchill's little number and no mistake. 'Dan,' he says to my uncle, 'Dan, the English think they have us banjaxed again, but I'm wise to their little ways. We're going to say nothing. We'll keep our powder dry and we'll live to fight another day.'"

"Not many would have thought of that, Father. That took some thinking, I'd say."

"None better at thinking, Superintendent, than Dev."

"There were no flies on Dev, eh, Father?"

"The fly was never born, Superintendent, that would dare go within a million miles of Dev. And to this day, that speech is under lock and key. It's in Dev's will, of course. No one is to set eyes on that speech until the day the country is finally united, when Clohessy's *Lubricum* will be back on sale and the speech will be given. RTE is to put it out — just after the Angelus."

"Oh, that will be a great day, Father."

"It will, Superintendent. So aren't we living still?"

"We are, Father."

"And aren't we fighting still?"

"We are, Father."

Glory-O
Glory-O to the bold Fenian men

Father Fahey

"When I was a young boy I didn't go out with the girls. I stayed in and did my chemistry."

Father Finbar Fahey surveyed the faces seated behind the laboratory benches. They in turn gazed back with expressions of schoolboyish blandness, behind which were reactions of disbelief, incomprehension, derision and, for a few, the thought that chemistry might be a welcome distraction from having to contemplate the unfathomable mystery that was the female sex.

Father Fahey loved everything about chemistry. He was in awe of the fierce passion of sodium as it tore the oxygen out of water molecules to liberate hydrogen, the pieces skipping across the surface of the water and bursting into flames as the hydrogen ignited. He was transfixed by the demonic appetite of fluorine, as it wrenched the hydrogen out of water and turned it into that most corrosive of fluids, hydrofluoric acid. He was cheered by all reactions, exothermic and endothermic and even those with no pretensions to the calorific. He was entranced by the way carbon atoms could be strung together almost infinitely, holding one, two or three hands out to each other as they danced the gavotte of life. He even had affection for those atoms that declined to enter any chemical reaction whatsoever, the noble gases helium, neon, argon and xenon, seeing, in their reclusiveness, their desire to remain pure and free from all attachments, something of his own priestly vows of poverty, chastity and obedience.

As a young seminarian in Maynooth, he had once tried to argue that chemistry should be seen as part of theology. The action of the chlorophyll molecule in transmuting light into life, the way that atoms and molecules welded together to produce all the riches and beauties of the earth – all should be seen as a sort of prayer in praise of the creator. He was quickly disabused of such notions and warned that any more of such heretical nonsense would have him sent packing. A spoiled priest would bring disgrace on any family, so he went back to orthodoxy.

The lesson he was teaching was the production of hydrogen using zinc and dilute sulphuric acid – always a favourite with the younger boys. They gazed in fascinated glee at the liquid bubbling in the stoppered flasks and then cheered as Father Fahey passed a lit taper over the glass tube coming out of the stopper and saw the flame leap up.

"Who can tell me what is coming out of the flask?"

Two boys put their hands up.

"Yes, Murphy?"

"Gas, Father."

"It is indeed a gas, but what sort of gas?"

No hands were raised.

"It is hydrogen. Hydrogen is the lightest gas and the lightest of all elements. You will come to understand, boys," continued Father Fahey, "that the reaction of many acids with many metals will produce hydrogen. Now boys, as good scientists, you must write up everything you have done in the experiment and draw a diagram of the apparatus you used."

Pens and pencils were applied to paper as they wrote down, with varying degrees of accuracy, what they had done. They copied diligently the equation that Father Fahey had written on the blackboard, knowing that it would disappear from their minds as soon as they left the classroom.

$$Zn + H_2SO_4 = H_2 + ZnSO_4$$

The bell rang for the end of the lesson. As the boys were leaving the laboratory, Father Fahey beckoned to Clancy.

"Clancy, could you serve mass at Hallingham tomorrow?"

For a moment Clancy hesitated. It meant getting up before six, but then thoughts of the breakfast came to him. There was no breakfast like a Hallingham breakfast.

"Yes. Father."

***

Father Muldoon looked down from the window in his room as the huge motorbike, its rider all in black leather, thrummed along the path towards the school gates. He felt a familiar surge of disapproval at the doings of the prelate from Borris. What did a priest want with a motorbike like that? A boy had told him that it was called a Brough Superior and when it was made it was the fastest motorbike in the world, with an engine of a thousand cc's. Whatever cc's might be, that machine had far too many of them. He would have a word with the Archbishop. Father Finbar Fahey would be lucky to have more than a few dozen of those cc's left by the time the Archbishop had finished with him.

Father Finbar Fahey, in the opinion of Father Muldoon, was too full of himself altogether. Couldn't sulphurous fumes be smelt coming out of that laboratory of his any day of the week? Who is the man for sulphurous fumes? The Devil himself, that's who. Didn't Saint Luke say that the day Lot left Sodom, fire and sulphur rained down from heaven and destroyed them all? Father Finbar Fahey is playing with fire alright. And isn't he a second cousin to Frankie Moneybags Fahey, who calls himself "the Catholic Turf Accountant", but whose odd are put to shame by any Protestant bookie you could name. Blood is thicker than water, so they say, and Fahey blood is thicker than most. What would you expect from those who come from that nest of vipers, Borris-in-Ossory, County Laois?

And his masses were indecently fast. Wasn't he supposed to be able to say mass in twenty-one minutes? A good speed of mass would have you out of the sacristy door on the dot of seven and back in the room, cup of tea in your hand and rashers sizzling in the pan, by the stroke of half past. Maybe a minute or so sooner, with a short epistle and gospel. For a twenty-one minute mass he must have galloped through the *Gloria* and *Credo* faster than Lester Piggott on Never Say Die. Needless to say, Father Finbar Fahey was cute enough to make sure he always had a good server. A good server can cut minutes off your mass time. The boy Clancy was top class – lightning with the cruets and bells and had all the responses off pat. Pity there weren't more like him. With some servers at the school you wondered whether you would ever get off the altar.

***

Clancy waited at the school gate for Father Fahey. He quite liked serving at mass, especially if there was something for him at the end. Weddings and funerals were best. With weddings, the guests were usually drunk and the sky was the limit. He once got five shillings from the father of the bride and another half crown from the best man, and, if he went with the priest to the reception, he could stuff his face. Funerals weren't usually so profitable. He might get a shilling from the chief mourner and more, maybe even half a crown, if he went to the burial. Funerals were supposed to be sad, but he didn't often feel sad, because the person who died was old and he didn't know them. Only once was different. It was the funeral of a baby. The father carried the little white coffin himself. Clancy saw tears streaming down his face. He had never seen a man cry before.

Clancy heard the deep, throbbing note of the Brough Superior before it appeared. His mother had been apprehensive the first time he told her that Father Fahey was going to take him on a motorbike, but had told herself that a priest would drive slowly. Clancy knew otherwise, but he had been assured by Father Fahey that Saint Columbanus, the patron saint of motorcyclists, whose embossed medal hung from the handlebars, would protect them. The priest handed him a helmet and, once it was on, they were off.

They sped through the suburban streets, leaning hard into the corners and accelerating away. To Purley and on to the Godstone Road, through Kenley, where the priest gave a wave to the police station. "The Sergeant there is an old school friend of mine." Then through Whyteleafe, the speed increasing all the time as Father Fahey weaved in and out of the traffic. Clancy clung firmly to his back, a little scared, more than a little exhilarated. They turned off at Caterham onto an undulating country road, their speed hardly decreasing. Finally, they stopped in a little clearing by the side of the road. Father Fahey dismounted and unzipped his leathers, to reveal a full clerical suit and collar. He remounted, and they proceeded sedately, turning into a long drive as Hallingham Convent School for girls came into view.

It was an imposing red building, set in rolling countryside. Clancy's mother had found out that the Duke of Suffolk's daughters went there. He was one of the premier Catholic dukes of England, she told him, but he only had daughters, who couldn't become duke. He mentioned this to Hearne, who suggested he might 'chat up' one of the daughters and marry her, so he could become duke. Docherty said he'd heard they were all ugly, but Hearne retorted that nobody that rich could be ugly. Clancy put an end to any nuptial speculations, saying that he never saw any of the girls when he went there. Only nuns came to the mass.

As they dismounted, a diminutive nun with a cheerful, ruddy face came hurrying up to them and curtseyed.

"Welcome, Father."

The accent was country Irish. Father Fahey smiled in acknowledgement and the nun led them towards the chapel. They went into the sacristy and Clancy saw the vestments had been laid out for them. He buttoned up the black cassock and then slipped the white cotta over his head. Father Fahey had donned the long white alb and stole and was tightening the cincture round his waist. He held up the chasuble, before slipping it over his head and onto his shoulders. Green silk and gold thread shimmered in the early morning sun coming through a window. They waited for a few minutes and then a bell rang. The priest picked up his chalice and paten and Clancy led him out of the sacristy and on to the altar. Clancy gave a sideways glance at the front pews, occupied by the nuns, dressed all in black, except for the stiff, starched, white wimples that framed their faces. He wondered if that meant they could only see what was directly in front of them, like horses in blinkers.

The mass went at Father Fahey's usual brisk pace, priest and server in quick-fire response. *Gloria, Credo,* epistle, gospel, cruets, bells and *Hoc est enim corpus meum* were disposed of and then things slowed for communion, as every nun came to the altar rails to receive the host. After that it was almost no time to *Ite missa est,* then back to the sacristy.

They went into the large breakfast room, with its stone-pillared window overlooking the school grounds. One wall was largely occupied by a massive marble fireplace, while facsimiles of old-master devotional pictures hung on the others. They sat down at the polished mahogany table, which was laid out with solid silver cutlery and bone-china plates, cups and saucers. The door opened and the same nun who had curtseyed when they arrived entered with a tray bearing plates of porridge that she put down, saying "There" to each. Clancy noticed how red her hands were.

"I haven't met you before, Sister. What's your name?" said Father Fahey.

The nun blushed slightly.

"Sister Imelda, Father."

"And what do you do at the school, Sister Imelda."

"I work in the kitchens, Father. We're all from the country there."

"I think I recognise that accent. Where are you from, Sister?"

The nun appeared surprised.

"Balinasloe, County Galway, Father."

"Ah, Balinasloe, I know it well," said the priest. "I have cousins in Clifden. Have you family there still?"

She shook her head.

"They are all gone now, Father. I have one brother in America, another here in England. Then I have a brother, a priest, in South Africa and two sisters, nuns, in Bechuanaland."

"Three nuns and a priest. That's a great Catholic family, Sister. I suppose you don't see them very often."

"Hardly at all, Father. I haven't seen my brother in America these twenty years and the ones in Africa are only allowed back every five years or so. I just have to pray for them instead."

The priest nodded.

"I'm sure your prayers will help to keep them safe, Sister. Give me their names and I will say a mass for them."

Clancy saw the nun's face light up in a smile that, if he knew the word, he might have described as beatific.

"Oh, will you, Father? That would be grand. I'll go and write them down for you."

She went out the door and each turned their attention to the thick, creamy porridge.

Just as they were finishing the porridge, the door opened again and Sister Imelda came in carrying a tray with two large covered plates on it. She was followed by another nun carrying a tray on which were a silver teapot and hot water jug, a rack of toast, a bowl of butter pats and three different marmalades. As the covers were removed, Clancy gazed in wide-eyed appreciation at the plate before him. Two crisp rashers of back bacon, a fat sausage, two fried eggs (two!), surrounded by mushrooms, tomatoes, black pudding and fried bread. It was what he had come for.

Priest and server ate in silence, paying the feast its proper due. Father Fahey was helping himself to a third cup of tea and another slice of toast when the door swung open and a nun swept in. The priest immediately stood up and motioned Clancy to do likewise.

"Good morning, Father Fahey," said the nun in crisp tones that were distinctly upper-class English.

"Good morning, Reverend Mother," said Father Fahey.

Reverend Mother was a member of one of England's oldest recusant noble families. Her porcelain skin and finely chiselled features, hardly lined, spoke of centuries of breeding. Daughters of the line were expected either to attend Court as ladies-in-waiting, before finding suitable husbands, or else to join an upper-class convent, often, as with Reverend Mother, the one they had attended as girls. She enjoyed a life of privilege, saw no contradiction between it and her faith, and addressed the lower ranks of clergy in the same manner as she had servants in her ancestral home.

"Do sit down," said Reverend Mother. "Father Fahey, I have a request."

"Yes, Reverend Mother?"

"When you come here next week, I would like you to say mass for the success of Sir Alec Douglas Home and his party in the forthcoming general election."

The priest looked startled.

"Pardon, Reverend Mother?"

"I thought that was quite clear, Father," came the reply in even crisper tones. "We can't have the Bolsheviks getting in."

Father Fahey was even more startled. He knew very little about English politics, but he hadn't heard anything about Bolsheviks in Croydon, and certainly not in this very leafy part of Surrey. He thought the leader of the main opposition Labour

Party, Harold Wilson, was in favour of something called "the white heat of technology", which sounded rather like chemistry, so he was, if anything, partial to that side.

"Bolsheviks, Reverend Mother?"

"Yes, Father, Bolsheviks. Look what happened in Spain."

"Spain, Reverend Mother?"

Reverend Mother gave Father Fahey a look that she normally reserved for the most obtuse novice nun.

"Yes, Spain, Father Fahey. Hundreds of priests and nuns were murdered in Spain by the Bolsheviks."

The priest struggled to reply.

"Ah, yes, Reverend Mother. Holy martyrs, all of them, God rest their souls. Dreadful people, Bolsheviks. Do you think it could happen here?"

"Why give them the chance? Who knows what might happen if they got in? I think we would all prefer not to be martyred in our beds."

The priest was feeling the full force of an aristocratic recusant, who had been told from childhood all that could happen if the wrong people "got in".

"Of course, Reverend Mother. No one wants to see martyrs in England again."

"Thank you, Father Fahey," said Reverend Mother and added, "I shall look forward to attending your mass next week," as she rose and swept out of the room.

Father Fahey was still looking at the door after Reverend Mother had left, when it opened again and Sister Imelda came in. She put all the breakfast things onto a tray and then pulled a piece of paper from a pocket in her pinafore.

"These are my brothers and sisters, Father."

Father Fahey perused the paper and Clancy saw it took a second or two before he realised what she meant.

"Now, I see, Sister, that you haven't put yourself down."

Sister Imelda blushed.

"I thought it was just for them, Father."

"Not at all, Sister. It is for the whole family."

He took out a pen and added her name.

"I shall say the mass next week," he said and gave Clancy a sly wink.

"Thank you and God bless you, Father," said Sister Imelda as she carried the tray out of the room. Clancy thought she looked an inch or two taller than when she came in.

A Religious Education Lesson

Clancy assembled the pennies into five neat piles of twelve and pushed the remainder to the side. They would go in next week. He put up his hand.

Father Muldoon nodded towards the raised palm.

"Yes, that boy, Clancy."

"Five shillings for the Kintups, Father," said Clancy.

"Five shillings for the Kintups," repeated Father Muldoon. "What have the Heavenly Host to say to that?"

Clancy turned his eyes to the back of the classroom. Gallagher, a boy who flaunted his piety and boasted that he was going to the White Fathers Junior Seminary next year, was slowly rising to his feet, a crestfallen look on his face.

"Four shillings for the Heavenly Host, Father."

"Four shillings for the Heavenly Host," said Father Muldoon, rather sternly. "I hope you can do better next week." Gallagher's face fell further. The priest continued. "Come out both of you with your money."

Clancy put the pennies into a bag and brought it to the priest's desk.

"Now boys," said Father Muldoon, after he had counted it, "put your satellites in."

Clancy had been surprised, not to say disconcerted, when Father Muldoon had appointed him as collector for the Kintups. Nevertheless, he had applied himself diligently to cajoling the pennies out of his classmates. He looked with some satisfaction at the Kintups chart. The three inner orbits were already filled with ten satellites, a shilling for each. The day's five would go into Orbit 4. When they had filled Orbit 6, three pounds would go off to the Foreign Missions. He marked the five new satellites as red circles at intervals on the orbit and carefully drew small aerials on each. He looked across to the Heavenly Host chart and saw that they had only just filled Orbit 3. Gallagher could hardly restrain his envy.

Clancy felt a surge of satisfaction, not just from winning the space race, but also from imagining all the black children he was helping to become Catholics. When they died they would be able to go to Heaven, unlike their poor, unbaptised brothers and sisters, who were doomed to languish in Limbo.

Father Muldoon leant back in his chair. There were not many aspects of the modern world that he appreciated, especially those he encountered in England, but he had to admit that the satellites were a grand idea. Competition between the Kintups and the Heavenly Host and the enthusiasm of young boys for everything to do with space had made collections soar. Every year he raised money for the Missions from the pupils and this year was going to beat the school record for Foreign Missions by a mile. Never mind that Kintups spelled sputnik backwards and they were named after the doings that the godless Russians had sent into the heavens. He would love to see the faces of the Russkies when they found out that their beloved sputniks were helping to send the Catholic message to the pagans.

He picked up a small booklet that was on his desk and held it up before the class.

"Boys, you all have your copy of this little book, *Pocket Stories of the Saints*. It tells of the way Blessed Saints loved and served Our Lord and His Holy Church. I want you to read it and then write about a particular saint who you think is an example to you in your daily conduct and in the practice of your religion. You may begin now and I will collect your books at the end of class."

Clancy leafed through the booklet. He was familiar with some saints – Saint Patrick of Ireland and George of England, and the Apostles and Disciples – Saints Peter, Paul, Matthew,

Luke and John and a few others, but the ones in its pages were mostly unfamiliar. Most of them seemed to be female and many of them didn't seem to offer much in the way of example for him, such as Saint Angela, "Friend of girls" or Saint Gertrude, the Abbess. "Sometimes men and women are so holy that Our Dear Lord comes to talk to them. He likes to bring His Blessed Mother with Him, too." They hadn't come to talk to him, probably because he wasn't holy enough. Rather a lot of saints also seemed to come to a grisly end, like Saint Agnes:

Saint Agnes

Agnes was only twelve when the Roman soldiers arrested her. They were killing all Christians in those days. But first they dragged her to the statue of a false goddess.

"Offer prayers and incense to Minerva," they ordered her.

Instead, brave little Agnes lifted her arms and prayed aloud to Jesus Christ.

So they put handcuffs on her. She was so tiny that the cuffs slipped off her wrists.

Then they whipped her cruelly. They said they would stop if she gave up Jesus Christ. Even the pagans wept to see her tortured that way.

Next they dragged her through the streets for the people to laugh at. Instead, some of them tried to save her.

Then a young man asked her to marry him. "I will save you if you do", he promised.

"I belong to my Saviour alone," she answered. With one stroke of the sword, the soldiers killed this brave little girl.

Her Feast is: January 21st.

He pondered becoming a martyr. On the one hand you went straight to Heaven; on the other, it would hurt – a lot. There wasn't much prospect of becoming a martyr these days, unlike in the time of poor little Saint Agnes. Murderous bands of Roman soldiers did not patrol the streets of Croydon and English

Protestants seemed to have given up the habit of burning Catholics at the stake or hanging, drawing and quartering them, as had happened to Blessed Edmund Campion.

As for getting married to escape martyrdom, he needed to give that more thought, because another theme had emerged as he read on. Sainthood and marriage didn't seem to go well together.

Saint Rita.

When Rita was a little girl, she wanted to be a Sister.
Instead, her Mother and Father made her marry a cruel, bad-tempered husband.
But though he was unkind to her, Rita was a good wife. She had twin boys whom she loved very much.
But her husband had many enemies. One day, some of these men killed him. Her sons, now young men, were very angry. "We will kill the men who murdered our Father," they cried. This is revenge and it is wrong.
Rita did not want them to commit mortal sin. She loved them. But she prayed to God to let them die rather than to commit a murder. Shortly after, God let them die. But first they confessed and received Holy Communion so that they went to Heaven.
Then Rita became an Augustinian nun.
During her life and after her death, she worked many miracles. The Spaniards, because of her wonderful deeds, call her The Sweet Saint of the Impossible.

Her Feast is: May 22nd.

Clancy thought about his own mother, a cheerfully devout woman from County Mayo, who made sure he went to mass on Sundays and Holy Days of Obligation and always said his evening prayers, with decades of the Rosary and the mysteries – Joyful, Sorrowful and Glorious – in Lent. Would she want him to die if he was going to commit a mortal sin? Up till now, the thought had never occurred to him, and, thinking about it, he was almost sure she wouldn't, but reading about Saint Rita had put a scintilla of doubt in his mind. What did "The Sweet Saint of the Impossible" mean? He decided to stop thinking about it.

Reading on he came to Saint Brigid of Ireland.

Saint Brigid

When Brigid was a very little girl, Saint Patrick converted the Irish. She was a very beautiful little girl. Many young men wanted to marry her.

"I shall be a nun," she thought. But she never knew she was going to be the first of millions of Irish nuns throughout the world.

"Make me ugly," she prayed to God. "Then I can love You alone." God heard her prayer and she became very ugly.

With joy she became a sister, a nun. And as soon as she did, God made her more beautiful than ever.

She built a lovely little convent. She tended the cattle herself. Other young women heard about her. They came and asked to join her and be nuns too. Then little girls came to be taught. The sick came to her and asked her to care for them. Often, she sold everything she had and gave the money to the poor. So the Irish called on her for help from all over the country.

So all over Ireland she went. She built convent schools and hospitals everywhere.

And when she died, all Ireland loved her. They made her the Patroness of the Green Isle.

Her Feast is February 1st.

So Saint Brigid was responsible for all those nuns he saw on the streets of Castlebar, when they went to Ireland to visit his grandparents. They always went around together. Women would nod to them and men doff their caps. A lot of them were old, so they were quite ugly. Had God made them like that so they could be good nuns? He wondered, too, about the boys in the third and fourth forms of the school, who seemed to have been afflicted with spots all over their faces. Had God made them ugly, like Saint Brigid, so that they were unattractive to the girls they were always talking about? He thought that was quite likely.

Even Saint Brigid, Irish though she was, wasn't the example he was looking for. Then he saw something rather different.

Saint Mary of Egypt
WHO HAD BEEN A SINNER

When she was a very little girl, Mary of Egypt was a great sinner.
Almost everyone heard about her. For she was very beautiful. She led many people into sin. She was very bad.
One day, a crowd of people took ship for Jerusalem. The king had just found the Cross on which our Lord was hung. Mary went along because she thought it fun to travel. She did not care about the Cross.
But when they came to Jerusalem, she went with the rest to the church. Inside was the Cross. She tried to enter. She could not. Some unseen force held her, as if she were chained.
Suddenly, she knew how wicked she was. She turned and saw a picture of Our Lady. "Mary," she cried, "Mary Magdalen saw the Cross. Please let me stand beside that other sinful woman."
And she walked into the church. She knew that her sins had nailed Jesus to that Cross. She fell on her knees and cried and cried, repenting of all her sins.
Then she went out into the desert. For years she lived alone. She prayed. She did penance for her sin.
In the end, a holy man found her body on the sands.
He buried the sinner who had become a saint.

Her Feast is April 9th.

Which saint to choose as a model? On balance, he thought he would rather not be a martyr. He didn't want to get married, so he wouldn't have children and so he wouldn't have to want them to die if they were going to commit a mortal sin. He didn't want to become any uglier than he was and he definitely couldn't become a nun. He put pen to paper and began to write.

Saint Mary of Egypt was a very bad sinner, She committed many bad sins like...

He looked up and gazed out of the classroom window, trying to imagine what those sins might have been.

Brompo

Father Brompton was short and plump, with a jolly face and a tonsure of bald pate, fringed with a circle of greying hair. Clancy thought he looked like Friar Tuck in the Robin Hood programmes on TV. He always wore a cassock, his feet, just visible beneath, moving with quick, short strides, giving him a waddling gait. He was usually surrounded by a gaggle of first-year boys, who always referred to him as Brompo. They followed him not just because he treated them kindly and listened to what they had to say, but because he taught the one lesson they enjoyed rather than endured – history.

Clancy hadn't learned much history at primary school. It wasn't needed for the eleven plus. What little he did learn was mostly about kings and queens. Henry the Eighth had six wives, or was it Henry the Sixth had eight wives? What did it matter? Either had far too many. He had mentioned it to his father, who was from Galway and remarked curtly that English history was just one damn king after another. Brompo didn't teach kings and queens – not the English variety, anyway. He taught ancient history – the Egyptians, the Babylonians, the Minoans, the Mycenaeans, the Greeks. Clancy and the rest of the class found them fascinating, exotic, almost alien, as if they had come from another world.

Brompo had become a priest because he didn't want to disappoint his mother, who came from a many-priested Irish family and felt that she would somehow be in dereliction of her duty if she did not send at least one son for ordination. So he was packed off to the junior seminary aged twelve and only occasionally returned to the family home after that. His mildly observant – in every sense of the word – English father always seemed surprised whenever he did return, and expressed a vague hope that they would see more of him, to which his mother would tut tut, and remind him that their son now had a higher duty to the Church.

His indestructibly sunny and optimistic nature enabled him to transcend the inanity, stupidity, pettiness and arbitrariness of much of seminary life. The occasional beatings with a tawse he shrugged off as spiritually strengthening, in emulation of Christ, who suffered far more for us all. His gradual separation from his family was part of the same process. "Leave all and follow me," was what Christ had enjoined his disciples and, to be a priest, he would have to do the same. He had a simple faith, unburdened by any questioning, much less doubt. All attempts to construct an intellectual basis for faith he considered to be a waste of time. Who could comprehend the mystery of the divine? It was impossible. Theology he found utterly boring and he only ever scraped through when examined. Prayer, by contrast, he found easy, especially since he suspected that God had much the same opinion of theology as he did.

Shortly after the war, as a young priest, he had found himself sent to Egypt as a military chaplain. It was there that his fascination with ancient history began. His first view of the Sphinx and the pyramids ignited a passion that never dimmed. His open manner and easy charm endeared him to the captain of a Nile cruise boat and he was invited to take trips whenever he wanted, with the excuse that he could minister to the spiritual needs of any Catholic on board. He became familiar with the magnificent temples that lined the river – Karnak, Philae, Kom Ombo, Hatshepsut and the many others, all the way downriver to Abu Simbel. He would wander round the Valley of the Kings, chatting to any archaeologists working there and trying to imagine himself as Howard Carter opening the tomb of Tutankhamun. He acquired a large collection of books on Egyptology, became well versed in the illustrations of tombs and temples and learned to decipher hieroglyphs, with their tales of great battles and deep devotion to the gods.

Once bitten by the Egypt bug, he moved on to the other ancients – the Babylonians and the Akkadians, the Minoans and the Mycenaeans. He immersed himself in their histories and, thanks to the military, he managed to visit sites all over the Middle East and the Mediterranean. In his room at the school he had, displayed on a table, a collection of curios and artefacts that he had picked up on his travels. Above the table was a photograph of Brompo sitting on the throne in the palace of Knossos.

There was one bit of Catholic doctrine that, contemplating the wonders of the ancient world, had given Brompo pause for thought – original sin. He found it hard to believe that the creators of those magnificent buildings and marvellous artefacts were never destined for Heaven. Why had God so exalted their artistry, yet would never let them enter his presence? So he made a virtue out of his blithe dismissal of theology and constructed an alternative, in which these ancients somehow prefigured the coming of the Redeemer. Their works and their sublime skills surely brought them closer to the divine and would free them from languishing forever in Limbo. The Pharoah Akenaten was clearly the first monotheist and the Minotaur, dragging the innocent off to his lair, was just another incarnation of the Devil. The Egyptian *Book of the Dead*, or, as he preferred, its other title, the *Book of Emerging Forth into the Light,* with its tale of the journey of the spirit through the ante-room to judgement, on to judgement itself, then to assumption to live among the gods, was too like the Christian vision to be simply coincidence.

Brompo was notoriously absent-minded and disorganised. He was always forgetting boys' names, mislaying possessions and never remembering which boys he had asked to serve his masses, so that sometimes two or three would turn up and at other times, none at all. Not that these things disconcerted him or the boys. That was just Brompo.

His knowledge, enthusiasm and genial nature meant that he could enthral any audience with tales of the ancient world, which is why he was only allowed to teach first-year boys. It was assumed that, by the time they were in the middle school, any interest in history, and, with it, his rather unorthodox views on religion, would have largely faded away. Generations of first-year boys, however, continued to be fascinated, and Brompo always did what he could to keep up their interest. He would invite groups back to his room after school and regale them with tales of pharaohs and kings and show them things he had found on his travels. On his first visit, Clancy pointed to a brown piece of what looked like stone that had curious signs inscribed on it.

"What's this, Father?"

"That is a Sumerian cuneiform clay tablet. The Sumerians used them like we use paper today, to keep records. They wrote on the wet clay and dried them in the sun. You can pick it up.

Now who can tell me where the Sumerians lived?"

Clancy was about to answer when Hearne beat him to it.

"Mesopotamia, Father."

"Quite right. Mesopotamia, which means the land between the two rivers, and they are?"

This time Clancy got in first.

"The Tigris and the Euphrates, Father."

As Clancy held the tablet he could almost feel himself standing under the warm Babylonian sun. He looked at the inscription and imagined it might be a decree by a king to his subjects.

"What does it say, Father?"

"It's a record of corn being stored in a barn."

Brompo took down several books from his large bookshelf and handed them out for some of them to take home. Clancy got one called *Knossos, the Lair of the Minotaur*.

"You must bring them back to me next week, after you have read them," he said, but Brompo could never remember what he had given to whom and relied on the honesty of the boys to return them. He almost always did get them back, mostly because others boys wanted to read them and would chivvy those with them to return them.

As half term approached, Brompo finished a lesson on the Hittites by asking,

"Who wants to come with me to the Brit Mus next Saturday?"

Many hands went up.

"Right," he said, "we shall all meet at the school at ten o'clock sharp. Any boy not here by ten will be left behind. Wear your school uniform. You will have money for the train to Charing Cross and the bus and take with you a packed lunch. Is that clear?"

There was a chorus of "Yes, Father."

On Saturday morning, Clancy made the school with five minutes to spare. He threw his bike into the rack and joined the others. Led by Brompo they marched in a gaggle down to South Croydon station. Talking loudly and excitedly among themselves, they piled on to the train. The few other passengers in the carriage hastily retreated to another. At Charing Cross they took a bus to Bedford Square. "On to the Brit Mus, boys," said Brompo after a cursory count of heads. They walked along Great Russell Street and Clancy saw for the first time the imposing classical facade of the British Museum.

"We'll go to the Egyptian gallery first," said Brompo as they went through the entrance. The gallery was high and long, populated by huge statues. The priest pointed to what looked like a lump of grey rock on a plinth. "Who can tell me what that is?"

Clancy peered at the stone and could see it had some sort of inscriptions on it.

"Is it the Rosetta stone, Father?" said Hearne.

"Correct. Now who can tell me why the Rosetta stone is here?"

"It's got different sorts of writing on it, Father," said Hearne, "so they could translate Egyptian."

"Correct again." He pointed to the stone. "At the top you can see a lot of symbols. They're called hieroglyphs and they are what the Egyptians used to write in their temples and for important monuments. In the middle, is what's called demotic script, that they used for every day and at the bottom is Greek writing. They are all saying the same thing. Until we found the Rosetta stone nobody knew what hieroglyphs meant, but we can still understand Greek, so we now know what the hieroglyphs were saying."

Brompo then pointed to a massive statue of the chest and head of a man in a headdress.

"That is Rameses the Second, one of Egypt's greatest pharaohs. He reigned for over 60 years from 1279 BC. He won many battles and built some of the most important temples in Egypt, so he is known as Rameses the Great. Some of the statues in those temples are much, much bigger than the one here. His Greek name was Ozymandias. Does any one of you know the poem 'Ozymandias' by Shelley?"

They all shook their heads.

"The poem tells of a traveller finding a huge statue of Rameses in the desert, long, long after the pharaohs had all disappeared. On the pedestal he reads the words:

My name is Ozymandias, King of Kings;
Look on my Works, ye Mighty, and despair!

"Shelley is saying that even the mightiest of rulers could never challenge Rameses. Go where you will in the world, boys, and you will never find works to equal those of Rameses the Great."

They went round the other Egyptian galleries and the boys took a particular, ghoulish delight in examining the various caskets of mummies.

"Are the mummies really still in there, Father?" asked Gallagher.

"Yes," said Brompo, as several of the boys laughed in horrified fascination.

"Now, boys," continued Brompo, "I want you to make notes on what you have seen here and then we shall go to see the Elgin Marbles."

"What are the Elgin Marbles, Father?," said Docherty.

"The Elgin Marbles come from the Acropolis in Athens. Don't you remember? I showed you a picture of the Acropolis in class."

Several heads nodded.

Clancy asked why they were in the British Museum, rather than still on the Acropolis.

"Lord Elgin rescued them," replied the priest, "The Turks, who ruled Greece at the time, were using the Acropolis to store gunpowder. If he hadn't rescued them they might have been blown to pieces."

Heads nodded again. As they left the Egyptian gallery, Clancy noticed that there seemed to be fewer in their party. Worsely, in particular, was not with them. He decided not to mention it to Father Brompton, who was busy talking about the pharaoh Kufu, who built the Great Pyramid.

"Onwards to the Assyrian galleries, boys," said Brompo, after they had made the tour of the Elgin Marbles. "We will see the giant lion sculptures."

Clancy felt a sudden pang of hunger. He reached into his satchel and pulled out his sandwiches. Waiting just inside the door of the gallery, out of sight of the others, he wolfed down a sandwich in what seemed only a matter of seconds and then walked through the door, but, to his surprise, there was no sign of his party.

He could see nothing indicating where the Assyrian gallery was, nor any attendant who might help him, so he set off to find it. He trudged through galleries of Greek and Roman artefacts and beautiful objects from the Middle East and Asia and even to one that displayed something called the Sutton Hoo treasure, which he was intrigued to find had come from Suffolk. When he eventually found the Assyrian gallery there was no sign of Brompo and the others. He decided that he had better report himself missing.

He went to the information desk in the Museum entrance. A uniformed attendant adjusted his glasses and looked down on him.

"Yes?"

Clancy hesitated, embarrassed.

"Please sir, I wonder if you can help me. I need to find my school party."

The attendant scrutinised the badge on his school blazer.

"Is it the Campion school in Croydon?"

"Yes," replied Clancy, astonished.

"With Father Brompton are you?" said the attendant.

"Yes," said Clancy, even more astonished.

"Don't worry, sonny," said the attendant, smiling broadly, "We know Father Brompton. He always loses some on his way round. It was half a dozen last time. You're the first so far. Oh look, here's two more, if I'm not mistaken."

Clancy turned to see Worsley and Robinson walking towards them.

"Are you two with Father Brompton as well?" said the attendant.

"Yes," said Worsley, not at all embarrassed.

The attendant pointed to some benches.

"You can wait over there. I expect he'll be along soon."

"What happened to you?" said Clancy as they sat down.

"We went for a fag," said Worsely.

"What?"

"My brother told me that Brompo never notices if you go missing. He says there's a place outside the whatitsname." He turned to Robinson.

"The Reading Room," said Robinson.

"That's it, the Reading Room, behind the staircase. You can smoke there and nobody can see you. And you can look up girl's dresses when they go up the stairs."

"Did you see any?" said Clancy, before he could stop himself.

"Nah. It's only old geezers that go up there," said Robinson, with more than a hint of disappointment in his voice.

About a quarter of an hour later Brompo arrived, with his now diminished retinue in a long, straggling row behind.

"Three more for you here, Father," said the attendant.

"Thank you, thank you, Mister Benson," said the priest, beaming. "So good of you. I know I can always rely on the Brit Mus to collect our waifs and strays. We're all here, are we? Good. Now come along, boys, we need to hurry. We mustn't miss our train."

Saint Patrick's day

His mother pinned the bunch of shamrock to the lapel of Clancy's school blazer. It had come, as every year, from his grandmother in Mayo, in a little box with a picture of a leprechaun and stamps with a map of Ireland and something that looked liked *pingine* written on them. Pingine, his mother had explained, was Irish for pennies. Irish, he reflected, was an odd sort of language. It seemed to be what he was always told children were supposed to be – seen but not heard. It was on stamps and all the street signs, but he had never heard it spoken on the streets of Castlebar when they went back in the holidays. When he bought a *Beano* and the newsagent asked for fourpence, he had said "Don't you mean four pingine?" but the newsagent looked baffled, shook his head and said, "No, fourpence."

"Do I really have to, Mum?" he said, as his mother had stepped back, admiring how nice he looked in his school uniform.

"You know March the seventeenth is the feast day of Saint Patrick, Michael. Don't you want to celebrate Ireland's patron saint?"

Clancy wasn't sure. He hadn't minded wearing the shamrock when he was at primary school, because there would be several other kids in his class doing the same, but Campion was different. Although there were other boys in the class who had Irish parents, they all supported England at football and seemed to look down on anything Irish. He had a feeling that he would be embarrassed – the only boy in the class with a bunch of bedraggled foliage on his lapel.

He was right. As they trooped into assembly, several of his classmates sniggered as they caught sight of the shamrock. Even his friends, like Hearne and Docherty, couldn't suppress a smirk. That was enough. He unpinned the shamrock and put it carefully in his pocket. He would need to put it back again when he went home or else his mother would ask what had happened to it.

Father Muldoon sported a luxuriant garland of shamrock on his cassock, sent by cousins in Carlow. He looked round the class and was not surprised to see none of the boys with it. Too many Irish in England kept their heads down when it came to their patron saint. It was as if they were ashamed of where they had come from and didn't want their children to know about their native land. Too many of those children lapsed from their Catholic faith – or, even worse, became Protestants. Some of them even thought of themselves as English, but what sort of patron saint did England have? If you had trouble with dragons, Saint George would be your man, right enough, but didn't he come from somewhere like Turkey? The English didn't even have a saint they could call their own, so they had to have a Turkey. No wonder they all turned Protestant. Ireland didn't have to look abroad. Saint Patrick was the man to keep Catholic boys to the one true path. The more they knew about him and his glorious works, the more steadfast they would become.

"Boys, who can tell me what today is?"

Many hands went up.

"Yes, Gallagher?"

"Saint Patrick's day, Father."

"It is Saint Patrick's day and, as you all know, he is the patron saint of Ireland. In Ireland, Saint Patrick's day is a Holy Day of Obligation, when all good Catholics are obliged to go to mass, but in England it is not. Saint Patrick's day is celebrated in

America, in Australia and all over the world, but in England you hardly hear a word about it."

In Father Muldoon's opinion, the reason was that the English bishops were a lily-livered lot, all too willing to cringe if some Protestant English toff raised an eyebrow. Any mention of Saint Patrick and you see them there, heads down, pretending to pray. The Pope needed to put some backbone into them and give Saint Patrick his rightful place.

"Let me tell you about Saint Patrick, boys. He was born in the north of England, only it wasn't England then. The whole of England was part of the Roman Empire, which, thanks to the emperor Constantine, was Christian. When he was not much older than you he was captured by pirates and taken as a slave to Ireland, which was then entirely pagan. He was there for six years, looking after sheep and cattle, and all that time his love for God and his church grew greater and greater. Eventually he escaped, but he was determined one day to come back to Ireland to convert the Irish to the one true faith. So he set himself to study and was ordained a priest and then caught a ship to Ireland. The Irish flocked to hear him when he preached." He pointed to the shamrock on his chest. "Who can tell me what this is?"

Clancy felt he had to raise his hand.

"Yes, Clancy?"

"Shamrock, Father."

"Quite right, Clancy, it is shamrock. It only grows in Ireland and it has three leaves on the end of each stalk. Saint Patrick used it to explain the mystery of the Holy Trinity, which was causing more than a few that he was trying to convert to scratch their heads. He said it was simplicity itself. Just as there were three leaves on a single stalk, so there were three persons in one God. That convinced them. He converted thousands at a time, including kings and queens, and founded many monasteries and convents and soon the whole of Ireland was Catholic. He did another thing as well. Can anyone tell me what?"

No hands were raised. Father Muldoon shook his head at the display of ignorance.

"He banished the snakes from Ireland. No snake has dared show its face there since Saint Patrick sent them packing, no doubt back to England."

Clancy was impressed. The idea of shamrock and the Trinity might be stretching things a little, but a saint who could banish snakes was one to be taken seriously.

"There will be Benediction in special honour of Saint Patrick after school," continued Father Muldoon, "which I will be taking. We will also be singing 'Hail Glorious Saint Patrick, Dear Saint of Our Isle'. Make sure you are all in good voice."

Clancy wasn't sure about his voice, but he knew the words by heart. His mother sometimes put it a record of it on the gramophone, sung by a priest, much to the annoyance of his father.

Hail, glorious St Patrick, dear saint of our isle,
On us thy poor children bestow a sweet smile;
And now that you're high in your mansions above,
On Erin's green valleys look down with your love.
On Erin's green valleys, on Erin's green valleys,
On Erin's green valleys look down with your love.

Father Muldoon, too, knew the words by heart. 'Hail Glorious Saint Patrick' was the hymn to put Protestants in their place. They had nothing that could match it. Nor had they anything to match his other favourite, 'Full in the Panting Heart of Rome'.

Full in the panting heart of Rome,
Beneath th'apostle's crowning dome,
From pilgrims' lips that kiss the ground,

Breathes in all tongues only one sound:
God bless our Pope, God bless our Pope,
God bless our Pope, the great, the good.

'Full in the Panting Heart of Rome' was sure to send every Catholic heart soaring to the heavens. The Archbishop of Canterbury would be quaking in his boots if he heard it. The English bishops should sing both of them every day. That would put some backbone into them. There were too many carpers altogether in England where Saint Patrick was concerned – Father Finbar Fahey for one. Hadn't he been heard talking some nonsense in the school common room the other day, saying there had been two Saint Patricks and the one that did the conversions was not the one everyone thought? Just the sort of thing you would expect from that nest of vipers, Borris on Ossory, Count Laois. He wouldn't get away with that sort of talk in Ireland. His parish would be scandalised and his bishop would have very stern words to say indeed. He would be reminded that giving offence to pious ears was taken very seriously in Ireland. Everyone knows that there was only one Saint Patrick and that before he came to Ireland there were very few that were Christian and when he died there were very few that weren't.

That was something that needed celebrating and few knew how to celebrate better than the Irish. Father Muldoon's thoughts turned to the evening. The place to be was the South Croydon Irish Centre, where many a glass would be raised to the saint. The Casement Boys ceilidh band would be in full swing and the singing and dancing would go on well past midnight. Superintendent O' Driscoll had promised to keep the likes of that officious bluebottle, PC Perkins, well away from the celebrations, so that no one would be bothered making their way home. A great time was sure to be had by all.

Patron saints

It is clergy night at the South Croydon Catenians. Dinner (mock turtle soup, lamb cutlets, potatoes and cabbage and Spotted Dick) is finished and whiskies are being served. Father Muldoon is seated next to Superintendent O'Driscoll of the Metropolitan Police, Z-Division (Croydon).

"I'm off to Epsom tomorrow, Superintendent. I always go for the Derby. You're not a racing man yourself?"

"I'm not, Father, and besides, we're too busy on the day. Every pickpocket and his brother will be there for the Derby. Our lads will have their hands full."

"God bless their efforts. I shall feel all the safer knowing that Superintendent O'Driscoll and his boys are on the case."

"We'll do our best to see you and all the punters are looked after, Father. What do you do when you are there? Do you have a bet or two?"

"Just a little one, Superintendent. I always like to have a shilling or two on the race. It adds to the fun. I like to see the Irish horses in the Parade Ring, before the race. Proud and mighty, all of them. They show the English horses the way home. All an English horse ever sees is the rump of an Irish horse disappearing in the distance. And I like to see the jockeys too. Most of them Irish, of course. English jockeys hardly know one end of a horse from the other."

"What about Lester Piggott, Father?"

"Lester Piggott is a very fine jockey, no question. Wasn't his grandfather from Sligo?"

"Was he, Father? I didn't know that."

"Not many do, Superintendent. He keeps it quiet, so I'm told."

"Oh, I suppose he would. He wouldn't want to let on to the other English jockeys."

"I don't think he would give tuppence for the English jockeys, Superintendent. They're none of them in his class. English jockeys are only fit to be sat on the also-rans. If you put all the English jockeys in a sellers' plate, you would be lucky to get five pounds for the lot."

"I won't be bidding, myself, Father, that's for sure. By the way, did I see you going into Mayday Hospital the other day? I was there to have the auld corns fixed. You do a lot of walking if you're a policeman."

"You might see me in the Mayday any day, Superintendent. The school gives me time off regularly to visit. I've been going these many years."

"And very welcome you must be, Father. I suppose you must know a thing or two about medicine by now?"

"I do, indeed, Superintendent. Ministering to the sick and dying is as good as any medical school. I can often tell what's wrong with someone just by looking at them. A doctor said to me only the other day, 'If I didn't know better, Father, I would have said you were a medical man.' Now doctors can do wonders these days, but there is one thing greater than all the operations and potions of this world and that's the power of faith."

"I'm sure that's right, Father."

"It is, indeed Superintendent. The power of faith and the last rites of the Church are better than any medicine. Many's the time I've gone into Mayday, past the wards full of the sick and dying, most of them Protestant, of course. Half of them bound for Hell, I'd wager."

"What about the other half, Father?"

"Who can say, Superintendent? God must have somewhere to put Protestants, I suppose. I've gone there to see a poor soul whose life has been totally despaired of. The relatives are all sitting around, sobbing and waiting for the end. I say the prayers and do the anointing and, like as not, in half an hour the patient is sitting up, taking tea and chatting like you and I."

"Would that be a miracle, Father?"

"Only the Pope can say that for certain, Superintendent. I just say it's the power of faith. Saint Jude will have a hand in it as well."

"Saint Jude, Father?"

"Saint Jude is the patron saint of lost causes, Superintendent. If all hope is abandoned, then Saint Jude is your man. Not enough is made of patron saints these days, in my opinion. A word in the right saint's ear can work wonders."

"Is that right, Father?"

"It is indeed, but you must choose your saint. Take Saint Francis of Assisi now. You never get anything but first-class service from him. A prayer to Saint Francis of Assisi is as good as money in the bank. The answer always comes by return of post, without fail. Saint Francis of Assisi will never let you down. I wish I could say the same of Saint Benignus, though."

"Saint Benignus? What's he the patron saint of, Father?"

"He's the man for socks."

"Socks, Father?"

"You know when you have a drawerful of socks and you can't find two the same. Father Dermot Duignan, he was in my year at Maynooth, he's a PP down in Clare now, swore blind that a word to Saint Benignus and you would have a matched pair in your hands in a couple of ticks. I tried it half a dozen times at least and was left standing there like a fool, with just one sock in my hand every time. I don't like to say this about a blessed saint, Superintendent, but I reckon he's sleeping on the job. There's good people praying to him to find their socks and Saint Benignus is taking forty winks. I don't know why the Pope gave him socks at all."

"I suppose the Pope must have his reasons, Father. Is that Frankie Fahey the bookie I see, coming over here?"

"It is indeed, Superintendent, coming to apologise for the whisky he's foisted on us, I would hope. 'Spirit of the Highlands'. What sort of whisky do you call that? I bet it was brewed and bottled a long way from Scotland. The Japanese, I'm told, have taken to making cheap whisky like they make cheap everything else."

"How are you, Father. Grand to see you again."

"I'm grand, Frankie. How's yourself?"

"Grand, too, Father. Our Knights of St Columba have just had their first meeting. I'm off to see the Archbishop soon. I'm hoping he'll say high mass for us in the cathedral."

"That's grand, Frankie, and the wife too? Is she well?"

"Philomena is in great form, Father. She's off with the parish to Lourdes next week. Miracles or not, it's always a fine thing to go to Lourdes. The parish has arranged for everyone who goes to receive a plenary indulgence and a special Lourdes medal. Oh, is that his honour, Justice Daly, over there? I heard he's just been appointed to the bench. I must have a word."

"That's Frankie Fahey for you, Superintendent. Buttering up the judges now. There's no end to his wiliness."

"I've been think about what you were saying, Father. Do you think we could have Saint Francis of Assisi for the patron saint of Croydon Police? We could do with a little help in catching thieves and murderers?"

"I would say there was very little chance there, Superintendent. Saint Francis is awfully busy already. He's the patron saint of Italy and has all them Italians to look after for a start, and you know how them Italians kick up a fuss about every little thing that happens to them. And then there are all the birds and the bees and the animals, of which he was specially fond. There has to be fair do's for saints, Superintendent. The Pope is very strict on fair do's for saints. He makes sure the work is fairly shared. There's no point in getting to Heaven if you have to spend all your time looking after us down here."

"Oh I see that, Father."

"Besides, what would happen if you did get Saint Francis of Assisi? Saint Francis would do the business all right. You'd have every thief and murderer in London behind bars before you could say Jesus, Mary and Joseph, and then you'd be sitting there with your feet up and the kettle on."

"Wouldn't that be grand, Father."

"Oh would it now, Superintendent, would it now? Have you thought of the consequences? Say what you like about the English, but they're cute enough when it comes to money."

"You're right there, Father."

"None cuter, I dare say, than the ratepayers of London."

"I'd say you weren't wrong there, either, Father."

"And what are the ratepayers of London going to say to themselves, Superintendent, when they see what's going on? They are going to say 'Why are we paying for the boys in blue to sit with their feet up drinking tea *when Saint Francis of Assisi is doing all the work*?'"

"Do you think they'd say that, Father?"

"Oh, they'd say a lot more, Superintendent. The ratepayers of London are not famous for making free with the contents of their wallets. They'd say 'Thanks for everything, Superintendent O'Driscoll. Here's the watch for your thirty years' service.' And then they'd hand you your cards and allow you to put your feet up and drink tea at your own expense. And then where would you be? Haven't you two girls at the Ursuline convent down in Wimbledon?"

"I have, Father. The apple of their mother's eye – and mine too, of course."

"Two of the finest Catholic girls in England, I have no doubt. Quality is always worth paying for, but quality like you get from Ursuline nuns does not come cheap, so I hear."

"It does not, Father. Many a time we've had to scrimp and save."

"Worth every penny, of course, but if you're on the dole you would have to take them out of the convent and send them out to be skivvies. I expect Mrs O'Driscoll would have something to say about that."

"She would, Father, she would. Words would be said."

"'Superintendent O'Driscoll,' she would say to you, *'Superintendent O'Driscoll,I did not bring two fine Catholic girls into this world to be skivvies to the likes of the English!'"*

"Oh, spot on, Father, spot on. You must be a mind reader. Those would be her very words."

"So they would be, good woman that she is. So, instead of Saint Francis of Assisi, I have another patron saint who I think will do the job for you – Saint Plodraigh."

"Saint Plodraigh, Father? Remind me what he did."

"He was a monk in Saint Kevin's time. He was looking after the holy vessels in the monastery one night, when a pair of brigands came looking to rob it. Brave Saint Plodraigh tried to stop them, but they showed him no mercy. They cut the head right off him and left it lying on the ground. The other monks found the head the next morning and it was still talking. It told them what had happened and where to find the thieves."

"Was that a miracle, Father?"

"I'd say it was, Superintendent. They found the brigands lying in a drunken stupor, with their ill-gotten gains all around them. They were marched off smartly and given their just deserts. Just deserts is what you got in those days. Not like today. The way things are going in England, Superintendent, you will soon be getting no more than a ten-shilling fine for murder. I don't know what has got into English judges these days."

"You're right there, Father. They're too soft altogether. We're working with one hand tied behind our back. There's nothing like a good hanging to put the fear of God into the villains round here."

"Fear of God is a marvellous thing, Superintendent, but sometimes you have to try a different tack. So I think you could do yourself a lot of good by sticking with Saint Plodraigh. His name may not be in lights like some saints you could think of. He may not have all the fancy cathedrals and basilicas named after him, but I'm told he is very effective in his own quiet way. A word in his ear, followed by a decade or two of the rosary, and you can be sure of feeling your miscreant's collar in no time. And Saint Plodraigh doesn't ask for credit. You never hear anyone saying 'Thanks be to Saint Plodraigh!' No, Saint Plodraigh lets you take all the credit. Keep on his right side and you'll catch criminals by the bucketload — and be paid handsomely for it. Isn't that what you want a patron saint for?"

The other St Patrick

Father Finbar Fahey felt himself swinging between high elation and deep misgivings. He felt as he would if he had just pulled off a particularly tricky chemistry experiment. He was in his room, putting the finishing touches to his article that he hoped would be published in the *Irish Journal of Ecumenical Studies* and that he was sure would put more than a few cats among pigeons in the fustian world of early Celtic scholarship. His thesis was that the cult of Saint Patrick was the creation of later hagiographers, writing long after the events, bolstered by Patrick's self-serving account of his life in his *Confessio*. Early fifth-century Ireland, far from being entirely pagan, already had a growing number of Christians before Patrick began his mission. Patrick had simply capitalised on this tide, specialising in converting nobles and the wealthy, particularly wealthy women, from whom he received many gifts.

He was sure that the historical enquiry was pointing one way. He was drawing on the work of the late Professor Thomas O'Rahilly, who in 1942 had given a lecture entitled 'The Two Patricks' that claimed that much of what was ascribed to Patrick was actually the work of Palladius, who had been sent to Ireland in 431 by Pope Celestine I. Precious little thanks did Professor O'Rahilly receive for his efforts. The ructions resounded from Dublin to Donegal, almost eclipsing ructions elsewhere in the world, as cleric and scholar alike condemned his impiety. Intrigued, Father Fahey had immersed himself in study of those times and come to the conclusion that Professor O'Rahilly had not gone far enough. Patrick was not only a johnny-come-lately, but a bit of a con man and quite possibly a swindler as well.

The more he read of 'The Two Patricks', the more convinced he became. The name Palladius, as Professor O'Rahilly had pointed out, was used by academics, but the annals suggest he was also called Patricius or Patrick. He was sent by Pope Celestine to minister to the Christian Irish as their bishop. Christianity had already taken strong root several decades before, due to missionaries from Britain, with such figures as Saint Ciarán of Saigir, who had been the bishop of Ossory. Father Fahey had a particularly soft spot for Saint Ciarán, since he himself came from Borris on Ossory. He considered that much of the groundwork for the wholesale conversion of Ireland had been laid by Palladius/Patrick, who brought together the existing Christian communities and built churches in many parts of the south of the country.

Later historians, even up to the present day, had tried to write Palladius/Patrick out of history by claiming that the second Patrick had returned to Ireland on his mission in the year 432, finding Ireland almost entirely pagan, and died in 461. However, as O'Rahilly comments, there are well-attested records of more than a dozen bishops who had worked with Patrick, dying decades into the sixth century, forty to seventy years after Patrick's supposed death. That seems unlikely. Instead O'Rahilly suggests that the two Patricks had been conflated into one. Palladius/Patrick's mission lasted from 431 to about 461 and the true date of the second Patrick's arrival was almost certainly decades later than normally assumed, around 461; he died in 492 or 493. These historians also downplay the fact that Patrick was put on trial by his fellow Christians for unspecified financial misdeeds. Patrick himself glosses over the event in his *Confessio,* claiming that he returned gifts from wealthy women and did not take payments for baptisms or ordinations. It is by no means clear that he was believed. Did Patrick, like many a self-glorifying evangelist since, use God to get rich?

Why then the cult of Patrick? Father Fahey had thought long and hard about the question and had come, very reluctantly, to the conclusion that neither Irish Church nor state were any longer capable of separating fact from myth – or would want to. Questioning national icons, especially one so firmly ensconced in the national psyche as Saint Patrick, was a mug's game. Anyone who did so would be roundly abused by everyone from TDs in the Dail and clerics in the pulpits to the brewers of stout and the growers of shamrock and would receive precious little support, even from those who agreed. Better to keep heads down and use the acknowledged uncertainties of dates and events to allow "Saint" Patrick his little-deserved renown. As the reporter says at the end of one of his favourite films, *The Man Who Shot Liberty Vallance*:, "When the legend becomes the fact, print the legend."

That evening he was due to go to the to help with the Saint Patrick's night party in Saint Mary's church hall. Nurses and staff from the Mayday hospital would prepare the food and drink for any Irish who had nowhere else to go on the night. Most were older men, some retired, others still working, usually on the many building sites around Croydon, all bearing the scars of hard work and even harder drinking. The Guinness would flow ad lib. It had to be that way, as he knew, otherwise very few of them would come. He would, as usual, try to talk to them. Some would be glad of a bit of conversation, others would prefer to nurse their pints in silence, perhaps musing on things long past. They had been decades in England and most had never married. Their families, like many in Ireland, had long since been dispersed to the four corners of the world, so there was no point in returning. This was all the home they had. Father Fahey said a silent prayer for them and added, as he did every day, one for his brother, Martin, who had been killed on a building site in Manchester, ten years before.

The Strap

Father Muldoon spotted his quarry walking unsuspecting along the corridor between classrooms.

"Come here, Clancy."

Clancy felt a familiar apprehension, knowing he must be guilty of something, but not knowing of exactly what.

"Yes, Father?"

The priest looked Clancy up and down before continuing. His expression told the boy that he was not impressed by his appearance.

"Clancy, I have been told by a prefect that you were seen leaving this school without wearing a cap."

Clancy racked his brains desperately for an answer. He couldn't just deny it. That would make any punishment worse.

"My cap doesn't fit any more, Father."

Father Muldoon shook his head scornfully.

"Is your head so swollen with self-importance that no cap will fit it, Clancy?"

"No, Father."

"Can I remind you, Clancy, that wearing a school cap, blazer and tie while going to and from school is a requirement for all boys from this school. Are you not proud of this school and proud to wear its uniform?"

"Yes, Father."

"I understand that a new cap costs twenty-two shillings and sixpence. Are you saying that your parents cannot afford to ensure that you are properly dressed for this school?"

"No, Father."

"I'm sure they are only too willing to make sure that you are a credit to them, good, hard-working, Catholic people that I know they are. I shall write to your parents suggesting that they take you to the school outfitters and fit you with a cap big enough for that swollen head of yours."

Clancy felt his face flush with embarrassment. He could think of nothing to say.

"Now Clancy," continued the priest, "your punishment is two of the strap. Make sure it doesn't happen again. I will not be so lenient next time."

He pulled out a notebook from his cassock pocket, scrawled on it, then peeled off a leaf and handed it to Clancy.

"Make sure you go after school and bring this chit back to me, signed, first thing tomorrow."

"Yes, Father."

***

Clancy nervously joined the queue of boys outside the strap room after lessons finished at four. He had been at the school for over a year, but this was his first time for the strap. Not so for most of the others. They jeered when he told them that he had got it for not wearing a cap, and jeered again when he said he had only got two.

"You're an idiot," said Elms, a third-former. "Everyone knows Muldoon's on the warpath. He gets like that every now and again. I'd stay out of his way if I were you."

A bit late for that, thought Clancy. He asked what the others were there for. There was the usual collection of talking in class, cheek and missing homework.

"I got six for cheating in a French vocab test," said, Elms. "I stuck the answers on the back of Lacy, who was sitting in front of me, only he turned round and Muggridge saw it. He was going to give Lacy six too, only I said he didn't know anything about it."

"Lacy would have bashed you up if you hadn't," said McDowell, another third-former. Elms shrugged. Clancy asked McDowell what his crime was.

"Breathing," said McDowell.

"Breathing?" said Clancy, not sure if he had heard aright.

"Yeah, breathing in Greek. Lovelace gave me four."

"How could he give you the strap for breathing?" said Clancy

"And what'd he give you if you stopped?" said Elms.

"You thickos don't know how lucky you are," said McDowell, "In Greek every word that begins with a vowel has to have a breathing. It's a little squiggle above the letter. If it goes one way it's like the word begins with an 'h'. If it goes the other way it's silent. Every time you forget to put a breathing on a word, Lovelace gives you a stroke. He calls it the 'breathing treatment'."

There was general agreement that this was a particular injustice, not that they imagined that there was anything they could do about it. The other thing they couldn't do anything about was which strap master was on duty.

"I hope it's DeAth," said Elms, "He only flicks the strap. You hardly feel it."

"I heard he doesn't believe in corporal punishment, which is why the school said he had to do it," said McDowell.

"Anyone get eight?" asked Elms.

They all shook their heads.

"And no double-eights?" said Elms, to general amusement. Double-eight was the nuclear option, given for only the most heinous of offences, though nobody was quite sure what they might be.

"You'd have to hit a master to get double-eight," said McDowell.

"I think you'd get expelled for that," replied Elms.

Heads nodded in agreement. You probably would be expelled if you hit a master.

"What if you hit a priest?" said McDowell.

There was silence for a few seconds while they contemplated this possibility.

"You'd get expelled and excommunicated," said Elms.

Heads nodded again. You definitely would be expelled *and* excommunicated if you hit a priest.

Clancy tried to keep his fear from showing in front of the other boys, who all seemed less fearful, though he wondered whether it was just bravado. He looked down the corridor and saw a tall, upright figure approaching.

"Oh no," said Elms, "It's Flogger."

Crispin Aubrey St John Flinders, the Senior Strap Master, known less than affectionately as Flogger, looked along the queue for the strap room, noting the presence of several of the usual suspects, before unlocking the door and entering. He took down the Strap Register from a shelf and entered the date at the top of a new page in his immaculate copperplate writing, the result of long, tedious hours spent practising calligraphy at his minor public school. Its ethos of muscular Christianity and a disdain for all things intellectual was thought to be the ideal grounding for a career in the military. In the early summer of 1939, Flinders had found himself in the RAF, just before war was declared. He had, as he acknowledged himself, a good war, mostly spent in planning bomber raids over Germany, and rising to the titular rank of Squadron Leader, without ever actually flying a plane.

After the war, as a regular officer, he remained in the RAF. He met and married a girl whose Irish Catholic parents had a morbid dread of "mixed" marriages and only consented to the union if he converted, fearing that otherwise their grandchildren might fall prey to the Devil and all his works and pomps. He had no problem with conversion. He had rather liked the Catholic padres he had met, much preferring their often alcoholic bonhomie to the prissy C of E types that hung around the mess. The Catholic traditions of arcane ritual and unthinking obedience to superiors also suited his military temperament. When his time in the RAF came to an end, his parish priest found him a place in a Catholic teachers' training college and so he became a school-teacher.

His chosen subject was geography. He took a particular pleasure in maps. He could not see a map without planning a raid. He would mentally choose the route for the Pathfinders to drop their flares so that the bombers could follow in. He would plan bombing approaches, dependent on weather and wind direction. He would note the high points where anti-aircraft batteries might be located and the flatter areas where enemy airfields might be situated, so that he could plot a home route for the bombers.

Once a year he would demonstrate to the boys in his fifth-form class how, if he had been in charge of the Luftwaffe, he would plan and execute a raid on the school, bringing in Heinkels and Dorniers from bases in Holland, over the North Sea and along the Thames to Greenwich, then striking south-west until they saw the Brighton Road, which would then give them the best angle of approach with, in his estimate, a 90 per cent chance of destroying the target, Blessed Edmund Campion School. It was agreed by boys who attended that this was the highlight of the year.

His military training made him a natural choice for Strap Master. He had always believed that corporal punishment was in the natural order of things and was pleased that mortification of the flesh, by self or others, also had a special place in Catholicism. It was his duty to impose discipline that was strict and sure. He had never shirked from that duty.

Clancy watched as, one by one, the boys in front of him in the queue came out shaking and blowing on their reddened hands.

"He's in a bad mood," said McDowell, while Elms said nothing as he walked away, but alternately blew on his hands and then jammed them up under his armpits. Clancy reached the head of the queue and felt himself begin to tremble. He heard the word "Next" and walked, almost in a trance, into the room. He stood there in silence, until Flinders said, "Where is your chit, boy?"

"Oh, sorry Sir."

He pulled the chit out of his pocket. Flinders took it and wrote the details into the Strap Book. He then stood and picked up the heavy brown strap.

"Hold out your hand."

Flinders seemed to make not much more than a flick of the wrist, a long practised technique that inflicted maximum pain with minimum effort.

"Now the other hand."

With each blow Clancy felt a sharp, intense, spasm of pain and then came its throbbing aftermath as his hands reddened. Flinders signed the chit and handed it back. It was all Clancy's fingers could do to grasp it. He turned quickly and walked out of the room, so that Flinders would not see how his eyes glistened.

The next morning, before school started, he joined the other boys outside Father Muldoon's room, waiting to hand back their signed chits.

Father Wendell

Father Wendell was in love. He was always falling in love. That was why he became a priest.

The object of his *amor* was Archer, a sixth-former, destined soon for Oxford. Archer was tall, lithe and blond, everything that Father Wendell was not. He had that all-too-fleeting bloom of youth and his slightly aquiline features gave him just a touch of haughtiness. He was, thought Father Wendell, almost perfect.

Father Wendell was untroubled by his feelings. On the contrary, for him they were spiritually uplifting. He had long learnt that urges of the flesh need to be sublimated, not suppressed.

It was a lesson that took some learning. On ordination, he had chosen as his confessor a lantern-jawed, Scots Jesuit of impeccable doctrinal rectitude, who, while uber-Catholic, had something of the demeanour of a John Knox, but without his lightness of touch. He was set a rigorous programme of spiritual exercises that reduced Father Wendell within a short time to an emotional, as well as spiritual, wreck. It became apparent to the young Father Wendell that his confessor was, like too many Jesuits, an over-brained psychopath. He needed to look elsewhere for spiritual sustenance.

Art proved his salvation. Art in the form of the much-portrayed Saint Sebastian – that perfect body accepting the exquisite agony of the arrows for his faith. The transformation of pain and anguish into the sublime. The walls of his small room were adorned with prints of the saint by Botticelli, Perugino, Titian, Caravaggio, Mantegna and El Greco, as well as with photographs of his dear, departed mother and his long-estranged sister. At times, he preferred ecstatic, many-arrowed versions, like that of Mantegna, at others he found solace in contemplating the single arrow piercing the breast of Caravaggio's almost insouciant Sebastian. It depended on his mood.

His confessor now was an aged priest, half blind, almost deaf and teetering on the edge of dementia, who listened to everything said to him with the same serene expression, said almost nothing in reply, and whose honeyed words, *ego te absolvo*, came as balm to Father Wendell's soul.

As he prepared to go to his next lesson, his thoughts turned to the school play that, rather against his better judgement, he had agreed to direct. He had chosen 'Richard III' and then discovered that there was a dearth of acting talent amongst the boys who had volunteered to take part. The only one who did have some talent also had a distinct lisp. He wasn't sure how "Now ith the winter of our dithcontent made glorious thummer by thith thon of York" would go down with the audience of parents and relatives. He decided to cast his net wider. Compulsory auditions were called for.

His next lesson was English, with the fourth form. Father Wendell regarded himself as a theological progressive and was rather dismissive of the idea of Purgatory, but had to admit that, if it did exist, it must be very like teaching an unruly, hormonally-unbalanced pack of acne-ridden, adolescent schoolboys.

As he entered the classroom and stepped onto the dais, he was aware, as always, of the inaudible, simmering, inchoate resentment felt about everything by boys of that age. He needed to counter it, so he had chosen as the text for the lesson *The Ballad of Reading Gaol* by Oscar Wilde – full, as it was, of blood, guts and jealous rage, things bound to grab their attention from the first verse.

He did not wear his scarlet coat,
For blood and wine are red,
And blood and wine were on his hands

When they found him with the dead,
The poor dead woman whom he loved,
And murdered in her bed.

He had briefly contemplated explaining the context in which Wilde had written the poem, then decided against – not with boys of this age. They would simply giggle at something they saw as smut.

He set each to read a verse in turn. It went surprisingly well. The readings were more lively than usual and the class showed every sign of interest. Working his way through the class, he came inevitably, if reluctantly, to Kelly. Kelly was a large, ungainly creature, whose pudgy, pockmarked face always had a supercilious expression and who saw himself as both class clown and class bully. He began reading.

Yet each man kills the thing he loves,
By each let this be heard,
Some do it with a bitter look,
Some with a flattering word,
The coward does it with a kiss

Father Wendell was already anticipating the next line,

The brave man with a sword!

when he heard a snigger.

He looked up."Is there something funny, Kelly?"

Kelly was clearly trying to hide a grin.

"No, Father."

"So is there something about Wilde's poem that you don't like?"

Kelly's grin turned to a smirk.

"Wasn't he a poof, Father?"

There were a few sniggers from Kelly's cronies and audible gasps from the rest of the class. Father Wendell fixed Kelly with a hard stare. He knew this was a dangerous moment. Kelly, in his blundering way, was testing him, pushing on what he thought was the priest's weak spot. He could not give an inch. Order in the classroom was always easy to lose and hard to regain.

"What exactly do you mean by 'a poof', Kelly?"

Kelly looked around, as if for support, but the rest of the class kept their heads down. All that came out was "Erm, um, um..."

"Well, Kelly," said Father Wendell, "if you can't explain, perhaps we should consult the dictionary. How would you spell 'poof'?"

Kelly realised he had to answer.

"P-o-o-f, I think, Father."

Father Wendell opened the dictionary and flicked through the pages.

"Ah yes, here it is. I see there is an alternative spelling: 'poof, see pouffe', spelled p-o-u-f-f-e. Let's see what that is."

He turned a couple of pages.

"Yes, this is it. Pouffe, p-o-u-f-f-e, a padded footstool."

There was a sudden, explosive burst of laughter from the class. Kelly's smirk turned sickly.

It was Father Wendell's turn to smile.

"You may remember, Kelly, in the unlikely event that you were paying attention, that we have discussed the role of metaphor in literature in this class, but you need to help me here. Try as I might, I fail to see any connection, metaphorical or otherwise, between one of our finest literary stylists and a piece of furniture?"

Again the laughter was loud. Father Wendell turned the screw.

"And why a footstool, Kelly? Why not an armchair? Or a table? Or a sideboard? Or even – and here, perhaps, I can see the faintest of connections – a *chaise longue*?"

Kelly's expression had turned to bafflement.

"*Chaise longue*, Kelly, is French, a language with which, I understand from Mr Muggeridge, you are almost entirely unacquainted, despite supposedly studying it at this school for the last four years. It literally means long chair and a *chaise longue* is a low settee with a curved back at one end. The Victorians were very fond of *chaises longues,* Kelly. Oscar Wilde was photographed on one more than once and his friend, Mrs Pat Campbell, the actress, was said to have exchanged the hurly-burly of the *chaise longue* for the deep, deep peace of the double bed."

Father Wendell smiled again, this time more benignly.

"I imagine, Kelly, that you have yet to experience either."

Kelly, deflated, sat down amidst the laughter. The reading continued, to evident enjoyment.

The lesson ended. As Father Wendell left the classroom he felt elation, even if it was tinged with a tiny prick of conscience at having humiliated a pupil in his charge. Examination of conscience could come later. Besides, he knew from the class that, for all their resentment of authority, what they really wanted was order. They wanted him to be in control. Kelly was just a necessary casualty for a greater good.

He went through a door and down onto the path that ran alongside the school's playing fields and tennis courts. He was walking, still absorbed in his elation, when he saw something that made his heart almost stop. Archer had just walked off the tennis court and was crossing the path in front of him. Father Wendell stared, transfixed, as Archer strode with an easy, swinging gait, racquet in hand and sweater swung carelessly across the shoulders, the patina of sweat still on his face. As if aware he was being watched, Archer turned his head towards him. A faint smile appeared on his face and then an even fainter sneer, before he turned his head away, went up some steps and disappeared into the school building.

Father Wendell stood stock still, mortified. Then he turned and walked, head bowed, quickly towards the chapel. He entered at the back and knelt down in the nearest pew. The late afternoon sunlight streamed through a high window onto a couple of younger boys kneeling in the front pews, awaiting confession, doubtless wanting to be shriven of their masturbatory fantasies to avoid explaining to parents why they were not taking communion at Sunday mass. He felt in his pocket for an old, worn medal of Saint Sebastian, that he had picked up years ago in Rome, and squeezed hard. He felt the pain as the edges dug into the flesh of his fingers. He continued squeezing. The edges were not sharp enough to draw blood. They were not arrows, but at least there would be some bruising, some token of atonement. He tried to pray and the words of Saint Augustine of Hippo came to him.

> Too late have I loved you, O Beauty so ancient, O Beauty so new. Too late have I loved you! You were within me but I was outside myself, and there I sought you! In my weakness I ran after the beauty of the things you have made. You were with me, and I was not with you.

Could he ever be with Him? Father Wendell closed his eyes and a single tear ran slowly down his cheek.

School dinners

Clancy fought the urge to gag as he prodded the slimy lump on his plate with a fork. Was it fish? He couldn't be sure. A distinctly rancid smell was coming from the liquid that surrounded it. Two potatoes and what had once been carrots on his plate seemed to have given up the ghost and were slowly being dissolved in the liquid. Friday dinners were always the worst. Fridays, according to the Church, were days of abstinence from meat and that meant fish. Fish, thought Clancy, must be another of the penances that the Church insisted on imposing on the faithful. Every mouthful surely meant a few days off the time he would spend in Purgatory.

Looking around, he saw other boys at his table gazing disconsolately at their plates. "I'm not eating this crap," whispered Hearne, although a few of the hardier were hungry enough to start eating. Clancy was about to agree, but he saw Father Arundell, who was on refectory duty, looking down on their table. There was no choice. He picked up a piece of supposed fish on his fork and put it in his mouth. It tasted every bit as bad as it looked and smelt.

Friday dinners might always be the worst, but, as Clancy was all too aware, that was saying little. The school believed in the notion that food for schoolboys should be no more than fuel, to ensure that boys could remain conscious and did not expire on school premises. Notions of taste or enjoyment were irrelevant. To that end, it employed Nurse Connolly.

Nurse Connolly – she was always known as "Nurse", although nobody knew why; she had no medical qualifications that anybody knew of – was a chain-smoking, red-haired Offaly woman of about fifty, who ruled the school kitchens with a rod of iron. Fuelled as she was by Woodbines and whisky, her temper was legendary. Nobody – priest, master or boy – dared cross her.

Nurse Connolly was a firm follower of that strain of Irish Catholicism that considered all urges of the flesh to be potentially sinful and no punishment too harsh for transgressors. Hell itself might not be enough for some. That was why Ireland had Magdalene Laundries.

It was well known that young boys have no control over their appetite. Gluttony was one of the seven deadly sins, so those in charge of them were morally bound to ensure that food must be as unappetising as possible to protect the young and avoid the occasion of that sin. All food should be boiled – not fried or grilled – until it was reduced to a grey mush. The only vegetables allowed were potatoes, carrots and cabbage; the only meat was "meat" and the only fish was "fish", both as defined by the supplier.

Nurse Connolly supervised the cooking seated at her table in the kitchen with her familiars, Bridie and Rosie. Bridie came from the same town as Nurse Connolly and was of a similar vintage. She provided her with endless, disparaging gossip about the other kitchen staff, the boys and their parents at the school, the goings-on in her parish, the awful state of everything in England, and much else besides. Rosie came from somewhere in Connaught – she never said exactly where. She said almost nothing at all. Her main task was to provide Nurse Connolly with a new packet of Woodbines whenever she ran out.

Nurse Connolly was in the habit of pouring herself a regular tot of her favourite whisky, contained in a Lucozade bottle that she kept on her table. On some days she would offer tots to Rosie and Bridie; that was usually the cue for a song. A particular favourite was 'I Dreamt I Dwelt in Marbled Halls'.

She had a strict hierarchy of preference when it came to dinners. At the top was the Canon's dog, Malachy, an Irish Setter, whose mahogany-coloured coat she insisted one of the kitchen maids groom every day. Malachy ate only choice cuts of meat from a local butcher – not from the usual school suppliers – and had his own bowl and basket in a corner of the kitchen. Every day, a little after twelve, he would amble into the kitchen, look around in the supercilious way of setters, ensconce himself in the basket and wait expectantly for his meal. Woe betide the maid who made him wait. She would feel Nurse Connolly's wrath.

Next in her hierarchy were the priests, who supervised at dinner. (Any master unwise enough voluntarily to supervise was given what the boys ate and never volunteered again.) That day it was Father Arundell, who requested poached haddock, new potatoes and peas, which was what he got, more or less.

That Friday, the supplier had sent only half the ordered amount of fish. After consulting her bottle of whisky, Nurse Connolly peered inside one of the fridges and found some fish left over from a previous Friday – she wasn't sure which – and decided it would have to do. She set the kitchen maids to work, giving orders as the meals were prepared.

"Will ye wake up and do the job, Bridget Murphy, or I'll have ye back home before your feet can touch the ground," she yelled at a kitchen maid who was holding her nose and poking a wooden spoon at a large cauldron.

Most of the kitchen staff came from Ireland, recruited by Nurse Connolly on her trips home. The two exceptions were the "foreigners", Josefina and Maria, from Spain. Josefina, a passionate, dark-haired, dark-eyed young woman in her twenties, wore tight dresses which emphasised her ample bosom and which tended to ride up and expose a glimpse of stocking top when she bent over. She was an object of lust to all the adolescent boys at the school, but any unwise enough to take matters further would be repulsed by a tirade of Spanish oaths, both blasphemous and scatological, and would slink away, utterly detumescent. Maria, by contrast, was a short, dumpy woman in late middle age, whose main object in life seemed to be to act as surrogate mother to Josefina and prevent her from letting her temperament get her into too much trouble.

That day Nurse Connolly had been generous with the whisky and "I Dreamed You Loved Me Still", in differing keys and registers, could be heard above the clatter of cutlery and plates, just as Father Mostyn made one of his visits to the kitchens.

Father Mostyn was the most handsome priest in England. Beneath lustrous, wavy, black hair were long-lashed, deep blue eyes and a wide, sensuous mouth, all set in a perfectly symmetrical face with a flawless complexion. He was so beautiful that he caused trouble wherever he went. Parish priests to whom he was sent as curate would soon demand he be posted elsewhere, because Legion of Mary mothers were in a continual tizzy over him, children were neglected, husbands belittled. Women of the parish would insist on cloistering themselves in the confessional with him, dredging up all sorts of imaginary sins in the hope of prolonging their sessions, while others would send him presents, often books of a devotional nature, with coyly suggestive messages written inside. A convent to which he was sent as chaplain found that its nuns had begun to doubt their vocation. A bishop decided to appoint him as his personal chaplain and then insisted that they spend much time each day alone, discussing the finer points of Catholic doctrine, to the consternation of senior clergy of the diocese and the jealousy of other bishops.

Through all this, Father Mostyn went in a cloud of unknowing. He was serenely unaware of any effect he had on people. He accepted without question all the tenets of the Church. He had no problems with priestly celibacy and never felt tempted to break his vow. He always assumed that the motives of others were as pure as his own and would not listen to anyone who tried to tell him otherwise. That was the final straw as far as the

Church hierarchy was concerned. The full horror of the situation dawned. It was clear that Father Mostyn was that greatest of all dangers to faith, morals and the authority of the Church – a Holy Fool.

Things could not have been more serious. Where to put Father Mostyn? After much discussion, accompanied, if not actually aided, by masses, novenas and prayers from the more pious of the clergy, it was decided that he should go where he would have the least effect – a Catholic boys school run by priests who could keep an eye on him. So he was sent to Blessed Edmund Campion.

As he had no qualifications or experience in teaching, he was told to take the younger boys for subjects that required neither: religious instruction and Latin. He was also asked to supervise the kitchens, because none of the other priests cared to risk the ire of Nurse Connolly.

As always, Father Mostyn's entry to the kitchen caused a stir. Maids simpered and curtseyed. Nurse Connolly quickly doused her cigarette, hid the Lucozade bottle and rushed forward, gushing.

"How are you today, Father? Isn't it a grand day? Won't you have a little something to eat to keep you going?"

Father Mostyn always declined her offers. Not because he knew about the food from the kitchen. He had never tasted it. He had given up eating a midday meal as a small penance.

For Josefina, the effect of Father Mostyn was always electric. She stood rigid, almost catatonic, staring at him, and when he left she began to howl. He had looked at her and smiled, so she howled because she thought he was taunting her, flaunting his unavailability and knowing that no other man could possibly compare. She would have howled if he had not noticed her – because he *was* unavailable and no other man *could* possibly compare. She howled when she thought of her disastrous love life, of all the other men she had known – those lecherous, pawing no-goods who only wanted her for her body. Why couldn't they be more like Father Mostyn? She howled when she thought of Father Mostyn. Why couldn't he be more like those lecherous, pawing no-goods and want her for her body?

Whenever Maria saw Josefina start to howl she would rush up to her and throw her arms round her and begin to howl herself. The two would howl in harmony. From Josefina would come oaths invoking the entire panoply of Spanish saints, as well as Christ and the Blessed Virgin; from Maria, snatches of lullabies between sobs, while Nurse Connolly would be screeching like a banshee, Woodbine in one hand, whisky in the other, shouting instructions to all to get back to work, as a cloud of cigarette smoke and ash drifted over the open cooking pots.

In the refectory, only vague snatches of the goings on in the kitchens were audible and; Clancy paid them no attention. He pushed a spoon into his "pudding", a bowl of tapioca – gelatinous globules in a milky liquid; "frogspawn" to all the boys. He stared hard and imagined he saw tiny tadpoles emerging from the globules. He was still hungry. He had eaten very little of the fish. What was the greater penance – to eat or not to eat?

Mind your language

It is clergy night at the South Croydon Catenians Dinner (cream of celery soup, shepherds pie, peas and treacle tart) is finished and whiskies are being served. Father Muldoon is seated next to Superintendent O'Driscoll of the Metropolitan Police, Z-Division (Croydon).

"How has your week been, Superintendent? Busy as usual?"

"Indeed it was, Father. Criminals in Croydon don't take days off. How was yours?"

"Grand, Superintendent. I was up at Aintree for the weekend. I always like to go for the Grand National. There's no finer sight than seeing the horses go over Becher's Brook. I stay with Father Tom Gormally, another Carlow man. He has a parish near there."

"And I suppose you have a little bet or two. Father?"

"Just a small one or two, Superintendent. Father Tom Gormally is a very fine judge of a horse. His tips are practically money in the bank – and he knows something that the other punters don't."

"Does he now? What would that be, Father?"

"Saint Blathmac, Superintendent."

"Remind me, Father. Who was Saint Blathmac?"

"He was an Irish saint, martyred on the steps of his abbey by the Vikings. Not the first to be slaughtered by those heathens and he wasn't the last either. The English learned a lesson or two from the Vikings, so I'm told. Father Tom Gormally says the saint has taken up an interest in racing now he's in Heaven. He's the man to go to if your horse needs a second wind. A prayer to Saint Blathmac can put two or three lengths in the final furlong on any horse, says Father Tom Gormally– but only if the horse tries. Saint Blathmac can't abide a horse that doesn't try. If your horse won't try, then Father Tom Gormally says you might as well stick a ticket to the dog food factory on it before it even comes under starter's orders."

"He must be winning every week with Saint Blathmac on his side, Father."

"Not at all, Superintendent. If he did, the bookies would soon get wise. The bookies don't like winners. As soon as you have a few winners they start making excuses why they can't take your bet."

"Is that right, Father?"

"It is indeed, Superintendent. Bookies have their bread buttered on both sides. That's why you never see a poor bookie. If they got to know about Saint Blathmac, Father Tom Gormally would be banned from every racecourse in the country. He has to play it canny. He makes a losing bet every now and again, just to keep them guessing. That way he still makes a few bob. He gives half his winnings to the Legion of Mary and the other half goes to his church fund."

"Do you think it really works, Father?"

"It does indeed, Superintendent. I saw it with my own eyes at Aintree. A horse that was also-ran all its life cantered home at thirty-three to one after Father Tom Gormally had a word with Saint Blathmac. The Legion of Mary were in clover that day."

"I'd say they would be, Father. As a racing man, I suppose you go to a few other courses."

"One or two, Superintendent. Epsom for the Derby, and Cheltenham, of course. I like to go on Gold Cup day. Half of Ireland will be there. I'd never go to Ascot, though."

"Why is that, Father?"

"Because it's *Royal* Ascot, Superintendent. The Queen of England will be there in all her finery, with her carriages and people bowing and scraping and curtsying to her all over the place. And you have to wear a top hat. What Irishman would wear a top hat?"

"None that I know, Father."

"A top hat is the symbol of the English yoke under which Ireland lived for seven hundred years. No self-respecting Irishman would wear one. Did you know, Superintendent, that there was a time when Catholics were banned from Royal Ascot?"

"I didn't know that, Father."

"Banned entirely. If they caught a whiff of a Hail Mary on you, you weren't allowed in. Even now, if you went, you would be hard put to spot a Catholic. They're all keeping their heads down, so as not to let on. Priests have to get a dispensation from the Bishop if they want to go to Royal Ascot and they keep their coats buttoned up to hide the dog collar, if they know what's good for them.

"Talking of keeping your head down, Superintendent, I see Frankie Fahey is coming this way. Too late, he's seen us."

"Great to see you again, Father. How have you been?"

"Well enough, Frankie. And yourself?"

"Never better, Father. And you, Superintendent? Are you ready to join the Knights yet?"

"I hope to one day, Frankie. Police work keeps me awful busy for now."

"I'm sure it does, Superintendent. In the meantime, can I interest you in taking part in our sweepstake for next year's Cheltenham Gold Cup, The winner gets an all expenses trip for the day. All proceeds to the Knights' charity, of course."

"I'm not much of a racing man, Frankie. I wouldn't know what to do if I won."

"You could always give the ticket to Father Muldoon if you do. I'm sure he would like to go. I'll leave you the form. You can just fill it in and send it back to us with the cheque."

"The Knights' charity is doing well then, Frankie?"

"Going from strength to strength, Father, thanks be to God. I have another bit of news for you. I've been appointed Provincial Grand Knight of the Knights of Saint Columba – and that's not all. The Archbishop has asked us to go with him and the Cardinal to Rome for a private audience with the Holy Father. His Holiness, I understand, takes a special interest in the Knights of Saint Columba. He sees us as soldiers fighting with him for the Catholic faith. Ah, is that Tony Kennedy over there? They say he's in line to be Mayor of Croydon. I must have a word. Great to see you both."

"So he's off to see the Pope. Frankie Fahey must be going up in this world, Father."

"Pride comes before a fall, Superintendent. Frankie Fahey is too full of himself altogether. He'll be wanting to be called 'Sir' Frankie next and his wife will be calling herself 'Lady Fahey', I don't doubt. She's another that's full of airs and graces. Frankie Fahey isn't going to Rome for the sake of his soul. He'll be wanting to sign up the Archbishop and the Cardinal for his books. He'll have a finger then in every parish in the country and his pockets wouldn't be big enough to hold his takings. It wouldn't even surprise me if he tried the Pope himself. His odds would still be a disgrace and he would still be hounding poor innocent punters for the few pennies they owe. It's a wonder he isn't locked up already."

"Meanness isn't a crime, Father. If it were, the jails would be full to bursting."

"More's the pity. I don't like to say ill of anyone, as you know, Superintendent, but I'd say a few strings would have been pulled somewhere for the Pope to see the likes of Frankie Fahey."

"The Pope has a lot on his plate these days, right enough, Father. What do you think of the new Council?"

"A lot of it is hot air, from what I hear, Superintendent."

"Do you think so, Father. I heard they're saying that mass is going to be in English."

"Stuff and nonsense, Superintendent. That will never happen. English is no language for a mass."

"Why do you say that, Father?"

"English is the language for Protestants, Superintendent. All Protestants speak English. You never hear a Protestant speak Italian or French or Irish, do you? You couldn't say mass in English. It wouldn't sound right."

"At least the congregation could understand what was being said, Father."

"What has that got to do with anything, Superintendent? You don't go to mass to understand the words. You go because the Church says you have to go. God doesn't care whether you understand or not, as long as you go to mass. 'Remember to keep holy the Sabbath day,' as it says in the Third Commandment. It says nothing about understanding."

"So you would stick with Latin, Father?"

"If it was up to me, I would, Superintendent, but I suppose the Pope has all sorts shouting in his ear. If he says we have to have mass in another language, then I'd say it would best be Irish."

"Do you think mass could be in Irish, Father?"

"Of course it could, Superintendent. Irish is a Catholic language. Didn't you learn that at school?"

"It's a long time since I was at school, Father. We all learned Irish, of course, but I've forgotten most of it. I only have a few words left, a *cupla focal,* as they say. How is your Irish these days?"

"I had great Irish when I was at school. Superintendent. I was always top of the class for Irish. I did all my lessons in Irish and won prizes for it. I did all my examinations in Irish. I even did my mathematics examination in it. You got 5 per cent extra marks for doing it in them days."

"Is that so, Father? How do you do mathematics in Irish?"

"It's very simple, Superintendent. You do the sums and then you write at the end 'The answer is' in Irish."

"You'd be a fool not to, Father, if you got another 5 per cent."

"The pity is, Superintendent, that everything in Ireland isn't done in Irish. It should be, but the English stole our language."

"I have heard that said, Father."

"Stole it right out of our mouths. There were people in the West who could never say another word after the English came."

"Some of them are still a bit slow in saying things now, Father, from what I hear."

"A few of them managed to keep the language in the *Gaeltacht*, Superintendent. It's a grand language. You can do everything in Irish that you can in English and more besides. You can say things in Irish that you couldn't say in English."

"What would they be, Father?"

"I couldn't say them, Superintendent, could I?"

"Oh, I see that, Father, but there are very few that speak Irish in Croydon. If you say mass in Irish here, no one would understand it."

"Exactly so, Superintendent. You can be sure that very few in the congregation would understand the words of the mass, whatever language it was in. If it's a sung high mass, you wouldn't hear any of the words anyway, what with the organ and the violins and the choir and the like. So if it was in Irish, they needn't bother to try. Kneel down, head down and pray to your maker. That's all you need to do at mass. Let the priest get on with the words."

"I see that too, Father. What do you think about this idea of saying mass facing the congregation that I hear might be coming as well?"

"I don't think anything of it at all, Superintendent. Who do you think a priest would rather be looking at when he says mass? Almighty God in his holy tabernacle on the altar or a bunch of all sorts, from decent Catholics like yourself to ragamuffins and reprobates, half of them drunk if it's midnight mass at Christmas? No priest would want to say mass facing the congregation. It would put him off entirely. He wouldn't know whether he was saying the Gospel or the Epistle."

"I'm with you there, Father. Looking at some you see in congregations would put you in a bad mood for your breakfast. So what do you think of the chances that the Church will say mass must be in Irish?"

"A lot better than you might think, Superintendent. Archbishop McQuaid is a big Latin man, but if he can't have Latin I've no doubt that he'll plump for Irish. There's a lot of bishops and cardinals that listen to Archbishop John Charles McQuaid in the Council. It's a brave bishop that goes against Archbishop McQuaid. Dev will have a word as well, I'm sure. Dev is a great Irish speaker and he is very well thought of in the Vatican. Popes don't like saying no to Dev. I'd say it's odds on that masses will all be in Irish soon."

"Wouldn't that be grand, Father?"

"It would indeed, Superintendent. And it would be one in the eye for the English too. They think they can go round stealing other people's languages and spreading their own Protestant lingo, like it was jam on bread, but we'll put a stop to their little game. They'll see us all going to mass in Irish and they won't know what's going on. They'll be saying to themselves, what are the Paddys up to now? We'd better learn Irish to find out. They'll have to learn for the good of their souls or pack their bags for Hell."

Father Arundell

Mister Rodney, head of the school's sports, was an intimidating physical specimen and even more intimidating in his manner. He informed Clancy that he had been promoted to captain of Howard House junior cricket team, because its usual captain, McDowell, had twisted an ankle.

"Why do I have to be captain, Sir?"

"Because I say so, Clancy. Here's your team sheet."

The list had fourteen names in all, so that he had a few reserves. These were supposed to be the best cricketers in his house, but, surveying the list, Clancy wondered how bad some of those not on the list must be. He spotted Dempsey's name. Dempsey was podgy, ungainly, wore thick, National Health glasses, and was utterly uncoordinated. Looking at some of the other names, Clancy suspected that Dempsey might not even be the worst.

The six houses in Campion were all named after his fellow English martyrs, forty of whom were entitled Blessed and so were in the ante room to sainthood. Howard House was named for Philip Howard, Earl of Arundel, who unlike Edmund Campion and most of the others, wasn't hung, drawn and quartered, but died of dysentery in the Tower of London. That, thought Clancy, was a bit of a cheat for a martyr. Anyone could die of dysentery. A proper martyr ought to be hung, drawn and quartered.

The houses played every year for the Garnet Shield, named for another martyr, Thomas Garnet, a Jesuit, nephew of the more famous Henry Garnet, also a Jesuit, who was part of the Gunpowder Plot. Both were hung, drawn and quartered, but Henry's was surely the more glorious end. If you were going to be martyred, thought Clancy, it might as well be something worth being martyred for. Why couldn't the shield be named after Henry? After all, everyone knows about the Gunpowder Plot. They would be batting for Guy Fawkes.

This was their last match in the competition. Howard had lost all their matches so far, usually by wide margins. Southwell, on the other hand, had at least half of the school junior team in their side and had won all theirs, usually by equally large margins. Howard were going to be thrashed.

The pitch was a rather rough one on a side of the main playing fields. Clancy called the team together on the pitch before the match. Hearne was in the side, so he appointed him vice-captain, despite his objections. He then asked who wanted to be wicket-keeper. There was silence for several seconds before someone said, "I will."

The voice belonged to Digby, a boy in the second stream, who Clancy didn't know.

"Have you done it before?"

"Yes. At my primary school."

Clancy looked around. There were no other volunteers, so Digby got the job. At least, thought Clancy, Digby was big. There was an even chance that any ball beating the batsman would hit him, even if he didn't catch it.

Clancy said he and Hearne would open the batting and asked who wanted to provide the backbone of the batting at three and four. No volunteers, so he put their names in alphabetical order, except for Dempsey, who he put last. He asked if there were any fast bowlers to open. They all shook their heads. He asked who had ever bowled before. Half a dozen hands went up. It was a twenty-over game. He would give each an over or two to see how things worked out.

Clancy decided that, as captain, he needed to give the team a pep talk.

"Look, team, this is going to be a very tricky match. I think we may need to play for a draw."

"How are we going to do that?" asked Hearne, while the others looked very sceptical.

"Well," said Clancy, clutching at whatever straws that floated through his mind, "on the bowling, we'll mix it up, slow with medium, spin with seam. We won't give them a chance to settle down. And no fancy stuff when we bat. Forward defensive to everything. Get them frustrated."

The scepticism of his team only increased. He looked towards the school and saw the Southwell team coming out of the changing room. Their captain, Alexander, was swishing his bat to and fro, then waved it, arrogantly thought Clancy, as he saw the Howard team. From the other corner of the field Hearne saw a long, black figure approaching.

"Oh no, it's Arundell," he said. "I bet he's coming to give us one of his talks about playing the game."

Father Arundell was very tall and very thin and very English. He measured six feet seven inches in the vertical plane, but gave little trouble to any scales on which he stood. The scion of a minor recusant family, which expected at least one male member in every generation to enter the priesthood, he was always immaculately dressed in a well-cut clerical suit. He usually went bare-headed, but would occasionally don a black *capello romano,* rather than the biretta that most priests favoured.

He took a recusant's long view that, in the end, England would revert to the one true faith. The Church, after all, thought not in years, nor even in centuries, but in millennia. The turning point, he considered, was the Oxford movement, with the conversion of John Henry Newman. It was only a matter of time, though perhaps a long time, before the rest came with him.

Father Arundell bore all the traits of his Jesuit education at their Lancastrian citadel, Stoneyhurst College, although for reasons that remained obscure, even to him, he was not accepted into the order on his ordination. He had always considered himself better suited to education, rather than parish work, and had asked to come to the Blessed Edmund Campion because he felt that he had a particular affinity with the martyr from his schooldays. Stoneyhurst held, among its many relics, the ropes used to quarter Campion after he had been hanged and drawn. He had suggested to the Canon that he might like to ask Stoneyhurst if they would allow the relic to be loaned to Blessed Edmund Campion school, to be put on display, to remind pupils of the sacrifices made by their Catholic forebears. The Canon had demurred, saying it might be a little gruesome for some of the younger boys.

He brought with him many of the traditions of Stoneyhurst and did not bother to hide his opinion that they were much superior to those of the Campion school. As in the Jesuit practice, all written work for his classes had to be headed AMDG for *Ad Majorem Dei Gloriam*, meaning 'For the Greater Glory of God', and ended with LDS, for *Laus Dei Semper*, 'Praise to God Always'. He was also proud of Stoneyhurst's literary alumni. Chief among them was Father Gerard Manley Hopkins SJ, although Father Arundell found his poetry difficult, to the point of being incomprehensible, especially the one about five nuns in a shipwreck. What happened to the nuns? A priest, particularly a Jesuit, ought at least to have made that clear. He much preferred poems like Wordsworth's 'Daffodils'. Much better rhymes. Even more to his liking were the Sherlock Holmes stories of former Stoneyhurst pupil, Arthur Conan Doyle. One couldn't go wrong with a Sherlock Holmes.

Father Arundell detested any hint of indiscipline or disorder. He associated indiscipline and disorder with things that were not English and associated order and discipline with things that were English, the most important of which were Empire Day, Sir Winston Churchill and cricket, although he conceded that none were what they once were. Empire Day had been abolished several years before, in 1958, and replaced by Commonwealth Day, something that Father Arundell considered a regrettable lapse into the demotic. The Church was not a commonwealth, so he saw no reason why the British Empire should have lower standards. Churchill was clearly in his dotage, though his spirit was needed by the country more than ever, and, as for the state of English cricket, the less said, the better.

Father Arundell taught French, or, more exactly, taught a certain idea of Englishness through the medium of French. His favoured French texts for teaching were translations of Rudyard Kipling, Robert Louis Stevenson and Arthur Conan Doyle. His speaking tone was imperious, making few concessions to the native accent. His model was the wartime broadcasts of Churchill to France – *"Français, c'est moi, Churchill, qui parle."* He required boys in his class to adopt similar barking tones when reading French texts aloud, tones they also used when speaking on holidays with their parents, baffling any French who heard them.

Father Arundell considered himself in charge of cricket at the school. He did not coach or organise games. He left those things to the sports masters. Rather, he dispensed advice to the school's teams, particularly to the First Eleven, based largely on his own experience of the game. As a schoolboy, he had been an indifferent batsman. His height meant that he was vulnerable to balls that skidded along the ground. As a bowler, however, while not particularly fast, his height meant he could make balls rise sharply off a good length. As a result, he was a valued member of the Stoneyhurst team for his ability to render opposing batsmen unconscious from balls that rose unexpectedly.

His family had donated the Garnet Shield to the school. He had named it after Thomas Garnet, rather than Henry, because Thomas was a fellow Stoneyhurst alumni and also because he considered the Gunpowder Plot to be rather vulgar and unseemly, not something any Catholic gentleman should ever contemplate being involved in.

His principal interest in cricket at the school, amounting to a passion, was the First Eleven cricket pitch. This was situated in the middle of the school playing grounds and was out of bounds to anyone not engaged in its maintenance. During the season he inspected it every day to make sure it was watered and the grass cut to regulation height. No weed was ever allowed to sully its pristine surface, on pain of instant excommunication and extraction. He checked it regularly for any bumps or dips, and every day in the season a dozen boys were instructed to push a massive heavy roller back and forth twenty times over the pitch to maintain its perfect flatness. No boy, or even master, was allowed to tread on it without Father Arundell's permission. It was generally accepted to be the best pitch in the district. A groundsman from Surrey Cricket Club had said it was as good as those at the Oval.

Father Arundell looked down at Clancy and the team.

"What team is this and who is captain?"

"It's Howard House, Father, and I'm captain," said Clancy.

"Ah," said Father Arundell, evidently not clear who Clancy was, "and who are you playing?"

"Southwell, Father."

"Ah," said Father Arundell, more emphatically. He was quite clear who Southwell were. "Some fine young cricketers in the Southwell side, so I hear. Promises well for the first eleven. I suppose that makes Howard underdogs, but never fear. The race is not always to the swift nor the battle to the strong. Be of good cheer, Howard. *'But his Captain's hand on his shoulder smote, "Play up! play up! and play the game!"'* That's the spirit, isn't it, captain?"

He looked down at Clancy.

"Yes, Father."

He turned and started walking towards the middle of the field, saying,

"Play up! Play up! and play the game. That's the spirit."

Clancy watched him as he strode away. He was never quite sure whether Father Arundell was saying something and meaning nothing or saying nothing and meaning something. He doubted he would ever know.

Father Arundell made his way to the First Eleven pitch where he was to supervise the last rolling before a very important match the next day. Edmund Campion had moved up the Surrey schools cricket league and was due to play its first match in the top league against Selwich College, a public school with a long cricketing history, including several mentions in *Wisden*. A small grandstand had been erected and a number of dignitaries, including the Archbishop, had been invited to celebrate the occasion. Father Arundell cast his eye over the pitch and decided it needed just a little more rolling to bring it to tip-top condition.

Clancy and Alexander watched as the umpire, Stephenson, a lanky sixth-former with a supercilious manner and half a moustache, tossed the coin.

"Heads," said Alexander.

Heads it was.

"We'll bat," said Alexander.

Clancy felt he had to open the bowling and that he had better bowl as fast as he could. The result was a long hop, three yards to the left of the wicket.

"Wide," said the umpire.

The batter, Alexander, smirked. Clancy tried again. This time the ball was delivered more centrally and both he and Stephenson had to duck as it zinged past their ears on its way to the boundary.

"Four," said the umpire, waving his hand.

"Wasn't that a six?" said Alexander.

"Four," said Stephenson sternly. "No questioning the umpire."

The rest of the over resulted in three more boundaries. The other two balls were so bad that Alexander disdained even to hit them.

Hearne bowled the next over. He was taller and rather better coordinated than Clancy, so his bowling bore more resemblance to what might be expected in cricket. However he was bowling to Haigh, one of the school's best all-round athletes, who was even more savage than Alexander in his treatment of Hearne's efforts. Twenty runs came off that over. Clancy tried his tactic of mixing bowlers, slow with medium, spin with seam, but nothing made any difference. The ball was sprayed everywhere and all the fielders did was run to the boundaries to fetch the ball.

At the end of the nineteenth over, Southwell were 204 without loss. Clancy called Hearne over for a tactical talk.

"This is embarrassing," said Clancy. "Can't we at least take a wicket?"

"How?" asked Hearne.

"Try a new bowler?"

"We've tried everyone who said they could bowl."

Desperate times need desperate measures, thought Clancy.

"What about someone who says they can't bowl? That might confuse them."

Hearne shook his head. The burden of captaincy was clearly getting to Clancy.

"Who?"

"What about Dempsey?"

Hearne tried – and failed – to suppress a laugh.

"You are joking?"

"Why not. It's the last over, anyway."

Hearne shrugged.

"Have it your own way."

Clancy called Dempsey over and tossed him the ball, which he dropped.

"You're bowling the next over."

Dempsey looked terrified.

"I don't know how. I've never done it."

"It's easy," said Clancy. "You've seen us do it. Just turn your arm over and send the ball down the wicket."

Dempsey's terror did not abate.

"I can't. I mean..."

"Come on, Dempsey," said Hearne. "You're our last chance for a wicket. Do it for the House."

Dempsey sighed deeply, then picked up the ball.

"Alright, I'll do it, but don't blame me for anything that happens."

The last over started.

Dempsey waddled up to the wicket and, with an action that was part throw, part shot putt, sent the ball high in the sky in the general direction of the batsman. Alexander started laughing and took a step back, preparing to hit the ball out of the field. As he did so, he stepped on his wicket.

"Out," said the umpire, raising a finger.

Alexander shook his head in disgust and started walking off the field. Dempsey blushed as Clancy patted him on the back, and the other Howard fielders gave him a round of applause.

The next batsman, Morgan, was another with a big reputation, who was miffed that Alexander and Haigh had hogged the fun to themselves and, with the rest of his team, had roared with laughter when Alexander got out. He took a peremptory guard as Dempsey waddled into bowl. Morgan looked with contempt and left it as it bounced well wide on the offside. Just as it was almost level with the wicket it hit a large divot in the pitch and took a violent turn to the right, just clipping the stumps and dislodging a bail.

"Out," said the umpire, and raised a finger again.

Morgan looked at the stumps in disbelief and then trudged back. Dempsey blushed even redder as Clancy and Hearne both patted his back and the rest of the team applauded vigorously.

"You're on a hat trick, Dempsey," said Hearne.

Dempsey looked blank.

"What's that?"

"Three wickets in three balls," said Clancy.

"Oh," said Dempsey.

Southwell's next batsman, Herlihy, hardly had time to get padded up before he was in. He hurried out to the crease, didn't bother to take guard and faced Dempsey. Dempsey's ball hit ground less than a third of the way down the pitch. Herlihy grinned and marched forward to hit it, but, in his haste to get on, he had not tied his bootlaces properly. He tripped over them, and as he sprawled on the pitch, the ball hit him square in the groin. He was wearing a box, but he still yelled with pain, as the onlookers fell about laughing. As the ball trickled further down the wicket, Digby, the wicket-keeper, pounced on it and whipped off the bails with a loud shout of "Howzaat!"

"Out," said the umpire, raising his finger yet again.

When Herlihy managed to stop groaning, he glared at the umpire.

"That's not fair! Can't you see I'm injured?"

"You were out of your crease," said the umpire. "You've been stumped."

Herlihy rose to his feet and, still glaring at the umpire, trudged reluctantly back. The Howard fielders all crowded round Dempsey, congratulating him.

"A hat trick with your first three balls. I bet that's never been done before," said Hearne.

Dempsey's face turned crimson and his glasses began to steam up. Dempsey finished the over with two wides, a "high" and three balls that barely reached the batsman, who took no further chances with Howard's secret weapon and simply blocked them.

It was now Howard's turn to bat. Clancy and Hearne walked out, with Clancy deciding to take the first ball. "Remember, let's frustrate them. Forward defensive to everything," he whispered, as they reached the wicket.

Southwell's opening bowler was Haigh, who Clancy thought must be tired after scoring an unbeaten century. He began to have doubts as Haigh disappeared in the distance to start his run and then came thundering in to the wicket. Clancy was steeling himself to go forward when he felt the ball whistle by him before he could move. He decided to change tactic and go back to the next ball. This time he just managed to move his bat as the ball clipped its edge and shot between wicket-keeper and slip on its way to the boundary.

"Four," said the umpire with a wave.

The next ball, he managed to nudge towards square leg and yelled at Hearne, "Run!" as he started from the crease. Hearne had no intention of facing Haigh and yelled back "No!" but it was too late. Clancy was more than half way down the pitch as a Southwell fielder threw the ball back to the wicket-keeper.

"Out," said the umpire.

"Who is?" asked Clancy.

"You," said the umpire, pointing at Hearne. "You didn't run."

A look of relief appeared on Hearne's face as he walked cheerily back. Next in was Digby, who managed to dodge a few balls from Haigh and Southwell's other bowler, Sullivan, who was almost as fast, before Sullivan bowled him. The rest of the Howard innings was a tale of woe. At the start of the seventh over, they were 23 for nine. Clancy had managed to cling on, mostly by luck. Last man in was Dempsey, who looked even more terrified than when asked to bowl. Clancy tried to calm his nerves.

"Just try to stop the ball hitting the wicket."

Dempsey was uncalmed. Haigh, still on his long run, came galloping in and bowled. Dempsey, eyes shut, swung wildly. There was a loud crack and the Howard team watched, open-mouthed, as the ball soared into the sky towards the middle of the field. As it finally came to earth, the umpire raised both arms:

"Six."

The Howard team cheered and clapped. Once again, Dempsey had defied the odds.

The ball hadn't finished its journey. It kept rolling until finally it came to a stop in the middle of the First Eleven pitch, as the heavy roller was making a run. Father Arundell was the first to spot it and yelled at the boys pushing the roller, "Stop! Stop!" but the massive roller had momentum and, once it was going, it took several yards to stop. It came to a halt just as the ball disappeared under it.

Father Arundell appeared shocked. He went down on his knees and looked for the ball, but nothing was visible. He barked an instruction:

"Pull it back, but very, very slowly."

The boys pulled, but the roller didn't move. They pulled harder and still no movement. There was a well-known problem with the roller's axle. Sometimes it would jam. This was one of those times.

"We need more to pull it, Father," said one of the boys.

Father Arundell nodded. He barked at the Southwell fielder who had come to collect the ball, "Bring your team over here now. Immediately!"

The boy ran back and within seconds the Southwell team were running towards the pitch, leaving Clancy and Dempsey, still at the crease, wondering what was going on.

"You boys push from that end," said Father Arundell, pointing at the Southwell team, "and you others pull."

They heaved and pulled, heaved and pushed, feet slipping on the grass, until suddenly the roller began to move. There was an indrawing of breath as they saw the ball was entirely buried in the pitch. Father Arundell knelt beside it, making hurrumphing noises as he examined it.

"Does anyone have a knife?"

"I've got a penknife, Father," said one boy.

Father Arundell took the knife and very carefully cut round the ball before levering it out. What was left was a ball-shaped hole. Father Arundell gazed at it in horror. At that moment Clancy arrived. He saw not only the hole, but skid marks over much of the pitch, left by the boots of the Southwell team as they were pushing. Even to his untutored eye, the pitch looked unplayable. Father Arundell, now back on his feet, was staring at the pitch, as if in shock, still harrumphing.

"Let's go and finish the game," whispered Alexander to Clancy, as they were both wondering what to do next. Clancy nodded. He didn't exactly relish the idea, but thought it best to leave Father Arundell to his private grief.

As they got back to their pitch they saw Stephenson, the umpire, sitting on a bench, reading a book.

"We want to finish the game," said Alexander.

Stephenson looked surprised.

"It is finished. You abandoned it."

"No, we didn't," said Alexander. "We went to help Father Arundell."

Stephenson shook his head dismissively.

"Did you, or did you not, walk off the field, leaving the batsman there?"

"Well, yes, but..."

"But nothing," said Stephenson. "You abandoned the match, so it's awarded to Howard."

Clancy thought Alexander would explode.

"That's stupid! How can you give it to them? We were 206 for three, they were twenty something for nine!"

Stephenson shrugged.

"That's the rules. You abandon the match, you forfeit it. I don't make the rules. If you don't like them, go and argue with the MCC."

Alexander was speechless. He gestured angrily to his team to follow him and they marched off towards the changing rooms. Clancy watched them go.

"What do you think?" he said to Hearne.

"I think we won," said Hearne.

Clancy agreed.

"A win is a win. We'll take it."

The Union

Docherty picked at the oleaginous, reddish object on his plate with a fork.

"What's this supposed to be?"

"Corned beef," said Dempsey.

Dempsey was fat, owlish and entirely undiscriminating in what he ate. He appreciated food only by quantity. The more there was of it, the better. Clancy and Docherty, neither of whom could bring themselves to eat what was on their plate, looked at him doubtfully as he munched.

"How do you know?" said Clancy.

"It looks a bit like corned beef, doesn't it? What else could it be?" said Dempsey, between mouthfuls.

"It could be anything," said Docherty. "Does it taste like corned beef?"

Dempsey continued chewing while he considered, "Not exactly like other corned beef, I've had. It's a bit mushy."

"Mushy?"

"Yeah, you know, mushy, like er..."

"Mushy?"

"Yeah, that's it, mushy."

"If it doesn't taste like corned beef," said Clancy, "what does it taste like?"

Dempsey considered further.

"I dunno. Kippers, maybe."

Clancy and Docherty stared at him in disbelief.

"Kippers?" said Docherty, "How can something that's supposed to be beef taste like kippers? Kippers are fish."

Dempsey seemed surprised.

"Who says? They don't look like fishes. They're just flat things. How are they supposed to swim and, anyway, where do they catch kippers?"

Clancy and Docherty looked each other and shook their heads. There was no point in discussing the zoological classification of kippers with Dempsey.

"How can you eat this crap?" said Docherty. "You can't actually like it."

Dempsey shrugged.

"I didn't say I liked it, but I've got to eat something at dinner time, otherwise I'd be starving by tea time."

Clancy thought a modicum of starvation might do Dempsey good, but stopped himself saying it.

"I don't care whether I starve or not. I hate school dinners," said Docherty.

"So do I," said Clancy, "but what can we do about it?"

"If you don't like dinners, then why don't you go on strike?" said Dempsey.

There were a few seconds of silence.

"What do you mean, go on strike?" said Docherty.

"Get everyone to stop eating dinners till they get better. My Dad's a docker. If they don't like something they all go on strike. They stop working till they get what they want. They do it all the time."

Clancy shook his head.

"How are we supposed to get everyone in the school to stop eating dinners?"

"You've got to get them in the Union, of course," said Dempsey.

"What Union?"

"*The* Union. There's always got be a Union. The Union's for everyone. Then, when you've got them in the Union, you have to have shop stewards to do the organising and then, for the strike, you have to have pickets on all the doors to make sure nobody goes in. If someone does go in, that's crossing the picket line and they're called scabs and they get chucked out of the Union."

As Father Mostyn entered the kitchen, Nurse Connolly hurriedly snatched the Woodbines from the mouths of Rosie and Bridie, before extinguishing her own and pushing the Lucozade bottle to one side.

"Ah, hello Father. Are you come for your dinner? I have a nice pork chop ready for you."

As always, Father Mostyn declined the offer. "No thank you, Mrs Connolly. I'm not eating lunch today," which was just as well, because Nurse Connolly had already eaten the chop in question herself.

Josefina eyed him with seething resentment. He had ignored her the last two times he had come into the kitchen and now he appeared to be ignoring her again. He must be doing it, she thought, because he was afraid desire would overcome him if he looked at her. Her mind swam with ideas for revenge. Next time he came, she would wear her lowest-cut blouse and tightest skirt, the one that rose up and showed stocking top and suspenders when she bent over even a little bit. She would flaunt herself and laugh in his face, knowing that he, as a priest, could do nothing as he wrestled with his lust. Then that momentary feeling of triumph as she knew he could do nothing was replaced by anguish as she knew he would do nothing. Maria put a comforting hand on Josefina's shoulder as she tried to repress a howl.

Nurse Connolly always made sure that Father Mostyn had no idea of what went on in the kitchens and she liked to leave him with no doubt as to who was in charge.

"Will you peel those potatoes properly, Brigid Murphy," she yelled at one kitchen maid. "They've so many spots left on them anyone would think they had measles."

"Make sure you stir that custard well, Oona O'Connell," she barked at another. "The boys can't abide lumps in their custard."

Father Mostyn looked on admiringly, glad that his role as Kitchen Supervisor was made all the easier by Nurse Connolly. He cast his eye round the kitchen and noticed Malachy, the Canon's Red Setter, lounging in his basket while supping from his bowl.

"Malachy is looking in very fine form today, Mrs Connolly. What is he having for his dinner?"

"Oh, he's in grand form, Father, and so he should be, with what we feed him. He's having chopped liver and chicken today. He's very fond of chopped liver. You always see a grand wagging of the tail when chopped liver is on the menu."

"I don't think he's ever looked better, Mrs Connolly," said Father Mostyn, "all thanks to you, and I know you take just as good care of the boys. What are they having for pudding today?"

Nurse Connolly gave him her most ingratiating smile.

"It's their favourite today, Father, prunes and custard."

"That sounds delicious, Mrs Connolly. What sort of prunes are they?"

Nurse Connolly looked at him, puzzled.

"They're grand prunes, Father. The best. Only the best is good enough for the boys."

"I'm glad to hear it," said Father Mostyn. "I can't remember when I last ate prunes. Where do your prunes come from?"

Nurse Connolly was even more puzzled. She looked at Bridie, who grunted something.

"Ireland, Father," said Nurse Connolly. "We're famous for our prune trees, so we are. You can't beat an Irish prune, so they say."

It was Father Mostyn's turn to be puzzled. He had a vague idea that prunes were some sort of dried fruit, but, naturally, he deferred to Nurse Connolly, who pulled out a large tin.

"Take a look for yourself, Father. Aren't these grand prunes?"

She gave one to Father Mostyn, who examined the small, hard, knobbly object held between his thumb and forefinger.

"I can see this is a very fine prune, Mrs Connolly. I suppose you have to cook them well, don't you?"

Nurse Connolly nodded vigorously.

"Oh, very well, Father. There's not many that know how to cook a prune like we know here. We boil them for two or three hours. That cooks them well enough. There's nothing finer, in my opinion, than a well-boiled prune."

Father Mostyn smiled his beatific smile.

"Excellent, Mrs Connolly, don't let me detain you. I'm sure the boys are looking forward to their prunes and custard."

He walked out of the kitchen and Josefina let out a single howl.

"What's this supposed to be?" said Docherty, as he and Clancy peered at the mess of yellow and brown in their bowls.

"Prunes," said Dempsey.

"How do you know?" asked Clancy.

"It's got stones in it." came the reply.

"It's got stones in it. Is that the only way you can tell it's prunes?" said Clancy. "What does it taste like?"

"Ermm..."

"Don't tell me," said Docherty. "Kippers?"

Dempsey shrugged.

"Sort of."

Docherty shook his head despairingly.

"Kippers and custard. That's got to be the pits. Why do we put up with it?"

At that moment the refectory door opened and the boys all stood up as the Canon entered. The Canon gave a slight nod of acknowledgement and motioned with his hand for them to sit down, before going through the door to the kitchens.

Dempsey scooped the last bit of custard from his bowl.

"I told you what to do if you don't like the dinners. Go on strike."

"You told us we needed the Union to go on strike," said Clancy. "We don't have a Union."

"Well, you'll have to join one," said Dempsey.

"Join what?"

"There's loads of them," said Dempsey. "Transport and General, Engineers, Boiler-makers, Garment-makers, you name it, there's a union for it."

"What about your Dad's Union?" said Docherty.

Dempsey shook his head.

"It's a closed shop."

"What does that mean?"

"Only dockers can join. Not schoolboys."

"All those others you mentioned. Are they closed shops too?" asked Docherty.

"I dunno. Some of them, I think?"

"They're all for workers," said Clancy. "What about schoolboys? Is there a Union for them?"

Dempsey shrugged again.

"Don't think so. You'll probably have to start one yourselves."

"How do we do that?" said Docherty.

The kitchen door opened and all stood up again as the Canon came back into the refectory, followed by Malachy. They nodded in acknowledgement together, the dog's nod being the slower and more deliberate.

"My Dad says you have to organise in a Union if you want to win a strike. That's down to the vanguard," said Dempsey, as the Canon left.

"I thought vanguard was a car, a Standard Vanguard," said Docherty dismissively.

"No. The vanguard my Dad is talking about is what he calls the militants. They're the leaders. They have to persuade others to join the Union, but they need to keep things secret until enough of them have joined."

"So who is going to be our vanguard?" said Clancy.

"My Dad says the workers always have to do it themselves. No one is going to do it for them."

"So we're the workers and we have to get the whole school into our Union in secret," said Docherty. "You must be joking. Someone will tell. Muldoon pokes his nose into everything. He'll go mad. We could get double-eight for this."

"My Dad says you don't need everyone to join. It depends on the cause," said Dempsey

"The cause?" said Clancy.

"Yes, what the strike is about," said Dempsey. "The whole school hates school dinners, don't they?"

"Yes," said Clancy and Docherty in unison.

"So my Dad says you don't need to persuade them about the cause. You just need enough members of the vanguard to mount the picket lines and then you should call the strike. Most of the school won't cross picket lines and you can call any that do, scabs. They won't like that."

The Sixth and Ninth Commandments

Father Muldoon adjusted his glasses and adopted his most serious expression. Gazing back at him were faces that ranged from the smooth and downy to the pimpled and semi-hirsute.

"Now boys, you have reached an age when I must talk to you about two of the most important commandments of Almighty God, commandments that are the occasion of sin for all those who do not believe in the one true religion and, I am sorry to say, for many who claim to be Catholics, but who do not act as good Catholics should. These are the sixth and ninth commandments."

Father Muldoon inwardly despaired as he contemplated the complete abandonment of these commandments in the moral and spiritual cesspit that was England. You only had to look at the pages of papers like the *News of the World* and the *Sunday People* to see degradation and sinfulness almost beyond belief, with lewd stories, pictures of scantily clad women and even Church of England vicars disgracing themselves. Only the racing pages retained a little probity. Their tipsters were first class.

Clancy could feel a frisson of prurient excitement run through the class as the priest continued.

"Who can tell me what is the sixth commandment?"

Gallagher's hand shot up, just ahead of several others.

"Thou shalt not commit adultery, Father."

"Correct, Gallagher. It is 'Thou shalt not commit adultery.' And who can tell me the ninth commandment?"

This time Hearne just beat Gallagher and the others.

"Thou shalt not covet thy neighbour's wife, Father."

"Correct, Hearne. 'Thou shalt not covet they neighbour's wife.'"

Another hand went up.

"Yes, Dempsey?"

"Please, Father, what does covet mean?"

The priest looked sternly in the direction of some sniggering, which stopped immediately.

"Covet means covet, Dempsey. If Almighty God had wanted to use another word He would have done so. It is for you to understand what He means, not for Him to explain Himself. Now, turn to your Catechism. You will see that the purpose of the sixth commandment is to safeguard the sanctity of marriage. What does it forbid? Docherty, will you please read paragraph 255."

Docherty rose to his feet, trying hard to suppress a smirk.

"The sixth commandment forbids not only adultery, but all looks, words and actions against virtue and chastity."

"What are the chief dangers to chastity? Robinson, read paragraph 256."

Robinson hesitated, as if not quite believing what he was reading.

"The chief dangers to chastity are idleness, intemperance, bad companions, improper dances, immodest dress, company-keeping and indecent conversation, books, plays and pictures."

"Now, Clancy," said Father Muldoon, "please read paragraph 273, which tells us what is forbidden by the ninth commandment."

Clancy turned over the page and read.

"The ninth commandment forbids all deliberate pleasure in impure thoughts, and all deliberate consent to impure desires."

The class waited for Father Muldoon to expound on the many dangers to their virtue that they might hope to encounter.

"As Almighty God commands you, purity and chastity must be your watchword, boys, as you go forth into this modern world, where temptation is all around you. In England, now, the Devil is up to his usual tricks everywhere. You see these shameless young Protestant girls in skirts that could hardly be called skirts at all. I'm told they even have a shameless name for them – miniskirts. No Catholic boy should have anything to do with a girl who would dress like that. And then there's this pop music, with people dancing to it like they were whirling dervishes. What's that long-haired bunch that everyone's talking about called?"

"The Beatles, Father," said several voices.

"Beatles? What sort of name is that? Are you all listening to Protestant creepy crawlies now?"

"Two of them are Catholics, Father," said Hearne.

The priest sat back, evidently surprised, almost shocked. He adjusted his glasses.

"Is that so? I'll ask the Archbishop to have a word with their parish priest. He'll give them a piece of his mind and tell them to stop prancing about like monkeys and get their hair cut and get proper jobs. What about the other lot, the ones with even longer hair? Are you telling me that they're Catholics too?"

"Do you mean the Rolling Stones, Father?" asked Robinson.

"I believe I do, Robinson."

The class looked at each other and shrugged or shook their heads. It seemed unlikely that Mick Jagger or Keith Richard were regular mass-goers. Muldoon continued.

"All those songs about loving and kissing and holding hands are pure licentiousness, boys. They encourage impure thoughts. They stir feelings that are the very occasion of sin. The Devil must be rubbing his hands every time those Beatles open their mouths. I trust no boy in this class would listen to them."

He stared at the class. The class stared blankly back at him.

"It's not just songs that are dangers to chastity, boys. The English newspapers are full of stories that can be sources of temptation. No Catholic family should take papers like the *News of the World* or the *Sunday People*. Even reading them could endanger your immortal soul. You should read papers like the *Catholic Herald* or the *Universe* instead."

Clancy thought about his own father, who took both the *News of the World* and the *Sunday People* – for the sport, he said. His mother read the *Catholic Herald,* but his father didn't, because he said there was no sport in it.

"No doubt you like to go to the pictures, boys," continued the priest, "but you must be very careful what you see. When you are a bit older you will be tempted by fancy advertisements to go to films with an X to their name. I am told that some of them display such depravity that the Devil himself would blush if he saw them. Think very hard before seeing any film, boys, and consult your parish priest. He will put you right."

Having disposed of press and cinema, Father Muldoon turned his attention to books.

"As the Catechism says, books can be just as bad. There are books written that plumb the very depths of evil. Books that no right-thinking person would ever want to read. That's why the Pope has the Index. The Index is a list of books that Catholics are banned from reading. In Ireland the banning of books is taken very seriously. The first thing they did after they threw the English out was to set up the Committee on Evil Literature. They make sure that no indecent book is ever allowed into Ireland and Ireland is all the better for it. One of them that you may have heard of, because such a song and dance of it has been made here lately in England, is called *The Country Girls* by a Clare woman called Edna O'Brien. I'm told that it contains such filth that no good Catholic has ever been able to finish reading it. I'm also told that not only the book, but the woman herself, has been banned by the good people of the County Clare. It's a pity that the English can't be persuaded to do the same, but that would be too much to expect. I hope that if any of you find such a book you will throw it straight into the dustbin."

Again the boys stared blankly back at him. No hand was raised for a question. Clancy wrote "Edna O'Brien, The Country Girls", in very small writing at the back of his exercise book and wondered, if he ever found a copy, how far he would get when reading it. Father Muldoon was still in full flow.

"In time to come, boys, many of you will get married, I trust to good Catholic girls, so that your children may be brought up in the one true faith. Purity and chastity are just as important within marriage as they are outside it. Preserving your chastity in this sinful world is not easy, but the Church gives you help and guidance. Gallagher, please read paragraph 257 of the Catechism."

Gallagher smiled unctuously before he read.

"The chief means of preserving chastity are: to be modest in our dress and conduct, to avoid the occasion of sin, to cultivate devotion to the Blessed Virgin Mary, and above all to seek the help of God through prayer and the sacraments."

"Let that, boys, be your guide. Have no truck with shameless Protestant girls with their miniskirts and their pop music and their indecent dances. You can dance all night with good Catholic girls who dress decently and then go with them to mass and communion in the morning. Always avoid indecent conversations or events. Only read good and improving books and papers. If you are afflicted by impure thoughts or feelings, think of the Blessed Virgin Mary. Make sure you go to confession and communion regularly and pray to God whenever you need help. If you do, you can be sure that your soul will leave this world as pure as when you were first baptised."

At break, a gaggle discussed the lesson.

"I didn't think much of that," said Worsley."He missed out all the good bits. He should have done more on adultery. My brother says married women are always at it."

The reaction was a mixture of fascination and derision.

"How does he know?" said Robinson. "How old is he? Sixteen?"

"Seventeen. He says that there's one married woman that's done it with three of the blokes at his work and he reckons that he could be next. He says that's what the people at his work told him – and he sees lots of the dirty mags there too."

"What dirty mags?" asked Dempsey.

Worsley gave him a scornful look.

"Mags dirtier than anything you've ever seen. They're a lot dirtier than any newspaper. You can't buy them in shops round here. You have to go up to shops in Soho to get them and they wouldn't let anyone like you in."

"So do they have people doing it in them?" asked Dempsey.

"Not half," replied Worsley. "My brother says you wouldn't believe some of the things they get up to."

"Have you seen them?" said Robinson.

"No. The blokes at his work won't give them to him. Besides, my Mum would flay him alive if she caught him with them. He's in enough trouble already because he says he's a Protestant now."

It took several seconds for this news to sink in.

"What do you mean, he's a Protestant now?" said Clancy.

"My Dad is a Protestant," replied Worsley, "so my brother says he can be one if he wants to. He says he likes being a Protestant. Protestants don't have to go to church on Sundays."

"What, never?" asked Dempsey.

"Hardly ever," said Worsley. "My Dad will only go if it's a wedding or a funeral or something like that. He says he doesn't like vicars."

Clancy thought about the chore of getting up for mass on cold winter Sundays, when he would much rather stay in bed. Despite all he had been taught, maybe there was something to be said for Protestantism.

"That stuff about Catholic girls not wearing miniskirts is crap too." said Docherty. "You should see the girls at Saint Anselms's. They get a skirt inspection at assembly, but by first break, skirts are up around their bums, knickers flashing everywhere."

"And I hear, some of them are at it with the boys behind the bike sheds," added Robinson.

"That's Secondary Moderns for you," said Hearne, sniffily.

"And what's all this stuff that Muldoon says about praying to the Blessed Virgin if you feel a bit horny?," added Worsley. "My brother says thinking about virgins always makes him horny."

"You can't say that about Our Lady," said Dempsey.

"It's not me, it's what my brother says," said Worsley. "He says girls don't want to be a virgins these days. Convent schoolgirls can't wait for it. Most of them don't hold out more than a week after they leave."

"How does he know?." asked Robinson. "I bet he's never done it with one."

"I bet he's never done it," said Hearne, as the others laughed.

"He reckons he's going to soon," said Worsley, becoming annoyed. "Him and his mates are meeting some girls from Saint Angela's in the Croydon Wimpy Bar. He says you only have to buy them a coffee and the knickers will come down."

This was met with general derision, although tinged with a little jealousy. Who knew what might happen after coffee in a Wimpy Bar?

Worsley continued.

"My brother says they're going to take them to this film to get them in the mood. It's an X."

"What's the film?" asked Clancy.

"I dunno. It's got a funny name. It's foreign."

"They won't be able to understand it," said Dempsey.

"That doesn't matter," said Worsley. "No one listens to the words in a foreign film. It's what you see. My brother says they're at it in the film the whole time."

"Has he seen it, then?" asked Hearne.

"No. He says that's what someone at work told him."

Fascinating as he found the subject of convent girls and their desires to be relieved of their virginity, Clancy had a more immediate question.

"Is wanking a mortal sin?"

All the others except Dempsey laughed.

"I bet if you asked Muldoon, he'd say it was," said Hearne. "He'd say you were off to Hell if you even mentioned it."

"Why do you ask?" said Dempsey.

Clancy began to blush.

"My Mum wants us all to go to mass together next Sunday. It's for her uncle. He died a year ago. She'll expect us all to go to communion. She'll start asking all sorts of questions if I don't. I can't tell her I've had a wank, can I?"

The others all nodded. Saying you've been wanking is not something mothers want to hear.

"Why can't you go to communion just because you've been a dirty little boy and had a wank?" said Worsley. "Why don't you just go? Who'll know?"

Clancy was surprised at how shocked he was at Worsley's suggestion. Fifteen years of a Catholic upbringing made the idea seem almost unthinkable.

"I can't do that. It would be…"

"Do you really believe that a bit of bread is really Jesus?" said Worsley.

"Well … maybe ... I dunno. Suppose it is."

"So you think it would be a sacrilege. You'll have to go to confession, then," said Dempsey.

Clancy grimaced. He has been trying desperately to hold off the inevitable.

"What do I say? I can't just say I've been wanking."

"You'll have to find another word for it," said Worsley. "There are loads of them. How about tossing yourself off?"

"That's just as bad," said Clancy.

"I've got one," said Robinson. "Firing a one-gun salute."

They began laughing.

"I've got another one," said Worsley. "Shaking hands with the wife's best friend."

Even Clancy was laughing, despite himself.

"You're not helping."

"Why don't you say what I say?" said Hearne. "Say you've been impure with yourself."

That produced guffaws all round. Clancy was astonished.

"Does that work?"

"Works every time," said Hearne. "It doesn't sound rude. It sounds..."

"Genteel?" suggested Clancy.

"Exactly. You had a genteel wank. The priest will hardly notice what you're saying. I bet you get no more than an Our Father and a few Hail Mary's."

***

Clancy decided to go to confession at Saint Aiden's in Coulsdon. He didn't want his parish priest to hear what he had to say. He entered the gloomy box and could only just make out the face of the priest through the grille. He started with a few desultory confessions of dereliction of duties and then swallowed hard.

"I have been impure with myself, Father."

Neither the priest's expression, nor the tone of his voice, changed.

"Did this action lead to loss of seed, my son?"

Clancy was surprised. He thought that was the point of wanking.

"Yes, Father."

The priest's face remained impassive and his tone unaltered.

"Is there anything else you would like to say to me, my son?"

"No, Father."

"Then for your penance say one Our Father and three Hail Mary's and pray to Almighty God for help in all things and ask for the intercession of His mother, the Blessed Virgin Mary."

As the priest began to intone the words of absolution, *"Ego te absolvo..,* " Clancy experienced a huge sense of relief and then, for no reason, Worsley's opinions of virgins and the priest's invoking of Mary became conflated in his mind. He felt a sudden tumescence. He tried desperately to put the thought out of his mind, but that only made things worse, as visions of sexually voracious convent girls floated before his eyes. Was this another sacrilege? Was he making a bad confession? Could he still go to communion on Sunday? Should he tell the priest? It was too late. The absolution had finished.

He opened the confessional door, knelt in a nearby pew and started his penance. He felt he must do more. Maybe, if he added another Our Father and a couple more Hail Mary's, that would be enough.

The Strike

Father Muldoon's mood was not improving as he cut the single rasher on his plate. Not only had he a sore head, but the school had forgotten to order bacon. One rasher was no notion of a breakfast. He was already in a bad mood, because his mass that morning had taken well over half an hour, thanks to a dolt of a server, Lennon, who kept mixing up the responses and nearly spilled the cruets. What Almighty God made of it, Heaven alone knew. He despaired of the English. What sort of nation was it that couldn't keep a school fed and sent boys to serve mass that didn't know their *Introibo ad altare Dei* from their *Ite missa est*?

To make matters worse, he had read in the *Catholic Herald* that mass was going to be in English, not Latin and not even Irish, and the priest would have to face the congregation, just like Protestants do. The Archbishop of Canterbury must be laughing himself silly.

Some priests might like it – Father Finbar Fahey for one. What would you expect from someone from Borris in Ossory? He would be rubbing his hands at the idea of parading himself before all the ladies of the parish, but how could you concentrate on saying the holy words *hoc est enim corpus meum* – or whatever it would be in English – with a pack of gormless parishioners staring at you? The way things were going you soon wouldn't know whether you were in a Catholic or a Protestant Church. It was all the fault of bishops from countries that no one had ever heard of. Johnny come latelys to the Catholic faith, most of them. Popes have been too soft on them. Archbishop John Charles McQuaid should have a word with the Pope. The Holy Father would soon put a stop to all that sort of nonsense, once he knew what was going on.

He eyed the unopened letter on his table balefully. Frankie Fahey was up to his tricks again. Hadn't he more money already than he knew what to do with? So why was he chasing every last penny? Did he think a poor priest had ten pounds or more in his back pocket, ready to give to a grasping bookie? And wasn't Frankie Fahey responsible for the state of his head after last night? The cheapskate Fahey thought he would curry favour and had presented the Catenians meeting with bottles of whisky that had some cod Scottish name, because he had been made an even bigger cheese in the Knights of Saint Columba. They must have come from the bottom of the barrel. You wouldn't get that sort of head from proper Scotch, like Teacher's or Bell's, however much you drank.

As he swigged his tea, something else was bothering him, something that he couldn't put his finger on. Something was up. He was sure of it, but he didn't know what. He had noticed a few boys whispering among themselves and going quiet when they caught sight of him. Nothing unusual in that, except it was the way they looked when they saw him. Not the usual suspects, either. He could see any devilment they might be up to a mile off. A chit for the strap soon had them pondering the error of their ways. It was some of the boys that usually kept their heads down and their noses clean that he was sure were up to something. He would get to the bottom of it.

Nurse Connolly found herself in an unusually buoyant mood that morning, as she eyed the bottle of her favourite whisky and the carton of 200 Woodbines that sat on her table. They had been sent by the school's food supplier after she had agreed to take a consignment of meat that had been rejected by Croydon Grammar School for Girls. Nurse Connolly could only shake her head in disbelief when she heard of it. Those Protestant girlies were too fussy altogether. The packets did not specify the sort of meat, but it would, she thought, make a fine enough stew when boiled for a sufficiently long time with cabbage and potatoes. Campion boys wouldn't turn up their noses at it. They knew what was good for them. She called Bridie and Rosie over and poured each a little tot of whisky, with a larger one for herself.

"Just the one, mind," she said as they downed their glasses. "It's a sin to have more than one before twelve."

Thus fortified she turned on her staff and set the orders for the day.

"Brigid Murphy and Oona O'Connell, stop your idling. Those spuds won't peel themselves. Assumpta Mahoney, those carrots won't get scraped and sliced by looking at them. Mary O'Brien, are you going to stand there all day catching flies in your mouth or are you going to cut up those cabbages?"

Josefina and Maria, as ever, ignored any commotion and continued with their usual task of cleaning the ranges and ovens and sweeping the floor. Nurse Connolly went back and sat down at her table, taking a deserved rest from her exertions. She passed a packet of Woodbines to Rosie, who took out a cigarette, lit it and passed it back. Nurse Connolly leant back in her chair, drew on her cigarette and contemplated things with some satisfaction.

In the mid-morning break Clancy, Docherty and Dempsey joined the others at the far end of the recreation ground for a meeting to finalise preparations. They had decided to take Dempsey senior's advice and keep things to a self-appointed vanguard, but inevitably there were leaks. A good number of the boys knew that rebellion over dinners was in the air, although most didn't know exactly what form the rebellion might take. That did not matter. Something finally was going to be done about the food. They knew enough to keep quiet so that news of it did not reach the ears of the staff. If Muldoon had got to hear of it there would have been ructions, but he seemed to be acting no worse than usual.

The middle school, the third and fourth years, was key. Clancy and Docherty were in 4A.

"4A is solid," said Docherty. "How about 4B?"

Dempsey nodded. "4B is solid, too."

"And 4C?"

Digby nodded.

"What about you third years?" said Docherty.

"We've checked and we reckon no one in our year will go in," said Mathews, who was in 3A, "but what about the first and second years."

"Don't worry about them," said Docherty. "We'll threaten to beat them up later if any of them goes in."

"Well, what about the sixth form, then?" said Mathews.

Clancy and Docherty looked at each other. They knew they couldn't intimidate sixth-formers, but before they could say anything, Worsley, who, as usual, had come to see what was going on, answered.

"Don't worry. They won't go in."

"How do you know?" asked Clancy.

"Because it's a day of fasting and abstinence for them."

"What?" said Clancy and Docherty in unison.

Worsley smiled.

"It was Stephenson's idea. My brother says he's a bit of a Bolshie. They know about the strike, but some of them are prefects, so they have to be careful. Stephenson found out that today is the anniversary of when Blessed Thomas Garnet was hung, drawn and quartered."

"Who?" said Docherty.

"The Garnet Shield that we play for in cricket," said Clancy. "It's named after him. He was a Jesuit."

"That's right," said Worsley. "And he went to Stoneyhurst, Father Arundell's old school. So Stephenson went to Arundell and said they would like to have a day of fasting and abstinence in honour of Blessed Thomas Garnet. Arundell was ever so pleased. My brother said he even smiled."

There was a low whistle of appreciation from the rest of the company.

"That is absolutely brilliant," said Docherty. "So are we all ready to go?"

They all nodded.

"Right, we agreed four pickets on both doors and we should have two at the end of the corridor to stop them even going to the refectory. The others spread the word in your classes. At 12.30 sharp. OK?" said Clancy.

They all nodded again, as the bell for the end of break sounded.

Father Muldoon, passing by an upstairs window, looked down and saw the group disperse. It made him more suspicious than ever that something was afoot. He needed to look into it.

***

Clancy, Docherty, Digby and Dempsey, picketing the main refectory doors, looked down the empty corridor with mounting glee. It was as if the whole school was of one collective mind. Almost none of the boys had attempted to go in to dinner. A couple of gangly fifth-formers, obviously oblivious to events, had turned up, but when told about the strike had burst out laughing, slapped Docherty on the back and went off cheering. Then Clancy saw two small figures coming towards them – first years. They stopped and looked up, timidly, at the pickets.

"Don't you know this is a strike?" said Docherty.

"Yes," said one, "but my Mum says I have to go to dinner every day and she'll ask me what we had."

"Tell her corned beef and prunes," said Docherty – the first thing that came into his head.

"We had that yesterday," said the boy.

Docherty didn't bother to ask him how could possibly know what he had eaten.

"Well, tell her toad in the hole and semolina, then."

"Toad in the hole and semolina," said the boy, doubtfully. "Have we had that before?"

"Yes we have – with real toads," said Docherty, trying not to sound exasperated. "What does it matter? Tell her anything you like."

"OK," replied the boy. "I think I'll tell her we had spam fritters and tapioca."

"Good," said Docherty and turned to the other boy, who was even smaller. "What about you? Do you have to tell your Mum what you ate?"

The boy blinked.

"I don't have a Mum. She died. My Dad works late. I only have bread and marge to eat when I get home."

The pickets looked at each other, not knowing what to say.

"OK, you had better go in," said Clancy, finally.

"Can Shaw come in with me?" said the boy, pointing to his companion.

Clancy looked at the others, who shrugged.

"Alright, just the two of you."

As the two went in and sat down among the empty tables, they heard loud noises coming from the kitchen.

"Holy Mother of God, where are all the boys? Have they been taken from us? Are they gone forever? What will we tell their mothers?" cried Nurse Connolly as she swigged another tot of whisky, the black of her eye makeup running down her face with her tears. Around her in the kitchen were steaming pots full of the day's dinners and piles of plates and dishes waiting to be filled.

"I saw plenty of them when I came in today," said Bridie morosely. "They're not coming in for their dinners."

"Not coming in for their dinners!," shrieked Nurse Connolly, her voice rising decibels in loudness and an octave in pitch. "Why wouldn't they want to eat all this lovely food we're cooking?" She slumped forward, banging the table with her fists and uttering loud sobs, then sat upright and began yelling at the staff.

"Someone's been putting things in the food. Someone's trying to poison them. That's why they're not wanting to eat it. Was it you, Brigid Murphy? I saw you putting too much salt in the potatoes the other day. What else did you put in them?"

Brigid Murphy shrank back from the verbal onslaught.

"No, Nurse, honestly, I didn't put anything in. Only the salt, as you told me. You didn't say it was too much."

"And what about you, Oona O'Connell?" yelled Nurse Connolly, "Didn't I see you spit in the cabbage yesterday?"

Oona O'Connell, a young woman of typical Irish country build, was not going to take the charge lightly.

"I did no such thing, Nurse Connolly. You're a disgrace for saying so."

That set Nurse Connolly into an even greater state.

"I'll tell you who's a disgrace. The pair of you, that's who. I've had enough of you both. There's any number of fine Irish girls that would give their eye teeth for your jobs. I only have to snap my fingers and they would be on the boat tomorrow. You can both pack your bags at the end of the week."

"I'm not staying another minute!," said Oona, indignation rising further.

Just then, Josefina, who had been listening intently, decided to intervene.

"The boys are not coming because your food is so 'orrible."

For a moment Nurse Connolly could not believe her ears, then she let go in a paroxysm of rage.

"What do you know about food, you jumped up floozy, you strutting Jezebel, you?" she screamed. "You spend all your time flaunting yourself and not doing what you're supposed to be doing. You can pack your bags, too."

Josefina was not to be outdone and screamed back at her with oaths and invectives, invoking the full panoply of Spanish saints and devils and suggesting various ways Nurse Connolly might rearrange her anatomy. At that moment, Father Mostyn, alarmed at what he had been hearing, came into the kitchen.

"Mrs Connolly, what is happening? Why are there no boys at dinner?"

Nurse Connolly gave an inchoate yell, while Josefina let out a howl, rushed up to Father Mostyn, flung her arms around his neck and burst into tears.

"She says I have to go. *Madre de Dios*. Please do not make me go."

As Father Mostyn staggered back, trying to disentangle himself, Maria rushed up and flung her arms round both of them. The more Father Mostyn tried to extricate himself, the more tightly Josefina and Maria clung. The trio careered on a rolling, teetering waltz around the kitchen, scattering pans and leaving a trail of smashed crockery on the floor, as Father Mostyn tried in vain to make himself heard above Josefina's howls and Maria's sobs.

The other kitchen staff stood stupefied at the sight. Assumpta Mahoney started crossing herself continuously, while Mary O'Brien had fished out a rosary from her apron and the Hail Mary's were gushing from her mouth.

"Now we see your true colours, you shameless hussy!," yelled Nurse Connolly. "It's priests you've been after all this time. You couldn't wait to get your filthy hands on one of God's own. Away with you, you scarlet harlot!"

Just as another pile of plates hit the floor, a voice was heard above the din.

"What in High Heaven is going on here?"

The voice was Father Muldoon's.

Richard III

Lights dimmed and, in the darkened room, the projector clicked and wheezed into life. On the screen, a medieval pageant – finely-attired ladies and gentlemen attending a king on his throne, muttering regal platitudes as he greeted his family. Then a sudden change of scene, as a dark, almost demonic, figure, leaning on the empty throne in the now empty room, moved rapidly forward, half limping, half hopping, and spoke:

Now is the winter of our discontent
Made glorious summer by this son of York,

The audience stared transfixed as Laurence Olivier's Richard, Duke of Gloucester, strutted, seduced and murdered his way to the throne of England, killing on his way brothers and nephews, accomplices and enemies, only to die in battle, his last, despairing cry:

A horse, a horse, my kingdom for a horse!

Father Wendell turned the lights back on.

"Now boys, that is the Richard the Third I want to see. Shakespeare, I'm afraid, rather over-egged the pudding with all sorts of little plots and prophecies that only confuse matters. His Richard could last four hours – rather more, I fear, than even your doting parents could put up with. Sir Laurence Olivier knows what an audience really wants – blood, treachery and villainy, with the evil-doer getting his comeuppance in no more than a couple of hours. That is what we are going to give them."

Faces with a range of mostly doubtful expressions looked back at him. Father Wendell was unperturbed. It was always thus. He was confident that it would be alright on the night, even though getting to that night was not going to be easy. He was a firm believer that somehow theatre always worked its magic and he knew also that those doting parents would be grateful at seeing anything that remotely resembled theatre and astonished that their offspring could be corralled into something as organised as a play.

First step: the casting. He surveyed those faces. Some had put themselves forward, eager to try acting, others he had picked out because he detected some trace of talent when teaching them. A few parts needed to be chosen carefully; the rest could be doled out like sweets. Who for Richard? He finally decided on Kelly. Kelly was something of a braggart and a bully, but, ever since the little incident with Wilde's *Ballad of Reading Gaol,* he had exhibited an unsuspected enthusiasm for literature and, Father Wendell thought, some acting talent. His bouts of bad behaviour were no more than an act, the usual mask for adolescent insecurity, and, in any event, they were suitable qualities for a tyrant king. His raging acne too was another disfigurement that could be added to the mix. Next, to choose Lady Anne, the widow that Richard so cruelly wooed. It was always tricky to get boys to play women, especially when they had to dress up. He looked around for the least acned, most symmetrical, face and settled on Elliott, a flaxen-haired fourth-former, who was already showing signs of what the cognoscenti called musicality.

So to Richard's victims. He pointed to Dempsey.

"Dempsey, you shall be George, Duke of Clarence. He was the brother of Richard, so, unfortunately for him, he was the first to be murdered, drowned in a butt of malmsey, which I believe is a type of sherry. You go pie-eyed to your maker. How does that sound?"

Dempsey blinked.

"Thank you, Father."

"Gallagher, I think you should be Lord Hastings, the Lord Chamberlain. Lord Chamberlains are traditionally rather unctuous characters, so I understand, but Hastings lost his head when he balked at Richard usurping his nephew, the young prince Edward. He seems to have been a bit of a martyr. Do you think you could play the martyr, Gallagher?"

Gallagher was notorious for his affected piety, always claiming that he was due to go to the seminary, but never actually going. Father Wendell had a loathing of piety. He regarded it as the Church's version of hypocrisy – the compliment vice pays to virtue. God surely had better things to do than listen to endless oleaginous supplications. Gallagher blushed.

"Yes, Father."

"Now who shall play the Duke of Buckingham, Richard's chief accomplice in all he did, until, finally, even he couldn't stomach the murder of the young princes and lost his head like all the others?"

He fixed his eyes on Archer. The delicious frisson of desire when he had first fallen in love had cooled a little to become a steady, pleasing ardour. It would come to a natural end when Archer left for Oxford and then there would be a chance for something new. He was always open to the spiritually uplifting joys of the new and there was a never-ending stream of possibilities in the boys of the school. The very fact that they were not to be touched, or even to know of his feelings, added piquancy to his desire. That desire was transmuted into the sublime as he contemplated those saints whose surging hormones propelled them to the heights of spiritual ecstasy, like his favourite female saint, Teresa of Avila, transfigured by ecstatic fleshly desires into feeling that Jesus was thrusting his golden spear into her, leaving her all on fire with a great love of God.

"Archer, I think you may be able to summon up the necessary malevolence to be Buckingham. Now, who shall be the other villains – the Cat, the Rat and Lovell the dog, who ruled all

England under the hog? Clancy, I have you down as the Cat, Catesby."

Clancy racked his brains, trying to remember what little he knew of history.

"Who was Catesby, Father?"

"Catesby was something of a thug, Clancy. He would do anything Richard wanted, no questions asked."

Clancy saw Kelly smirking. He did not like Kelly.

"And, at the end," the priest continued, "when Richard cries 'My kingdom for a horse,' he has to let him know that there is not a horse to be had."

Clancy nodded. That would wipe the smirk off Kelly's face.

Father Wendell looked at Worsley and pronounced him most suitable to play the Rat, Ratcliff. He then appointed the other parts, selected a couple of blond, blue-eyed cherubs from the first year to be the young princes and doled out copies of the play.

"I want to see you all on the stage on Wednesday after school. I shall accept no excuses. You are troupers now and the motto of every trouper is 'The show must go on.'"

***

Your beauty, that did haunt me in my sleep
To undertake the death of all the world,
So I might live one hour in your sweet bosom.

Father Wendell resisted the urge to put his head in his hands, Early rehearsals were not going well. Not that they ever did, but these were going particularly badly. Richard was attempting to woo Lady Anne, who was following the coffin of her husband, Prince Edward. Richard had organised the death of Edward and her father-in-law, King Henry VI. But instead of Olivier's quick-witted, devilish wooing, Kelly made the words sound as if he was reading a shopping list.

"Kelly, you are supposed to be telling Lady Anne that you are mad with passion for her, even though she is accusing you of killing her husband. To convince her that you would rather die than live without her love, that you would risk all to spend an hour in her sweet bosom, you are baring your breast and urging her to plunge the sword in, or else she must yield to your charms. I know this is Croydon, Kelly, but could you try to sound a little less suburban?"

Kelly nodded, closed his eyes, pursed his lips, took a deep breath, pulled at his shirt and began to orate. A shirt button pinged off and skittered along the floor, almost to Father Wendell's feet. Elliott's Lady Anne recoiled in fright but then recovered, fluttering eyelids and gazing back at him, a little too admiringly, Father Wendell thought.

"Better, Kelly, better, but let's see the devilry too. I know you have it in you."

Kelly affected what he thought was a devilishly irresistible expression. To Father Wendell it was little more than his usual smirk, but it would have to do for the time being.

"Carry on."

And if thy poor devoted servant may
But beg one favour at thy gracious hand,
Thou dost confirm his happiness forever.

There was silence; Lady Anne seemed enraptured. Father Wendell glared at Elliott.

"Lady Anne, it's your line."

Elliott shook his head.

"Sorry, Father. What is it?"

"Thank you, Elliott. Carry on."

Elliott looked puzzled.

"I'm sorry, Father, I've forgotten my line. What is it?"

It was Father Wendell's turn to shake his head.

"Your line, Elliott is, 'What is it?' Now let us finish this scene. There are a dozen or more to go."

They muddled their way through the rest of the scene, a line missed here, a transposition there, until Lady Anne departed, leaving Richard alone:

Was ever woman in this humour wooed?
Was ever woman in this humour won?

"Neither wooed nor won, Kelly" said Father Wendell. "I'm afraid you're something of an also-ran in the wooing stakes at the moment. We have much work to do. As for you, Elliott, do try to be a little harder to get. Your Lady Anne was practically falling into Richard's arms the moment the coffin was set down. Remember, he has just had your husband and father-in-law killed. That wouldn't make him the most endearing prospect."

***

Father Wendell clapped his hands.

"Now listen, cast. Let me remind you once again that this is a crucial scene in the play. King Edward is dead and his grieving widow, Elizabeth, is being urged by her kinsmen, Lords Dorset and Rivers, and by Richard's mother, the old Duchess of York, to bring her eldest son, the young prince Edward, who is now king, from Ludlow, where he is living, to London,so that he can be crowned. Enter Richard and his familiars. He appears to agree that the prince should come to London, but makes sure that he has only a small escort, so that he has little protection when he arrives. Most of the party then depart and Richard is left alone with Buckingham, when their true characters emerge and the fate of the prince is sealed. Everybody got that? Now let's begin."

Queen Elizabeth was being played by McGlyn, a rather plump adolescent, who made a suitably statuesque queen. His best quality, Father Wendell acknowledged, was a very loud wail, ideal for the speeches he had to deliver, which were mostly run-of-the-mill Shakespearean lamentations. With McGlyn in full cry, Father Wendell could just about make out a few phrases, like "Edward, my lord, thy son, our king, is dead" and "All springs reduce their currents to mine eyes" but that was good enough. Nobody listened to the words of lamentations. It was the tone that counted.

"Now, Richard, Buckingham and the others – in you go. You're here to cheer them up. As Richard says, 'none can help our harms by wailing them.' Enough of wails he is saying. The king is dead. Long live – well, we know who."

Father Wendell thought that Kelly rather overdid the bonhomie in greeting his mother and the others, but, on reflection, maybe that was to the good. Perhaps it was the glint in Olivier's eye, but his Richard III, supposedly a tragedy, always seemed to him to teeter on the edge of comedy – a comedy where Richard, far more than a pantomime villain, was a cackling, scheming manipulator, revelling in the chaos he creates and laughing at his final fate.

Greetings over and the rest of the company dismissed, only Richard and Buckingham remained.

"Now you both come centre stage and act like the conspirators you are. Buckingham, this is your chance. You realise what Richard really wants and you are willing to give him all the help he needs."

Father Wendell's eyes were on Archer as he came forward with the faintly condescending expression that he always found utterly irritating and absolutely beguiling. Archer turned to Richard in silky tones:

My lord, whoever journeys to the Prince,
For God's sake let not us two stay at home.
For by the way I'll sort occasion,

As index to the story we late talked of,
To part the Queen's proud kindred from the Prince.

Father Wendell winced at Kelly's near monotone reply:

My other self, my council's consistory,
My oracle, my prophet, my dear cousin,

"Kelly, I've explained to you that this is a crucial part of the play, where Richard tells us openly how far he will go. Parting the prince from his kindred leaves him helpless, at Richard's mercy. He doesn't need to hide things from Buckingham. Do you remember the way Olivier responds in the film? He is confiding; he is almost playful. Let me show you."

Father Wendell decided he would outdo even Olivier in coquettishness. He put his hand on Archer's forearm, emulating Olivier. Archer's eyes widened.

"*My other self*. They are soulmates, Kelly, nothing is hidden from each other."

He turned towards Archer, looking straight into his eyes, gave his arm a gentle squeeze and felt it stiffen.

"*My oracle, my prophet*. Buckingham goes further and says what Richard had only thought – or perhaps had hardly dared to think." Archer's eyes widened a little further. "There are no secrets between them now, though only they – and we, the audience – know what is to come. So Richard seals their tryst by saying, '*my dear cousin*'." Father Wendell paused, his hand still on Archer's arm, as Archer gazed back at him, almost unblinking, then continued. "He was welcoming him not into his actual family – he was, after all, in the process of murdering most of them – but a family bound to each other by a shared secret." He paused again. "They are twinned in their destinies. There is no going back. So now, let's repeat those two speeches and show the audience what they really mean."

Both nodded; Archer blushed slightly. Father Wendell wondered at the power of art to reconcile desire and submission. His thoughts turned to the previous week and a performance of Allegri's *Miserere,* the thrilling, almost orgasmic, top Cs of the soprano transforming the words of supplication: *Amplius lava me ab iniquitate mea: et a peccato meo munda me* – "Wash me thoroughly from my wickedness: and cleanse me from my sin" - into something approaching exultation in both sin and its expiation. He smiled inwardly.

Was ever someone in this humour wooed?
Was ever someone in this humour won?

***

"Now, cast, this is the *pièce de résistance,* the scene that will wow the audience – the ghost scene."

Father Wendell found the cast looking back at him rather quizzically. He went on.

"There are many ways to do the ghost scene, two of which we will definitely not follow. Shakespeare rather overdid things in what I might describe as an 'all-singing, all-dancing' spectral extravaganza. Olivier, on the other hand, let the side down, I'm afraid, with a very poor show of a few wailing wraiths who would hardly afright your maiden aunt. I think we can do better than either. I have some ideas for very ghostly lighting."

Clancy and several others were impressed. It was about time Shakespeare, not to mention Olivier, were taken down a peg or two.

"Let's see who we can leave out. If we take Shakespeare's list, he started with Henry VI, possibly the least impressive monarch ever to rule in this sceptred isle. He reigned for a very long time, almost fifty years, was crowned king of France as well as England, lost both thrones, lost the hundred years war against the French and lost his wits in the process. I think being damned by him would almost guarantee Richard victory. We can also dispense with those nonentities around Queen Elizabeth, Lords Rivers, Gray and the other one. Who does that leave us with?"

He consulted his text.

"Clarence? Yes, Clarence is a must. Being drowned in a butt of malmsey is, I believe, unique in theatrical history. I once saw a Richard III where the ghost of Clarence did not appear to have completely recovered from his ordeal and was distinctly merry. The audience appreciated it, although I'm not sure his fellow actors did. Lady Anne, she who was wooed, won and despatched, is another must. Every audience knows that Hell hath no fury like a woman beheaded. The two little princes must be there, of course. Nothing tugs at the heart-strings quite so much as infants meeting an untimely death. We must lay it on thick." He looked at the text again. "Hastings? Hmmm. Nobody ever feels very sorry for Hastings. You will have to work hard to get the audience's sympathy, Gallagher. Do you think you're up to it?"

Gallagher adopted his most pious expression.

"I hope so, Father."

"Good. Do say a little prayer before you go on. You never know. Someone may intercede for you."

Father Wendell turned to Archer.

"That just leaves Buckingham. You are the turncoat, Archer. First one side, then the other. How do you put it?"

The first was I that helped thee to the crown;
The last was I that felt thy tyranny.

"Then you have your appointment with the executioner. Some might think Buckingham got his just deserts. You might have to work even harder than Gallagher to win the audience. You will have to show that you really mean what you are saying, to display qualities like insight, contrition and, as we Catholics say, a firm purpose of amendment. Do you think those qualities are within you?"

Archer was taken aback, unsure of the degree of irony in the question – unsure, too, whether any of those qualities *were* within him. Their eyes met; Father Wendell smiled.

"Now, let's run through it."

***

A horse, a horse, my kingdom for a horse!

Kelly's Richard stood waving his sword. Clancy's Catesby responded.

Withdraw, my lord. I'll help you to a horse.

Father Wendell clapped once, loudly.

"Clancy, you have the air of a seedy dealer in horseflesh with a broken-down nag to sell, who thinks this is an opportunity to get it off his hands. Your lord and master is about to be engulfed by a horde of his enemies and, if he goes, you are next. Do try to put just a little urgency, maybe even desperation, into your voice. Now, try again."

Clancy's second effort was several decibels louder and half an octave higher in pitch. Father Wendell grimaced.

"I hear the desperation, Clancy, but I think it needs a little work."

***

"Careful with that sword, Kelly. I know it's only wood, but the way you are waving it about, you will put someone's eye out. And another thing – it's you who is supposed to be killed, not everyone assaulting you. No doubt Richard would prefer to have survived, but history says otherwise. Please let them deliver the fatal thrusts. Now, let's do it again. I'll let you kill a couple of them. After that it's no more king. Got it?"

Kelly assented, reluctantly, and after coming perilously close to eviscerating two other boys that he particularly disliked, succumbed and lay on the ground, legs and arms twitching violently, attempting to emulate the last moments of Olivier's Richard. Father Wendell shook his head.

"Two twitches are quite enough, Kelly. You are no Olivier, and even he rather gilded the lily, writhing all over the ground as he did. Most unbecoming of a king, if you ask me."

Kelly's face told of his disappointment. Father Wendell was unmoved.

"We now come to the final scene. The battle is over, Richard is dead and Richmond has won. Richmond, who, as I'm sure you all know, became Henry VII, does his bind-up-the-wounds speech."

Now civil wounds are stopped, peace lives again.
That she may long live here, God say amen.

"So everyone departs in a spirit of brotherly love. One of Shakespeare's less successful final scenes, I'm afraid. To be honest, most of his happy endings are rather soppy. I much prefer ones like Hamlet or Romeo and Juliet, where the stage is littered with corpses and there are lamentations all round. This one is particularly soppy. Richmond comes across as the most appalling goody-two-shoes, whereas he was really a nasty old miser. Shakespeare had to portray him like that because good Queen Bess was on the throne at the time and Richmond was her grandfather. It didn't pay to fall out with royalty in those days."

***

The evening of the first performance arrived. Father Wendell stood at the entrance of the school assembly hall, now arranged as a theatre, and greeted parents and families, many saying how much they were looking forward to their son's first appearance "in lights". Rehearsals had been the usual chaos, but he was confident that some sort of performance would ensue – enough, at least, to satisfy an indulgent audience.

He went in as the house lights dimmed and Kelly limped out to deliver his "winter of discontent" soliloquy. It went rather better than he had feared, although the combination of lights and makeup had hidden Kelly's acne, which, he thought, was a shame, because a pock-marked face added something to the sense of Richard's misshapen evil. He made a note to add more hunchback padding for the next performance.

Another pleasant surprise was that the costumes, cobbled together from a dozen dressing-up boxes, with tights borrowed from mothers and sisters, looked fetchingly Elizabethan. Father Wendell was amused at the various stages of manhood revealed by the tights, and was particularly impressed with Archer, as he strode across the boards, carrying all before him.

The play proceeded more or less on course, murder by murder. Most had to be committed offstage. No sufficiently large butt could be found for Dempsey's Clarence, so a stage-hand was deputed to make splashing sounds in a bucket in the wings. As Richard and Buckingham plotted, Lady Anne was wooed, won and discarded; Hastings beheaded; a Cardinal persuaded to pluck the prince out of Sanctuary; a bumbling Lord Mayor and the London populace exhorted to acclaim Richard king. Then the parting of the ways, as even Buckingham could not stomach killing the princes. Father Wendell, had similar reservations and felt that seeing the young princes being smothered onstage might be a little too much for their parents, so they too had to be despatched offstage.

As the play moved to its climax, out of the corner of his eye, Father Wendell noticed a hand, which he assumed belonged to the prompter, poking out from the wings and gesticulating as Richard was speaking.

Give me another horse! Bind up my wounds!
Have mercy, Jesu!—Soft, I did but dream.

He had an idea that something had gone wrong, but without the text in hand, he could not be sure. At the end of the scene he hurried backstage to find Kelly sitting down slumped, with his head in his hands.

"What happened?"

"He's missed out the ghost scene, Father," said the prompter.

"What?"

"I'm sorry, Father," said Kelly, looking up, distraught. "I don't know how it happened. I just forgot and went from one scene to the other."

Father Wendell took a deep breath and considered the options. As he had told the cast, in his opinion the ghost scene was very much the play's *pièce de résistance*. He had arranged for the ghosts to appear behind a light muslin screen, their whitened faces spotlight. The effect was satisfyingly spectral. It was unthinkable not to do it.

"We have to have a ghost scene. The play isn't the play without a ghost scene. We will have to put it at the end."

The cast looked at him, astonished.

"What do you mean, 'at the end', Father?" said Archer.

"I thought someone of your intelligence would know what 'at the end' meant, Archer. After Richmond has finished his final speech you must all go on and do the ghost scene."

The cast looked even more astonished.

"Don't worry," said Father Wendell. "They won't notice. I doubt if any of them have ever seen the play before. Besides, it's a much better ending than the dreary last scene. It will give them something to talk about."

***

Father Wendell stood outside the hall, greeting the audience as they emerged.

"Oh it was lovely to hear the boys speaking such lovely language, Father, even if I didn't understand all of it," said one mother.

"Thank you, Mrs…?"

"O'Halloran, Father. My boy Brendan was one of the crowd cheering when your man, the lord, was saying Richard should be king."

"Ah yes, Brendan. Splendid performance. Bound to go on to greater things next year."

"I loved it was so spiritual at the end, Father," said another mother. "It makes a nice change from all this bad language and kitchen sinks you see on television these days. Don't you think we need more spirits on television?"

"I do see what you mean, Mrs…?"

"Cleary, Father."

"Mrs Cleary. Spirits are in rather short supply everywhere, I'm afraid."

"How could he do it, Father?" said Mrs O'Halloran.

"How could who do what, Mrs O'Halloran?"

"That King Richard. How could he murder those two little boys?"

"Oh, he was a wicked, wicked man," said Mrs Cleary. "He must have been to murder the likes of those two little angels we saw on stage."

"I can assure you that those two are still very much with us, Mrs Cleary," said Father Wendell

"Oh they are, thanks be to God," said Mrs Cleary, "but those two little innocents he put in that tower aren't."

"I had to cry when I saw what happened," said Mrs O'Halloran. "I had to say an eternal rest for their souls."

"I'll say one too," said Mrs Cleary. "You can never have too many eternal rests."

Father Wendell thought he had better offer reassurance.

"I'm sure the little princes went straight to Heaven, like all innocent children. No need to pray for them. God would have opened his arms to them."

"I'd say you're right, of course, Father, but they say an eternal rest never goes to waste," replied Mrs Cleary. "Saint Peter can hand them out to another poor soul who has no-one to pray for them. That could be just the ticket to get them into Heaven."

"He would go straight to Hell, wouldn't he, Father?" said Mrs O'Halloran. "No Purgatory for him."

"Well, er, Mrs O'Halloran, who knows the limits of God's mercy?"

"The Devil would have him roasting in the fires of Hell before he could get his coat off," said Mrs Cleary. "I think the Devil himself would be shocked at some of the things that wicked King Richard got up to, don't you, Father?"

Father Wendell was always at a loss when confronted by simplicities of faith. He considered that he had long since transcended notions of retributive spiritual justice, so he had no idea how to reply. He smiled sweetly and turned to other parents who wanted to talk to him about their sons' thespian triumphs.

Easter

It is clergy night at the South Croydon Catenians. Dinner (cream of mushroom soup, pork chops, potatoes, peas and carrots and apple pie) is finished and whiskies are being served. Father Muldoon is seated next to Superintendent O'Driscoll of the Metropolitan Police, Z-Division (Croydon).

"It's Holy Week next week, Father. I expect you'll be very busy."

"Oh, I will, Superintendent. There's something to do every day. On Maundy Thursday we'll have mass in commemoration of the Last Supper and then Adoration of the Blessed Sacrament all through the night at the school chapel. I've organised a rota for the boys and their parents."

"That's very good of you, Father. Will they all come?"

"They will, Superintendent, if they know what's good for their immortal souls. On Good Friday we have Stations of the Cross and a procession round the school grounds, followed by a veneration of the relic of the True Cross. The Canon was given it when he was in Jerusalem with Allenby's army in 1917. It's the holiest relic in England, so they say."

"A relic of the True Cross – there's not much holier than that, Father. Are there many more like it?"

"There are a few, I believe, Superintendent. The Pope has one, of course, but the Canon's comes from Jerusalem, so it's one of the best."

"I'd say it would be, Father. It couldn't have gone far if it was still in Jerusalem."

"Just so, Superintendent. On Easter Sunday I'll be going to Sanderstead to say Solemn High Mass. Where will you be?"

"We always get mass at St Mary's in West Croydon, Father. They have a great choir there."

"So they do, Superintendent. I've heard them a few times myself. Canon O'Shaughnessy is very keen on choirs. He likes the sound they make, so he tells me."

"Canon O'Shaughnessy is a great one for choirs, Father. He sometimes conducts the choir himself. He's a great parish priest. The parishioners all speak very highly of him."

"So they do, Superintendent, even though he's had a few hurdles to overcome. He's a Laois man, I believe, from near Borris in Ossory. The less said about some others who come from that part of the world, the better."

"There's good and bad everywhere, Father – even in Croydon, though I sometimes wonder where all the good are hiding round here."

"Talking about good and bad, Superintendent, here's Frankie Fahey coming over. What does he want now? It won't be to apologise for the whisky. What's this one called? Inchmorangie. I'll wager it's never been to Scotland in its life."

"Great to see you again, Father. How have you been?"

"Grand, Frankie, and yourself?"

"Never better, Father."

"And the wife?"

"Philomena is in the pink too, Father, thanks be to God. She's off to Croagh Patrick next week for the pilgrimage."

"She'll be up for sainthood one day, Frankie. Is she doing it barefoot?"

"Sadly not, Father. She's a martyr to the bunions. The doctors have told her she is never to go barefoot. She's very disappointed, as you might imagine, but she's been very bucked by my good news, though at the moment it is very confidential. I trust you will keep it under your hat. I have been approached to be the next Supreme Knight of Great Britain. It will be a great honour."

"Congratulations, Frankie, you'll be moving in grand circles now."

"Oh, I don't know, Father, though I've heard from the Archbishop and the Cardinal to say how pleased they are, and the Pope is to be informed. Philomena, of course, is absolutely delighted, but, thanks be to God, I have to remain humble. The Knights is a charitable body. We treat rich and poor alike. Oh, is that Dermot Kelly over there? He's just been made a director of the Orion Bank, so I hear. I must have a word."

"Will you listen to that, Superintendent. A humble Frankie Fahey! The man has more brass than a bell factory, chasing after bankers. The way he's going he'll have more money than any bank soon. But enough of him. As you were saying, you're hard put to find much good anywhere in England, Superintendent, more's the pity, but I like to think we turn out our fair share from the school."

"That's very true, Father. We don't find many boys from Blessed Edmund Campion up before Croydon Magistrates."

"I should hope not, Superintendent. Our boys are good Catholic boys, all keen to make their Easter duties. Catholics all over the world will be celebrating the rising of our Lord from the dead at Easter, and in Ireland, of course, we are doubly blessed, with two Easter risings."

"I'm with you there, Father."

"As would any Irishman be, Superintendent. At Easter 1916 Ireland threw off the English yoke and breathed the free Catholic air."

"Weren't there still some Protestants left in Ireland at the time, Father?"

"There were indeed, Superintendent, but we showed them the door and they went, bag and baggage, up to the North, or back to England, where they belonged."

"Were they much of a loss, do you think, Father?"

"Not at all, Superintendent. There were plenty more jobs for Catholics after they had gone. Why would we fight for Ireland only to leave the Protestants in charge? What would the O'Driscolls of old say to that?"

"I'd say they would agree, Father. A good few of them did their bit for Ireland, so I'm told. How about your people?"

"They did a good deal more than a bit, Superintendent. You'll have heard of one of them, my uncle, Ernie Muldoon."

"Ernie Muldoon was your uncle? You must have some tales to tell, Father."

"I have indeed, Superintendent, tales that would make your spine tingle with pride. You'll know the song, 'The Bridge of Clavertigh', about how Ernie led the boys from the IRA in an ambush in Tipperary on a platoon of Black and Tans and sent the lot of them to Hell."

"I know it well, Father. I've heard it sung many a time."

We sing a song of Erin free,
Of Collins and Muldoon.
It was on the Bridge of Clavertigh,
That Black and Tans all met their doom.

"A great day for the cause, Father."

"One of the greatest, Superintendent. There weren't enough Protestant coffins for all of them and the Bishop of Cashel wouldn't let them use Catholic coffins, so they had to send to Belfast for more Protestant ones. It was a lesson the Black and Tans would never forget."

"I'd say they wouldn't, Father, and I think there would be plenty more tales like that about your uncle Ernie."

"There are indeed, Superintendent, almost too many to tell. Ernie was the terror of the B-Specials in the North. He and his boys would sneak over the border and take them on anywhere. One time they destroyed a whole barracks full. There was a wailing and a gnashing of teeth among Orangemen that day, I can tell you. And, good man that he was, Ernie would always make sure that they went to mass and communion after a raid – and confession, particularly if they had shot any Catholic cows in mistake for B-Specials."

"I suppose it was an easy mistake to make in the dark, Father."

"I'd say it was, Superintendent. Those Protestant farmers in the B-Specials had faces like a cow's backside."

"Didn't he have a hand in the Big House burnings too, Father?"

"He did, Superintendent. Ernie and his boys would turn up at a Big House with the flaming torches and any rack-renters and lords inside would soon make themselves scarce. You would see the bonfire in the next county. In the end, though, he put a stop to it."

"Did he, Father? Why was that?"

"The last house they were going to burn was Kilconnealy Castle, a great palace of a place, stuffed with the finest paintings, silver and furniture, and owned by Lord Lisdoonvarna, one of the very worst of the bunch. He and his ancestors had always lived high on the hog, while his tenants starved in misery. He knew full well what was in store for him, so he ran for England with his tail between his legs before Ernie and the boys got there. When they arrived it started to rain – a deluge, so I'm told, that put all the torches out. So Ernie decided to stay the night to make sure no harm came to the house. It didn't stop raining for a fortnight and by that time Ernie had decided he would stay longer."

"Was he squatting, Father?"

"He was squatting for Ireland, Superintendent. He was making sure Lord Lisdoonvarna never came back."

"How long did he stay there, Father?"

"For the rest of his life, Superintendent. He was allowed to stay by a grateful nation. Ireland always rewards her heroes. He lived there with his wife, Concepta, another fine example for the nation."

"Concepta Muldoon? Haven't I heard talk of her?"

"You would have done, Superintendent. She led the National All Saints Day novena, which every year prayed for the release from Purgatory of those Irish souls there. By the time it ended it was decreed that it had released all Irish souls then in Purgatory and had enough prayers in the bank for Irish souls to be exempt from Purgatory for the next ten years."

"I remember her well now, Father. Do you think she was a saint?"

"There's many that do, Superintendent. The Mammy was a member of the Archsodality of Our Lady of Kilconnealy, which prays for her beatification. The word from Rome is that the Pope looks kindly on the idea of the Blessed Concepta and has asked the Archbishop of Dublin to look out for a miracle in her name. You need a miracle so that you can be called Blessed."

"With all those Irish having her to thank for praying them into Heaven, I shouldn't think a miracle will be long in coming, Father."

"Let us hope so, Superintendent. Ireland is the land of saints and scholars, but we can always do with another saint."

"What did Ernie do after, Father?"

"Ernie was a Dev man, Superintendent. There was no shilly-shallying with Ernie. It was Dev all the way down the line, so there was a bit of business that had to be settled after we threw the English out. The Free Staters had to be shown the errors of their ways and Ernie was the man Dev relied on to show them. There were very few that would care to argue with Ernie."

"Wasn't he a great singer too, Father?"

"The very finest you ever heard, Superintendent. You can forget your John McCormacks and your Joseph Locks. Ernie had them all beat for a song. His 'Boulavogue' would bring patriotic tears to the eyes of the strongest of men and send them out, flag and Thompson gun in hand, all fired up to fight for Ireland's cause. We've never heard his like since. He was a great countryman, too. Are you a shooting or fishing man, Superintendent."

"I'm not, Father. There's not much chance of that in Croydon. The brother fishes. He always tries to get me to go with him when I go back to Roscommon."

"If Ernie, God rest his soul, were alive he would show you how, Superintendent. There was nothing Ernie didn't know about fly-fishing. Salmon and trout the length and breadth of Ireland swam in fear of his rod. I heard tell that fish jumped out of the river in fright when they caught sight of him on the bank. He was a great shot, too. They used to hold the All-Ireland Pheasant Shoot in the grounds of Kilconnealy Castle. One year, 1941 I think it was, he broke the Irish record for birds shot – 2,700 and a bit more, though carpers claimed that some of the birds were Chinese pheasants and shouldn't count for an Irish record. Ernie had no time for that sort of talk. A look from him and they soon stopped their carping."

"Oh Ernie knew what was what, alright. There are none left like him now, Father."

"There are not, Superintendent. When he died, mourners lined the roads all the way from Kilconnealy Castle to Dublin. Three bishops and 57priests attended at his Requiem Mass. Dev delivered the eulogy – in Irish, of course. Ireland has not seen a send-off like it since."

French lessons

"Every time I open my mouth, some fool speaks!"

Clancy ticked off another Muggerism amidst barely suppressed giggles in the rest of the class. It was something to do in French lessons, better than actually learning French.

"It's only been five minutes," whispered Hearne, who was sitting next to him. "I reckon we'll get a few more today."

Clancy tried to stop himself from grinning. The most he had ticked in any one lesson was five. He looked at Mr Muggeridge surveying the class for the miscreant, with his usual expression of exasperation that there were too many suspects on which to pin the blame, and thought there might be the prospect of beating the record.

Charles Augustine Muggeridge was every inch the Frenchman. He had been born to a French mother and an English father, who had moved to Paris in pursuit of his artistic ambitions. Unfortunately for Muggeridge *père*, he had no artistic talent and had frittered away a modest fortune in attempting to prove otherwise. His only son, Charles, brought up largely by his mother, a woman of sound, conservative and Catholic principles, had inherited his father's lack of artistic ability and had added to it a lack of discernible talent for any activity or profession that might allow him to earn a living.

With the family fortune largely gone, his mother despaired of his ever finding gainful employment in France and decided that only England held out any prospects. Everybody in France knew of English schoolboys' inability to ingest any but the most rudimentary elements of French grammar and vocabulary, so she reasoned that teaching French in an English school ought not to be beyond his ability.

After endowing her son with a diploma in pedagogy, purchased from a local institution, she enlisted the help of her local bishop, to enquire of his counterparts in England whether a suitable position might be found in a good Catholic school. Initially she had hinted at schools like Ampleforth and Stoneyhurst, but was told that those establishments tended to look sniffily at candidates with qualifications less than a degree from the Sorbonne. Eventually he was offered a post in an establishment called the Blessed Edmund Campion Boys Grammar School, located in Croydon, a place of which she had never heard. When she did learn more about it, she rather wished she had remained in ignorance.

Charles had a passable, though idiosyncratic, grasp of English, spoken with an accent compared to which Maurice Chevalier sounded like John Gielgud. He had almost no knowledge of English customs and mores, so his mother had taken the precaution of sending him to stay in a boarding house in London, three months before he was due to start at the school, to accustom himself to the country.

At first he had found everything bewildering. Then he remembered his father reading *Alice in Wonderland* and *Alice Through The Looking Glass* to him in English as a young boy. At the time, he had no idea what they were about, but now all became clear. They were not childish fantasies, but rather factual descriptions of England. Everything in England was through a looking glass – a mirror image. Cars drove on the opposite side of the road, which put him in peril every time he stepped off a pavement; in France a temperature of 30 degrees was a hot day, in England a cold day, and, as for the currency, he thought he would never understand it. Instead of the rational one franc equal to a hundred centimes, there was a panoply of units bearing seemingly arbitrary relations to each other. There were pounds, shillings and pennies, in multiples of twelve and twenty. He was never sure which applied to which. Then there was the array of coins, some of which seemed to have no reason to exist, like the thrupenny bit, equal to three pennies – why three? Why not five or seven or any number? And there was something called a half-crown, but no full-crown as far as he could see. Even the pennies could be divided into halves and something called a farthing.

Pounds could be a particular difficulty. Very early in his stay he had gone into a shop to buy butter. The assistant had asked him did he want a pound and he asked how much that was. The assistant pointed to a packet and Charles had remarked that it didn't seem much for a pound. Butter was much cheaper in France. The assistant had looked at him oddly and replied, "No, mate. Butter's two and six a pound. You get eight pounds for a pound." Eight pounds for a pound? To a mind accustomed to Cartesian rigour, that made no sense whatsoever.

Charles Muggeridge had now spent more than fifteen years living and teaching in England, but had made few concessions to his adopted country. He liked to think that, in the words of General de Gaulle, he embodied a certain idea of France. That was certainly true for the boys of Edmund Campion, though that idea bore little relation to any lofty Gaullist notion. Instead they saw him as the caricature Frenchman that had been portrayed in everything from film and TV to the pages of the *Beano*. Their object in his lessons was not to learn French – perish the thought – but to find ways of goading him into Gallic outbursts that they found funny.

The giggles from his first remarks had died down, though he couldn't identify the fool that had spoken.

"Now boys, turn to page 77 in ze book. I want you to translate ze passage you see. It is about life in France."

Clancy opened the book and scrutinised the text. It seemed to be all about *fermiers* and *paysans*, with an admixture of *vaches, poules* and *blé,* confirming his impression that the French were a bunch of yokels. The rest of the class seemed to have come to the same conclusion. There was a low moo from the back of the class. Mr Muggeridge pointed to Dempsey.

"Was zat you, Dempsey?"

"No, Sir."

"I heard you grin, laddie. I know it was you."

Clancy made another tick. Two. For several minutes there was silence as the boys worked, then came another moo, followed by several chicken noises from the other side of the classroom. Mr Muggeridge was becoming more agitated.

"Zat was you, Hennessey, wasn't it?"

"No, Sir."

"Yes it was. I will not 'ave you clucking me, laddie. Any more of zis and I will telephone your mother. In ze past I 'ave 'ad several *affaires* with your mother over ze telephone."

Clancy contemplated adding two more ticks but settled for one. Mr Muggeridge was primed. Time for the diversion.

Worsley raised a hand

"Yes, what is it, Worsley?"

"Please, Sir, who do you think will win the Tour de France?"

This was the trump card. For three weeks in every year it was guaranteed to win. Mr Muggeridge's main obsession was the Tour. His eyes almost glazed over at he thought of scrutinising every twist and turn of the Tour described in the copies of *L'Equipe* that were posted to him from France daily. He would bring a small transistor radio into the classroom and listen to the French broadcast of the race, with the volume turned down, as the boys did their exercises.

There was only one answer to the question.

"Why, Jacques Anquetil, of course. Now get on with your work."

Worsley, like every other boy in the class, knew that a follow-up was needed.

"I heard that Raymond Poulidor was going to win, Sir."

Mr Muggeridge regarded that with a mixture of contempt and surprise. Contempt that anyone could imagine that the peerless Jacques, winner of four Tours, could lose to an upstart like Poulidor, whatever the *sans-culottes* of the French public thought of him, and surprise that a boy like Worsley would have such knowledge.

"Jacques Anquetil will always win. He is ze king of ze time trials."

Worsley was not alone. He, Hearne and Clancy had got hold of a copy of the magazine *Cycling Weekly* that detailed all the stages and riders of the Tour, with opinions on likely winners. They intended to put the information to good use.

"He may be good at time trials, Sir," said Hearne, "but they're shorter this year. Poulidor could beat him over the mountains."

"I agree, Sir," said Clancy. "Mountain stages like Thonon to Briançon and Toulouse to Luchon look very tricky for Anquetil. I reckon Poulidor has the edge."

Gallic suspicions were aroused. Mr Muggeridge had never come across boys with this degree of interest in, let alone knowledge of, the Tour. What did they know of places like Briançon and Luchon? Their knowledge of French geography was abysmal. They had heard of Paris and that was about it. Besides, the English had no interest in the sport of cycling. The Tour hardly got a mention in the newspapers. Football was what they cared about, and perhaps rugby. Worsley, Hearne and Clancy were up to something.

"You three are a right pair. You are saying zis to distract me from your lessons."

Another tick. Four.

"No, Sir," responded Worsley. "We wouldn't do that. We just want to know who you think will win. We know Anquetil has won before, but some say he is over the hill and Poulidor will get him this time."

This was almost too much for Mr Muggeridge. No one should be allowed to traduce the great Jacques Anquetil in that manner.

"I 'ave told you a million times before, Worsley, zat I do not repeat myself. Jacques Anquetil will win. He is ze king of ze time trials."

Tick. Five.

"How does he keep going so long, Sir?" asked Hearne. "Does he have special food or something?"

Mr Muggeridge was still suspicious, but he had to admit it was a reasonable question.

"Cyclists 'ave to be very careful what zey eat. Zey must not get fat. Zere is one food zat all cyclists eat for strength and stamina and zat is eggs. Who can tell me what is ze French for egg?"

He pointed to a startled Dempsey.

"Er ..." said Dempsey, with perhaps a hint of an f at the end.

"Correct, Dempsey," said Mr Muggeridge, gratified that something at least had seeped into Dempsey's head. "The French for egg is *oeuf, un oeuf, nom masculin.* All you boys that do cycling should eat eggs to keep up your strength."

"Is that what you do, Sir?" asked Gallagher, ever anxious to curry favour.

"I do, Gallagher. I 'ave joined ze South Croydon Wayfarers Cycling Club and when Mrs Muggeridge sees me coming back from a ride she puts me on an egg."

"Bingo. That's six," whispered Hearne.

As they spilled out of the classroom after the lesson, they started laughing. "Could be seven-up next time," said Docherty - but then the laughter was stifled as they saw Father Muldoon coming towards them along the corridor. The entire class passed by him in silence, as he looked on with a baleful expression. Docherty broke the silence, as they turned into another corridor.

"He's still on the warpath, trying to get back at us for going on strike. He's giving chits to everyone. McDowell got eight for whistling in the gym. It wasn't even a loud whistle."

"Yeah, and I heard he gave all the under-14 football team six because one of them had dirty kit. He said the others should have told him to wash it," said Worsley.

"And he's now giving four if you have brown shoes instead of black," said Dempsey, "and if you have shoes without laces. He says they're only worn by spivs."

"He can't go on like that forever," said Clancy. "Anyway we won, didn't we. Nurse Connolly and her crew have been sacked. The dinners have to get better."

"They couldn't get any worse," agreed Hearne. "By the way, does anyone know what's happened to Mostyn? Nobody seems to have seen him lately."

Wolsey dropped a bombshell. "He's been sent to Nigeria."

The others looked at him in astonishment.

"Why, and anyway, how do you know?" said Clancy.

"My Mum knows Sir Douglas McKinsey. He's the chairman of the school governors. You know all the ladies like Mostyn. He told her that Muldoon had caught him in a clinch with Josefina, the Spanish tart that used to be in the kitchens. He said they couldn't have that sort of thing going on in the school. He said it would set a very bad example."

That brought hoots of derision.

"That's why Josefina got sacked," said Docherty. "Do you think Mostyn was actually doing it with her?"

"I bet he was," said Worsley. "My brother said he'd give her one if it was him."

That brought more derision.

"Well anyway," continued Worsley, unabashed, "he's been packed off to some mission in the middle of Nigeria, hundreds of miles from anywhere. He can do what he likes there and no one will ever know. That's the last anyone will ever see of him."

The Death of Winston Churchill

Father Arundell could never be considered, not by himself, still less by others, an emotional man. He took a magisterial view of mortality. Death comes to us all and, in the sight of God, no death has more significance than any another. Death was a release from this vale of tears. *Nunc dimmitis* was his watchword – Lord, now lettest thou thy servant depart in peace. Even so, he was surprised at how profoundly moved he felt when he heard of the death of Sir Winston Churchill, so moved that he decided, as he considered himself the embodiment of Churchillian principles at the Campion school, to speak to the school assembly that cold January morning.

The school hall was being redecorated, so assemblies were being held in the open air, on the recreation ground. Father Arundell began speaking as snow began to fall.

"Boys of this school, dedicated as it is to the blessed martyr, Edmund Campion, who died a proud Englishman, devoted to saving his country from evil, you will have heard today of the death of another proud Englishman, Sir Winston Churchill, who was also dedicated to saving his country from the evil that menaced it. All of us now should not only give thanks for his life, for without him we might all be living under the yoke of tyranny, but should see him as standing for all of the things Blessed Edmund Campion and this school also stand for."

The snow was becoming heavier. Clancy felt himself beginning to shiver. "How long do you think he's going to go on?" he whispered to Hearne, who rolled his eyes and shook his head.

"We can learn many lessons from the great speeches that Winston Churchill gave during the war," continued Father Arundell. "Your fathers, many of whom will have fought in the war, will confirm what I say. 'I have nothing to offer but blood, toil, tears and sweat,' he told Parliament, when the war appeared to be going badly. That, boys, is an essential lesson. Blood, toil, tears and sweat will take you on to victory in life's struggles. Anything less and you are admitting defeat – and no Campion boy worth his salt ever admits defeat."

The snow was now coming down with a blizzard intensity. The priest wiped it from his glasses and, as the oration continued, Clancy could see that it was starting to stick to his well-tailored black suit.

"'Never in the field of human conflict was so much owed by so many to so few,' Churchill said of the pilots in the Battle of Britain, who saved us from invasion. You boys, too, should think of yourselves as the few – the few of the one true faith who will, through being steadfast in the good fight, bring England back to the faith of our fathers."

Clancy was now shivering continuously and he began to stamp his feet to keep warm. Others in his class were blowing into their hands or rubbing them together. Through the swirling flakes, Father Arundell resembled a gaunt snowman, his words becoming less and less audible in the sound-deadening snow. "...their finest hour... you too can have your finest hour if..."

***

Father Muldoon looked with considerable satisfaction upon the three rashers that lay beside the fried egg, tomatoes and bread on his plate. They were Irish rashers, not the watery, stringy English sort. This was promising to be a good day – Irish bacon was back for breakfast and Winston Spencer Churchill was dead.

Ireland's greatest enemy since Oliver Cromwell had gone to get his just deserts. He'll find the Pearly Gates slammed shut if he dares show his face. All his fancy speechifying will get him nowhere. Saint Peter will know what to do with the likes of

Winston Spencer Churchill. Didn't he once say that if Hitler had invaded Hell, he would find kind words to say of the Devil? He'll be needing those kind words. He is probably even now taking tea with Satan himself, the two of them laughing about all the wickedness he got up to when he was on Earth. Maybe Adolf Hitler will pop in for a chat. The pair of them would have plenty to talk about.

He'll find plenty of Black and Tans there, too, to keep him company. Churchill despatched the Black and Tans, the dregs of England, off to Ireland to bomb and slaughter their way across the country, but Ireland was more than a match for them and packed them straight off to Hell, thanks to Uncle Ernie Muldoon and his boys in the IRA.

There will be many a glass raised in Heaven when they get the news - and many a verse sung to celebrate. The 'Bridge of Clavertigh' and 'Come Out, Ye Black and Tans' will of course be top of the songsheet. Heaven will be rocking when those two belters are being sung.

Come out, ye Black and Tans, come out and fight me like a man
Show your wife how you won medals down in Flanders
Tell her how the IRA made you run like hell away
From the green and lovely lanes of Killashandra

All the other great songs – 'Kevin Barry', 'Boulavogue', 'The Foggy Dew', 'A Nation Once Again' and 'Kelly the Boy from Killane' – will be heard too. Ernie Muldoon and Kevin Barry will lead the choir of angels and there will be many a patriot joining in, like Sean South from Garryown, Father Murphy from old Kilcormack, the boys of Kilmichael and the bold Fenian men. Michael Collins will be there. He had a very fine voice, so they say. Heaven won't have seen many days like it and, I'd wager, there will only be one better. That will be when the North comes back and all those Orangemen will have to toe the line, or pack their bags for England, where most of them belong.

***

Father Wendell flipped through the pages of the rather tattered copy of Winston Churchill's *My Early Life* that he had found in the school library. The great man had just died and hagiographical outpourings filled every newspaper, radio and TV station. He had expected to read that the usual combination of muscular Christianity and imperial bombast had shaped the early life of the future colossus. Instead the figure, in fact or fiction, that he thought the young Churchill most resembled was Bertie Wooster, admittedly with rather more derring-do and without a Jeeves to save him from the less sensible of his endeavours. There was too, he thought, an air of what the American critic, Susan Sontag, had recently called "camp" about his writing – the distant father who died young, the beautiful, adored, mother, "a fairy princess: a radiant being possessed of limitless riches and power," and the jocular, almost facetious, cadence of his prose.

Wodehousean tones seemed to be everywhere in the book. Born to immense privilege, the young Winston, grandson of the Duke of Marlborough, shared Bertie's ease in moving among high society and acquaintance with almost everyone who mattered, while looking askance at their actions and mores and often getting into hot water as a result.

My Early Life is packed with characters that had more than a passing resemblance to Wodehouse's comic knights, Roderick Spode and Watkyn Bassett, and would have received many a ripe entry in Jeeves' Junior Ganymede club book. General Sir Redvers Buller "was a characteristic British personality. He looked stolid. He said little, and what he said was obscure. He was not the kind of man who could explain things, and he never tried to do so." Not that it did his military career any harm: "He plodded on from blunder to blunder and from one disaster to another, without losing either the regard of his country or the trust of his troops." Another military man, Colonel Brabazon, possessed "a moustache which the Kaiser might well have taken as his unattainable ideal. To all this he added the airs and manners of the dandies of the generation before his own, and an inability real or affected to pronounce the letter 'R'." When informed by the stationmaster at Aldershot that his train had gone, he replied, "Gone! Bwing another!"

The idiosyncrasies and characters of upper class English society were the accepted way of life. After an undistinguished stint at Harrow school, Winston went to Sandhurst and then, as a subaltern, to India, where his main preoccupations were polo and punitive raids against rebellious tribes, many of the raids under the aptly named general, Sir Bindon Blood, a policy known as "butcher and bolt".

Father Wendell found himself amused at the young Churchill's ability to persuade a high-up contact – almost always a Lord or a General – to allow him to join every imperial scrap going, from the last cavalry charge of the British army, at Omdurman in the Sudan, to the Boer war. Like Bertie Wooster, he always seemed to get into hot water but somehow escaped.

Running through it all, Father Wendell detected, too, a nostalgia for an almost prelapsarian England of his youth, where everyone knew their place – and for some that place was splendid indeed. "In those days English Society still existed in its old form. It was a brilliant and powerful body, with standards of conduct and methods of enforcing them now altogether forgotten." Matters were given their due importance. "Lord Salisbury was accustomed scrupulously to avoid calling a Cabinet when there was racing at Newmarket, and the House of Commons made a practice of adjourning for the Derby."

Father Wendell never ceased to be impressed, as well as amazed, that a small ruling elite could, by a combination of arrogance, insouciance, entitlement and a dash of cunning, impose itself on much of the world. He contemplated, too, the irony of the situation of an elite that considered itself wise and benevolent, that was much given to leisure and ruled over a quiescent populace, lived an existence indistinguishable from decadence and was barely a step away from extinction. He smiled and wrote lightly in pencil on the frontispiece, *Sic transit gloria mundi.*

***

Mister Rodney, the school sports master, surveyed the class with a disapproving eye. Not that this class was different from any other. He surveyed every class in the school with a disapproving eye. His eye was seldom in other than disapproving mode. He was a former sergeant major and had served in several colonial conflicts, including Malaya and the Kenyan Mau Mau uprising. Accordingly, he had a rather jaundiced view of lesser breeds without the law, among whom he most certainly included Campion schoolboys.

"Pay attention, boys," said Mister Rodney. "It's snowing, so we can't go outside for PE and the gym is being used by another class, so we are going to have to do something else instead."

Gloom descended on the class. Clancy, like all the others, knew what something else meant – a geography test. Sports masters were supposed to have a second string to their bow for just such circumstances. It was almost always geography, because it was thought that it involved little more than colouring maps and memorising the capitals of countries, so any simpleton could teach it.

Mister Rodney puffed out his impressive chest and addressed the class.

"You will know by now that Sir Winston Churchill died today. Sir Winston was a great believer in the British Empiyah. When he was in, people stood to attention whenever the Empiyah was mentioned. Now look what has happened since he went. We've given it away and a right mess them fuzzies have made of things. I bet most of them are wishing that they was still in the Empiyah and someone like Sir Winston Churchill was still in charge. So we are going to have a geography test today and, in honour of Sir Winston, all the questions will be on the British Empiyah."

Gloom descended even further. There could be little prospect of escape.

"Right, boys, bend over your desks."

Mister Rodney was a firm believer in the maxim of guilty until proven even more guilty. He assumed that the boys would be unable to answer his questions, the punishment for which was a whack on the backside with a plimsoll he always carried. So, to speed up matters, the boys' rears would be in the appropriate position when the questions were asked.

He turned out to have a surprisingly wide knowledge of the geography of the Empire, particularly of those parts where he had served and had had occasion to chastise the natives. Questions on the Malayan Federation, the states of India and the tribes and languages of Africa were inevitably followed by plimsoll meeting buttock. Clancy found himself the last in line. He braced himself as Mister Rodney approached.

"Now, Clancy, can you tell me the capital of Tanganyika?"

Clancy felt a surge of relief. He knew the answer because he had been reading a book on Africa.

"Dar es Salaam, Sir."

Whack!

Clancy felt pain, followed by surprise and then indignation. Before he could stop himself, he blurted out.

"Please, Sir, it is Dar es Salaam. You can look it up."

Whack!

"Nobody likes a smart aleck, Clancy."

Finished with the test, Mister Rodney stood back and looked over the serried ranks of upturned buttocks, each still smarting from the plimsoll's wrath. He thought back fondly to his days of soldiering, shouldering the white man's burden, something these boys would never have to do. To remind them of their heritage, he had administered a lesson in the fickleness of fate and the arbitrariness of authority. It was the proper British way, the way things should always be. The patriot in him was stirred. He had done Sir Winston proud.

Heaven and Hell

The needle came down gently on the disc and the plangent notes of the *Kyrie* from Palestrina's *Missa Papae Marcelli* filled the room. Father Wendell leaned back in his chair, savouring the sumptuous tones coming from his stereo hifi – large Wharfedale speakers, powered by a Quad amplifier, 30 watts per channel, individual controls for bass, treble and middle tones – the only one like it in the school. The recording had been made of the Sistine Chapel Choir at the coronation of Paul VI, the latest pope in the line that the Church claimed stretched back to Saint Peter. How many had there been, he mused? At least two hundred and fifty. Marcellus II, whose papacy lasted only three weeks, would surely have been considered among the least significant, had Giovanni Pierluigi da Palestrina not ensured his musical immortality, his name resounding at every papal coronation since, while most of his fellow pontiffs, predecessors and successors alike, languished in the obscurity of history. Could there be jealousy in Heaven? Perish the thought.

The *Kyrie* was the last remnant of Greek in the Tridentine mass. How had those sibilant *eleisons* survived among the *Gloria* and the *Credo* and the *Agnus Dei* of the sonorous Latin? He often wondered, without finding an answer. Not that it mattered. He marvelled again at how the time-burnished words of the mass, Latin or Greek, melded with the music of Palestrina and then he gazed at the latest documents emanating from the Second Vatican Council on his desk and pushed them aside. It was as if the music was mocking the banality of their language, the triteness of their sentiments and the thoughtless vandalism of casting aside centuries of tradition. It was not why he became a priest.

Why *had* he become a priest? It was a question that he had often asked himself when younger, but now realised that there was no answer – nor could there be. Priesthood was not a destination but a journey – a mysterious quest for grace, that gift of God bestowed on those of faith, with no certainty of it ever being found or even what exactly it was. His vocation, he could see now, had begun with a fascination with the trappings of sight and sound – the decorated interiors of the churches, many gaudy, some magnificent, the gorgeous vestments, the gold and silver of the ciborium and monstrances, the many statues of the Virgin and saints, the graphic depictions of Christ's agony in the Stations of the Cross on the church walls.

There were, too, the processions, the music, the incense, the all-encompassing ceremonial. Then came an equal fascination with the sacraments – the power of the priest in the dark booth of the confessional, who could send him spiritually cleansed back into the light, and a sense of awe at the transubstantiation of bread into the body of Christ. Above all, he now realised, priesthood offered sanctuary. He knew his nature: the priesthood was the perfect home for it. No questions would be asked, no aspersions cast. For him, grace was not, as some would have it, a sort of spiritual balm, anointing the faithful and the submissive. Rather it was, at least in part, the acceptance of what one was, what had been gifted by God. The really grave sin was to deny it.

Vatican II invoked in him a mixture of despair and contempt. Despite all the hopes of reformers, all the high-sounding promises, the results were little more than Protestantism Mark 2, but, as Marx once remarked, second time as farce. It had none of the passion for renewal or the coruscating denunciation of abuses of a Luther, nor did its liturgy in English compare remotely with the resonance of the King James Bible or the Book of Common Prayer. Instead, it proposed stripping Catholic ceremonial of much of its glory and sense of mystery and replacing it with tepid recitations, purportedly to relieve it of much of that mystery and allow the faithful more involvement. But for him, that sense of mystery was precisely why the faithful came to mass – the sense of awe imbued by the architecture of church and cathedral, the arcane rituals of priest and servers, the Latin, understood not for its words but for its musicality, a background to thought and worship. The role of the priest was to help the faithful delve deeper into the mystery of faith. The whole edifice of Catholicism was built on Christ's promise to Saint Peter – "Thou art Peter and upon this rock I will build my Church." Questioning the role of priest as mediator between God and man was like admitting that the Church had made a two-thousand-year mistake.

Even worse, the Council seemed to him to be infused with a spavined puritanism, as if the Church could somehow be cleansed of all of its imperfections, and if that would in any way be a good thing. The Catholic Church always had, to say the very least, an ambivalent attitude to what it officially thought of as sin. Many of the great glories of European civilisation emerged from the murkiest of Vatican sources. The Renaissance popes, chief among them the Borgias and the della Roveres, were, to a man, murderers, adulterers, simoniacs and thieves. He was reminded of Harry Lime in *The Third Man*: "In Italy, for thirty years under the Borgias, they had warfare, terror, murder and bloodshed, but they produced Michelangelo, Leonardo da Vinci and the Renaissance. In Switzerland, they had brotherly love, they had five hundred years of democracy and peace – and what did that produce? The cuckoo clock."

Nor were these popes the exception, rather very much the rule. He had long thought that the history of the papacy was very much like Gibbon's description of history itself in *Decline and Fall* – "little more than the register of the crimes, follies, and misfortunes of mankind." To take one example among many, the first John XXIII, now expunged from the list of pontiffs in favour of the recently-deceased patron of the Council, was indicted on over fifty charges, most of which were eventually dropped in deference to the office. As Gibbon commented, "The most scandalous charges were suppressed. The Vicar of Christ was only accused of piracy, murder, rape, sodomy and incest."

Were these popes not chosen by God, like all the others? Were they not infallible, like all the others? Did they sponsor some of the greatest works of humanity, dedicated to the glorification of God, despite or because of their many and manifest failings? Could a pope who lived by all the precepts of the Church do the same, or are holiness and great art incompatible? Is great sin a necessary, even if not a sufficient, condition for the creation of great works? Does that justify both art and sin – and is the art its own forgiveness?

He recalled, on his first visit to Rome, walking from the Vatican in the spring sunshine down the Via Cola de Rienza, across the Queen Margerita bridge and into the Piazza del Popolo. Tucked away in the corner of the piazza was the basilica of Santa Maria del Popolo. As he entered, his eyes were dazzled by the architecture of the basilica, once an Augustinian church, that had been rebuilt and beautified by the popes of the high Renaissance – Sixtus IV, Julius II and Alexander VI – and graced by some of its finest artists – the high altar by Bernini, the choir ceiling by Pinturicchio, mosaics by Raphael. There had been buried Vannozza dei Cattanei, favourite mistress of Alexander VI, Rodrigo Borgia, and mother of his daughter, Lucrezia. There too, irony of ironies, Martin Luther, then an Augustinian friar, had spent his only night in Rome.

He had come to see for the first time what he considered two of the greatest works of the painter whose art seemed to him supreme – Caravaggio. Murderer, brawler, banished from everywhere he lived and more than a little mad he may have been, but for Father Wendell he had no peer. He stood in awe and wonder, looking first at the Crucifixion of Saint Peter and then turning to the Conversion of Saint Paul. Saint Peter is bathed in light, his expression a mixture of fear and resignation as he is nailed upside down to the cross and dragged off into the dark by a faceless figure. Saint Paul, caught as if in a spotlight, lies on the ground, hands raised, looking up towards his horse and another figure almost obscured in the shadows. The twin pillars of the Church, the one the rock on which it was built, the other on whose words it was forged, both prostrate in terror. *Chiaroscuro* – light and dark – what more apt metaphor for the Church?

The last chords of the Palestrina *Agnus Dei* faded as he turned his mind to other matters – the next day's English class with the fourth form. He had set them to read *Portrait of the Artist as a Young Man* by James Joyce, the text chosen, he had to admit, at least in part, for his own amusement. Now they were in the full throes of adolescence, with the pieties of their younger years clouded by masturbatory fantasies, he wanted to see how they reacted to Joyce's mixture of self-absorption and religious fervour. How would they take a dose of Hell?

***

"Please open your book at Chapter 3. This chapter, as you all should have read, is about the retreat that Stephen Dedalus and his fellow schoolmates undertake. Can someone please tell me what exactly do we mean by a retreat?"

Most of the boys looked at each other sheepishly. Eventually Gallagher put up his hand.

"It is a time for prayer and contemplation, Father, away from distractions."

"Thank you, Gallagher. That is part of it. Let me read you what the Rector, who is giving the retreat, says."

> A retreat, my dear boys, signifies a withdrawal for a while from the cares of our life, the cares of this workaday world, in

order to examine the state of our conscience, to reflect on the mysteries of holy religion and to understand better why we are here in this world.

He smiled inwardly. The Rector had described, almost as succinctly as was possible, the chief instrument with which Irish Catholicism entraps its adherents – the over-examined conscience. *Portrait* was surely its finest example in literature, with Stephen Dedalus continually obsessing about his "soul" and its fate, minutely questioning all his thoughts and actions and then attempting to escape with a less than believable foray into Dublin's red-light district – at age sixteen in ultra-Catholic Ireland? Hardly – before creeping back for another bout of flagellation of the soul. It seems never to have occurred to him that too much examination of conscience was worse, far worse, than too little.

Catholicism's other obsession, of course, was with death. He smiled to himself again. How would these boys, who had, like all young, an implicit belief in their immortality and had never given a moment's thought to their own death, react to the Rector's description of Hell?

"Kelly, would you please read out the passage on page 119, beginning 'Now let us try'."

Kelly, flustered, stood up and riffled through the pages until he finally found the passage. He blinked a couple of times and cleared his throat.

Now let us try for a moment to realize, as far as we can, the nature of that abode of the damned which the justice of an offended God has called into existence for the eternal punishment of sinners. Hell is a strait and dark and foul-smelling prison, an abode of demons and lost souls, filled with fire and smoke. The straitness of this prison house is expressly designed by God to punish those who refused to be bound by

> His laws. In earthly prisons the poor captive has at least some liberty of movement, were it only within the four walls of his cell or in the gloomy yard of his prison. Not so in Hell. There, by reason of the great number of the damned, the prisoners are heaped together in their awful prison, the walls of which are said to be four thousand miles thick: and the damned are so utterly bound and helpless that, as a blessed saint, Saint Anselm, writes in his book on similitudes, they are not even able to remove from the eye a worm that gnaws it.

Kelly looked around as he sat down. The rest of the class stared straight ahead.

"What are we to make of this vision of Hell?" asked Father Wendell.

Most of the class stayed mute. Gallagher, with his endless flirtation with a vocation, prided himself on a passing knowledge of theology.

"I thought Hell was the absence of God, Father. If you cannot be in His presence that would be punishment enough."

Father Wendell thought that a little too sophisticated for a fifteen-year-old. Did he have any real idea of what he was saying about the presence of God?

"Oh, come now, Gallagher. That sort of Hell doesn't sound much of a punishment, does it? Out of sight, out of mind, as they say. Wouldn't any soul there forget about God after a while and get up to more devilment? Don't you think that Joyce, through the words he gives the Rector, is saying that God would make sure that sin didn't pay? Would you like to read the passage on page 120 that starts with 'All the filth of the world.'"

Gallagher seemed to flinch as he picked up the book.

> All the filth of the world, all the offal and scum of the world, we are told, shall run there as to a vast reeking sewer when the terrible conflagration of the last day has purged the world. The

brimstone, too, which burns there in such prodigious quantity fills all hell with its intolerable stench; and the bodies of the damned themselves exhale such a pestilential odour that, as Saint Bonaventure says, one of them alone would suffice to infect the whole world.

Father Wendell nodded. Saint Bonaventure was never one to look on the bright side.

"Now that sounds more like it, doesn't it? The Rector leaves us in no doubt that God means what he says. God sends sinners to Hell *to be* punished, not *as* punishment. And remember, Hell is for all eternity and he leaves us in no doubt, too, what eternity means. Hearne, please read out the passage on page 132 beginning 'Now imagine.'"

Hearne turned the pages to find the place and stared at the page for several seconds before reading in a flat monotone.

Now imagine a mountain of that sand, a million miles high, reaching from the earth to the farthest heavens, and a million miles broad, extending to remotest space, and a million miles in thickness; and imagine that at the end of every million years a little bird came to that mountain and carried away in its beak a tiny grain of that sand. How many millions upon millions of centuries would pass before that bird had carried away even a square foot of that mountain, how many aeons upon aeons of ages before it had carried away all? Yet at the end of that immense stretch of time not even one instant of eternity could be said to have ended.

There was silence as Hearne finished. Father Wendell surveyed the faces. Some looked shocked, others were simply impassive.

"So I think we can say that there will be plenty of time for regrets in Hell. Stephen seems to accept it. Do we think he should?"

Clancy raised his hand.

"I'm not sure he should, Father. Don't you think it's a bit harsh of God to punish someone forever for just one sin?"

"You might think that, Clancy, but the Rector believes that God would not. Let's hear what he says." He searched through his marked copy. "Ah, yes. Here it is. He says if God could end all the miseries of the world by letting just one venial sin go unpunished he wouldn't do it, *'because sin, be it in thought or deed, is a transgression of His law and God would not be God if He did not punish the transgressor'.*

"So now, for this lesson and for your homework, I want you to write about how you think the Rector's words on Hell have affected Stephen and, perhaps, you could finish by discussing whether his words would have the same effect today."

Father Wendell surveyed the class. Some brows were furrowed; some eyes narrowed in concentration; no pens yet moved. He pondered for a few moments whether he should examine his own conscience further and then thought better of it. True, he was subjecting unformed and largely clueless adolescents to Catholicism red in tooth and claw, but that would be a useful antidote to the smutty fantasies that would otherwise occupy their thoughts. There was, he had to admit, a certain redemptive power in the idea of the Hell of eternal torments. He had seen more than one reprobate shocked into mending their ways by a dread of frying forever.

His eyes ran again over the Rector's words: *"God would not be God if He did not punish the transgressor,"* and found himself suppressing a laugh. The whole idea of Hell was absurd, comic even. He did not believe a word of it. God would hardly be so crass. What, beyond the purely sadistic, would be the motive for bringing souls into existence only for them to languish in eternal torment? So much for the God of love. On the other hand, he found it difficult to believe the alternative, that Hell was a deprivation of what Pius X had called the "beatific vision", an ecstatic communion of the individual with God. He had been reading Aldous Huxley's *The Doors of Perception* and the beatific vision sounded uncannily like some of the states induced by mescaline and other psychedelic drugs that Huxley described.

On any rational basis, Hell was incompatible with the idea of a loving God. But it was the very idea of a loving God that troubled him most of all. Where in this vale of tears was the evidence for God's love? Was it that God had created the world and had then remained forever indifferent to his creation, leaving humanity to its own devices, free to explore all aspects of its nature, good and bad? Was that the real insight of a Caravaggio – and of a Renaissance pope?

The World Cup

It is clergy night at the South Croydon Catenians. Dinner (pea and ham soup, pork sausages, potatoes and cabbage and apple crumble with custard) is finished and whiskies are being served. Father Muldoon is seated next to Superintendent O'Driscoll of the Metropolitan Police, Z Division (Croydon).

"What did the boys at the school think about England winning at the football, Father?"

"I think I'll never hear the end of it, Superintendent. They have been talking about it for weeks. I believe the rest of the country has been cheering too, but what for? The English team winning at English football in England. You would have to be born yesterday if you didn't think where was something fishy going on."

"Do you think the English have pulled a fast one, Father?"

"Fast or slow, never put anything past the English, Superintendent. Some of their team are even Catholics, to their shame."

"Are they, Father?"

"Weren't there two brothers in there that I hear are Catholics?"

"Do you mean the Charlton brothers, Father?"

"I do, and there may be others who prefer not to let on, so I'm told. It wouldn't do them any good if things came out."

"Isn't there one call Cohen, Father? He would be Jewish, I suppose."

"Is that so, Superintendent? I knew a Jew once – Manny Shulman was his name. He was a course bookie at Aintree. I always bet with him when I went. He was a gentleman and gave better odds than some I could mention. I told the Mammy, God rest her soul, about him. She was always a bit fearful about such things, the Mammy, and had to sign herself before she said, 'Is he a Catholic Jew or a Protestant Jew?' I had to smile. God bless her, she didn't know any better. I said, 'Mammy, all the disciples were Jews and then they became Catholics. There's no such thing as a Protestant Jew.'"

"You don't follow the football yourself, Father?"

"I do not, Superintendent, not English football anyway. Irish football was always my game. I was a member of the GAA since I was a boy. I've always abided by the ban."

"You'll find nobody over here that's heard of the GAA, Father, even when you tell them it stands for the Gaelic Athletic Association, and they've no idea that Irishmen are banned from watching or playing football."

"The ban on English games, or garrison games as we used to call them, is something every patriotic Irishman should respect, Superintendent. Canon Maloney, our parish priest in Carlow, used to say that it was a sin to play or watch an English game. Only a venial sin, of course. He said it would cost you a week extra in Purgatory. You had to confess it if you wanted to come out of the confessional with your soul all shiny and white. I'm a racing man, as you know, Superintendent, but Irish football is up there for me with the Turf. I always try to see a game in Croke Park when I'm in Dublin. Did you play it yourself?"

"I did, Father. I was in the junior Roscommon team when I was a young lad. They all said I was sure to be in the seniors the next season."

"Roscommon always have a great senior team, Superintendent. Did you not play for them?"

"I did not, Father. My family were very poor and I had no money. There were no jobs in Roscommon at the time, so I had to go to England for a job. It was 1941and the war was on. They were crying out for big, strong Irishmen. You had your pick of jobs in England that time. I worked for a while in a munitions factory in Cumberland and then I saw an advertisement in the papers for the Metropolitan Police and I never looked back."

"A million others like you, Superintendent, came over to England in their hour of need and won the war for them. Little thanks did they get for it."

"Oh, I don't know, Father. I've no complaints. The Police is a grand job."

"It is indeed, Superintendent, and they're lucky to have you. Tell me now, if you had a son would you let him play English football?"

"I doubt if I could stop him, Father, but I only have the two daughters. They play hockey. My eldest is very good. She's the captain of the school team."

"Hockey is an English game, Superintendent. The GAA ban it too."

"Do they, Father? I didn't know that, though I don't suppose the GAA can ban it in England."

"More's the pity, Superintendent, and it's a good job that they don't play Irish football in England or else the English would be up to their usual tricks. If there was a world cup for Irish football the English would find a way to win it."

"How do you think they could do that, Father?"

"The same as they always do, Superintendent – chicanery. I was talking only yesterday to Father Joe Gormley. He was in my year at Maynooth and he has a parish now in Manchester, near the big ground of their team."

"Do you mean Manchester United, Father?"

"The very one, Superintendent. Father Joe Gormley says some of them come drinking in his parish social club. He says after a pint or two they start spilling the beans about what the English team were up to in that World Cup of theirs."

"What did they do, Father?"

"The dirtiest of tricks, Superintendent. I'm told they played teams from two good Catholic countries."

"That's right, Father, Argentina and Portugal."

"Father Joe Gormley told me that he was told that the English would come up behind the other players and make lewd and blasphemous remarks about the Blessed Virgin Mary. The very idea would make Catholic blood boil. Any good Catholic would forget all about football when it came to defending the honour of Our Lady. It put them off their game entirely. One, I'm told, was so mad that he got himself sent off."

"That would be a dirty trick indeed, Father. Are you sure that's what they did?"

"Father Joe Gormley says it's straight from the horse's mouth, Superintendent."

"What horse would that be, Father?"

"I couldn't say, Superintendent The seal of the pint is a bit like the seal of confession. Father Joe Gormley would never let on who exactly said what after a few pints, but you can take it as gospel."

"Is that Frankie Fahey I see over there, Father?"

"It is, Superintendent. Too late, he's seen us. Will you look at the size of the Knights of Saint Columba medal he has round his neck. It's a wonder he can stand up straight. I suppose that's what he gets for being Supreme Knight or whatever he calls himself. He'll be wanting something, that's for sure – and the other thing you can be sure of, there'll be no apology for the whisky. What's this one called? Glenhaddoch. I'll wager it has never seen a glen in its life."

"How are you, Father? I trust you're well."

"Well enough, Frankie, and how are you and all the family?"

"We're all in fine form, Father, thanks be to God. Philomena is on a pilgrimage to Woldingham today. She's taking the Legion of Mary."

"She's booked her place in Heaven already, Frankie. Are you doing anything to join her?"

"As you ask, Father, I'm doing my bit. We have a special offer for you and all our clients on the Grand National. Sixpence in every pound of winnings will go to erecting a statue of Saint Eligius at Aintree."

"Which Saint Eligius would that be, Frankie?"

"He is the patron saint of jockeys, Father. He is particularly honoured around Aintree. The parish there has made a special novena for it."

"A saint indeed, Frankie. A statue is the least he deserves. More power to your elbow. And I suppose you've been doing well, too, with all the betting on this World Cup."

"Well now, Father, I wouldn't say that. England were the favourites and bookies never do well when the favourites win."

"You don't look as if you have a ticket to Carey Street in your pocket, Frankie."

"We have to be careful with our odds, Father, as I'm sure you know. Is that Monsignor Kelly over there? I must have a word. Very good to see you again, Father, and you too, Superintendent."

"Frankie Fahey is careful with his odds alright, Superintendent, so careful you couldn't tell them from thievery. I bet he had his fingers crossed hoping the Jerrys would win, but the English were too fly even for him."

"What about the Germans, Father? How did the English beat them? Surely they would not take much notice of anything the English team said?"

"Indeed not, Superintendent. Martin Luther and his like have said much worse things about the Blessed Virgin Mary than the English could dream of saying. Your Jerry is a tough nut to crack. Your Jerry doesn't like to give second-best to anyone, least of all the English. They've had enough of that already. You need much more than words to get the better of the likes of him."

"You're not wrong there, Father, though the English seemed to have managed it a couple of times."

"More by luck than by judgement, Superintendent, but you've put your finger on it. When they can think of nothing else to say, the English always talk about the war. And who do they always mention?"

"Would that be Churchill, Father?"

"Indeed, Superintendent, Winston Spencer Churchill, the scourge of Ireland. And who else?"

"Hitler?"

"Adolf Hitler, of course, and there's one other that completes the pack."

"Are you thinking of Stalin, Father?"

"I am, Superintendent, Joe Stalin. Did you know that Joe Stalin wasn't a Russian?"

"Is that so, Father? I always thought he was."

"Many do, Superintendent, but he really came from somewhere called Georgia."

"I thought that was in America, Father?"

"The Yanks have one, so the Russkies always want one too, Superintendent. It's tacked on to Russia somewhere, so I believe."

"Is it, Father? What has it to do with the football?"

"I'm coming to that, Superintendent. Father Joe Gormley explained it all to me. He says that one of the English goals didn't go in the net. Instead it was given by a man with a flag."

"The linesman, Father?"

"The linesman, the very man, Superintendent. Everyone thought he was a Russian, but he was really from Georgia, just like Joe Stalin. Now whatever they think of him in the rest of Russia, Joe Stalin is held in very high regard in Georgia. So the wily English, up to their usual machinations, let the linesman know that Winston Churchill always thought very fondly of Uncle Joe and surely he wouldn't want the spawn of Hitler to win.

All he had to do was wave his flag when the ball went near the German net. That did the trick."

"Very interesting, Father, but do you think it would stand up in court, as we say in the police?"

"The verdict is in and England won, Superintendent. What more proof do you want? Joe Stalin and Winston Spencer Churchill were as thick as thieves, and both tricky as a skulk of foxes. Adolf Hitler's fate was sealed when those two got together and it was the same with the football cup. The Jerrys should have had a word with Dev. He would have put them wise to all the little tricks the English get up to."

"I'd say he would have, Father."

"You can be certain of it, Superintendent. The Jerrys should have put Dev in charge of their team. Dev knows how to get the better of the English. He gave them a pasting in 1916 and showed them the door in 1921. He'd stand no nonsense from any English footballers."

"What do you think he would do, Father?"

"He would give them both barrels, Superintendent. First, he would have a word with the Archbishop of Dublin, John Charles McQuaid. He and Dev see eye to eye on everything. Archbishop McQuaid would line up the Irish saints in the German cause. There are plenty that have no love for the English – Saint Laurence O'Toole and Blessed Oliver Plunkett to name but two. There's plenty a saint can do on a football field when his dander is up. Then, two can play at a game of whispering in the ear. Dev would tell the Jerrys to whisper the names of Michael Collins, Sean South from Garryowen, Father Murphy, Kevin Barry, Kelly the Boy from Killane and the other Irish heroes. That would put the fear of God into the English team. They would be quaking in those fancy boots of theirs. The Jerrys would be able to walk the ball into the net."

"Do you think Dev would have wanted the Germans to win, Father?"

"He would have wanted the English to lose, Superintendent, and he did have a high opinion of the Jerrys. He always thought they were a very straightforward people, which is more than you could say for some."

"Do you think so, Father?"

"Certainly, Superintendent. Say what you will about him, you knew where you stood with Adolf Hitler."

"I suppose that's true, Father."

"Dev thought so, Superintendent. When Adolf Hitler died, he went down to the German Embassy in Dublin to sign the condolence book. When he arrived, he found the ambassador standing there and no book anywhere to be seen, so he insisted the ambassador found one."

"That's Dev for you, Father. He was always a stickler for form."

"Very true, Superintendent. Dev is the last of the old school. You can always rely on Dev to do the right thing."

The Dance

"Clancy, what's that you have in your bag?"

Clancy turned round to find Father Muldoon peering suspiciously at the faces that peeked from the top of his briefcase.

"It's an LP, Father."

"An LP? What sort of LP?"

Clancy hesitated, not quite sure what to reply, then decided he had best not obfuscate.

"It's called *Sergeant Pepper's Lonely Hearts Club Band*. It's by the Beatles," he added, knowing that would make things worse.

Father Muldoon's eyebrows rose to their full extension.

"Haven't I warned you against those Beatles, Clancy – and two of them born Catholics, so I'm told. Their parish priests should have put a stop to all their nonsense before they were out of short trousers." He pointed to the offending article: "Show me."

Clancy handed it to him and the priest's eyes narrowed as he examined it.

"Who is this Sergeant Pepper, Clancy?"

"I don't know, Father."

"What about his Lonely Hearts Club Band? Had you ever heard of that either?"

"No, Father."

Father Muldoon shook his head.

"You've bought something and you have no idea what it's about. I thought you were a bit more sensible than that, Clancy."

Clancy attempted an explanation, without much hope of succeeding.

"There is a song about Sergeant Pepper on it, Father."

"I've no doubt there are songs about all sorts of things on it, Clancy, most of which I'd prefer not to listen to."

He examined the cover more closely.

"Who are all these people?"

"The ones in the uniforms are the Beatles themselves and those others are their waxworks in Madame Tussauds."

Father Muldoon sniffed.

"The waxworks are a lot better looking. What about all the others?"

Clancy only recognised a few.

"I think that's Fred Astaire, Father, and that looks like Marilyn Monroe."

Father Muldoon sniffed again.

"Marilyn Monroe, the one in the films, the one that was always getting herself into trouble?"

"Yes, Father."

The priest's eyes lighted on another.

"I seem to recognise that face. Who would he be?"

"I think it might be Oscar Wilde, Father."

"That is not a name that should be mentioned in Catholic company, Clancy." He pointed to a bearded figure. "And here's another face I seem to have seen before. Who might he be?"

Clancy hesitated before replying.

"It looks like Karl Marx, Father."

"Karl Marx, the communist?"

"Yes, Father."

Father Muldoon recoiled in shock and shook his head in evident disbelief.

"Clancy, you are a member of the sixth form of Blessed Edmund Campion School. You are supposed to set an example to the younger boys at this school, yet you are carrying around pictures of sodomites and communists. What have you to say for yourself?"

Clancy hardly knew where to begin.

"It's not like that, Father. The songs are about other things. There's one about a girl leaving home; there's another about a meter maid. They're just about life, really."

Father Muldoon was unconvinced. He handed the LP back.

"Put it away and don't let me see it again."

***

"It's only out today. How did you get it?" asked Hearne, who, with Dempsey, Docherty and Worsley,was examining the Sergeant Pepper cover.

"A friend of my Dad's owns Dooley's record shop in Surrey Street," said Clancy. "He kept one for me. All his other ones have been bagged already."

"Have you played it yet?" said Dempsey.

"I haven't had a chance. I only picked it up this morning on my way in. They've been playing it non-stop on Radio London and Caroline, according to Dooley's, but the BBC said they weren't going to play 'A Day in the Life' because it's supposed to be about drugs."

"Nobody listens to the BBC anyway. The pirates are much better," said Hearne to general agreement. "Shame we won't hear them live again, though. Looks like you were one of the last, Mike."

Clancy pulled a face, half grin, half grimace. He had once managed to sneak into the Fairfield Halls in Croydon when the Beatles topped the bill.

"I couldn't hear them and hardly saw them. The girls were all jumping up and screaming. It was bedlam."

"Fairfield is crap for rock, anyway," said Worsley. "The Crawdaddy is much better."

"*Was* much better," said Hearne, "when the Yardbirds were there. You had Eric Clapton, Jeff Beck, Keith Relf, all that lot.

Now it's all got bigger. They don't do clubs any more – not in Croydon anyway – they only do theatres and the college circuit."

They all agreed. Rock was getting too big for its boots. "I'm into blues now," said Worsley. "There's a big American tour coming to Fairfield next month – Muddy Waters, Lonnie Johnson, Otis Slim, Sonny Boy Williamson, all the greats. I'm definitely going. Anyone else want to come?"

They all nodded. Blues was the coming thing.

***

Father Muldoon was only too well aware of the dilemma. The tide of licentiousness and profanity that was washing over a godless England had to be held back at the gates of Blessed Edmund Campion School, but, at the same time, things were changing fast. It was bad enough that the mass was in English and he had to face the congregation gawping at him while he was consecrating the host, but the dreaded pop music seemed to be taking over the world. Whether he liked it or not, the natural exuberance of youth could not be completely denied, let alone suppressed. What was to be done?

He said a little prayer for inspiration to Saint Anthony and picked up the latest copy of the *Nationalist,* just arrived from Carlow. The Mammy, God rest her soul, used to send it every week without fail, but she was gone now and his cousin Oona could be a little hit or miss with her posting, but it was always good to hear from home. He flipped through the pages. The *Macra na Feirme* column was there, of course. Ireland always drew her strength from the land. Dev always knew that. Dev was very sound on the land. Didn't he say the countryside would be bright with cosy homesteads? And wasn't he right enough? He turned another page to read a homily by Father Dermot O'Leary on Saint Jean-Marie Vianney, the Curé of Ars.

Father O'Leary was a born writer, no question. It was as if the saint himself was standing next to you. The Mammy was another great one for the Curé of Ars. The Mammy used to read him stories of how the Devil used to drag the poor priest round his bedroom by his feet, but the Curé of Ars was more than a match for Satan himself and sent him packing. Thousands used to queue for him to hear their confession and the Pope made him the patron saint of priests. That's why Father Muldoon, as a boy, had chosen Jean-Marie Vianney as his Confirmation name.

Looking down the page, another item caught his eye. "Carlow Showband for London tour."

> One of Carlow's top attractions, the Scallions Showband, is set for a tour of London next month. Lead singer, Charles (Carlo) Shaughnessey, told the Nationalist that they will bring their unique blend of ballads and patriotic songs to Irish Centres, church halls, pubs and other venues in London next month. "We have a number of dates lined up, mainly around Kilburn and Kentish Town, with others still to be finalised. We will be bringing a breath of the real Carlow to London." The band recently accompanied the choir of the Cathedral Church of the Assumption of the Blessed Virgin Mary in Carlow at a celebration of solemn high mass by the Bishop of Kildare and Leighlin, the Most Reverend Dr Peter Cullen.

Father Muldoon said another prayer to Saint Anthony, this time of thanks. He knew what to do. There was no point in swimming against the tide. He had to swim with it. Good Catholic boys had to be brought together with good Catholic girls and what would bring them together was good Catholic music from the Scallions Showband. He would organise a dance at the school and get the Scallions Showband to play. As for good Catholic girls, there was no finer source in Croydon than St Brigid's Academy, run by the nuns of the Daughters of the Cross, but getting them to come might be tricky. He would have to convince the headmistress, Sister Maria Immaculata.

***

First, he needed to see if the Scallions Showband was available. How to contact them? He had no idea but then thought that if they had played for the bishop in Carlow, perhaps the bishop could help. After much toing and froing on the telephone, he finally managed to get through to the bishop's secretary.

"You will have to talk to their agent," said the secretary, a Canon Mullery.

"What's an agent?"

"He looks after all their bookings. He's called Des O'Malley. I'd be careful when you talk to him."

The secretary gave him the number and Father Muldoon had again to navigate the vagaries of the Irish telephone system. Eventually someone answered.

"Mr O'Malley?"

"Who wants him?"

"It's Father Muldoon here, from Blessed Edmund Campion School in England. I was hoping to speak to Mr O'Malley about booking the Scallions Showband for our school dance."

Father Muldoon heard a rustling sound, as if papers were being shuffled, and some muffled voices. Then the same voice spoke.

"Sorry, Father, Des O'Malley here. I was on the other line. What can I do for you?"

"I understand, Mr O'Malley, that you handle bookings for the Scallions Showband and that they are due to come to London next month."

"Got it in one, Father. It's the Scallions first London tour. Lots of interest, as you would expect. I'm talking even now to a couple of companies about a record deal."

Father Muldoon had no knowledge, and even less interest, in record deals.

"I would like to book them for our school dance next month, the twentieth."

"That might be possible, Father. Let's see. The twentieth, that's a Saturday. Well, Father, you are in luck. Saturday is normally the big night, but I've heard that the Saint Aiden Centre in Battersea has just cancelled. They had a fire. Whole thing burned to the ground apparently. I do have a couple of venues on the waiting list, but clergy always come first with me. Say yes now, and the date is yours."

"Excellent, Mr O'Malley. The address is Blessed Edmund Campion School, Foxley Road, South Croydon. I will see you and your Scallions Showband on the twentieth. The dance will start at seven thirty."

O'Malley had to intervene quickly before Father Muldoon had put the phone down.

"Aren't you forgetting something, Father?"

"Am I?"

"Yes, Father, the fee."

"Fee? What fee?"

"The fee for the band, Father. Our standard fee is £100."

Father Muldoon was outraged.

"£100! You can buy a house in Carlow for that! This is for a Catholic school, Mr O'Malley. I thought you were a Catholic band."

"Well now, Father, don't upset yourself. We're all good Catholics this side of the water. We have a special rate for clergy and those in religious orders of £50."

"£50 is half a fortune. Is that the lowest you can go, Mr O'Malley?"

"It is, Father. By the time we have paid fares and hotels and meals and what have you, we would be doing it for nothing."

***

Sister Maria Immaculata had a very low opinion of the male sex and made few, if any, exceptions for the clergy, most of whom she regarded as being rather too fond of drink and gambling. She faced Father Muldoon with a stern, unblinking stare as she spoke in her polished, upper-class Dublin tones.

"Are you suggesting, Father Muldoon, that I send girls from this academy to some sort of Bacchanalian orgy?"

Father Muldoon did his best to mollify her.

"Not at all, Sister. Surely it's better for good Catholic boys and girls to meet each other before they go out into the world, to godless places like universities, where they will meet all sorts that could turn their heads away from the faith."

Sister Maria Immaculata's expression did not change.

"I am well aware of the dangers and temptations faced by our girls when they go to university, Father Muldoon. We take good care that they are well able to resist them."

Father Muldoon was impressed and intrigued.

"How do you do that, Sister?"

"We write to Catholic university chaplains informing them about girls from our school coming to their university and instructing them to contact them as soon as they arrive. We ask them to keep an eye on the girls and report back to us of any sign of backsliding from their religion, such as missing mass. Missing mass is always a sure sign of backsliding."

Father Muldoon nodded vigorously.

"I agree with you there, Sister. Once a boy starts missing mass, then he's on the slippery slope."

Sister Maria Immaculata's expression became, if anything, more stern.

"We do not have slippery slopes at St Brigid's, Father Muldoon. If we find that the behaviour persists at university then we write to the parents informing them of their daughter's failings.

When they come home at the end of term they are left in no doubt as to what is expected of them. Very few do not mend their ways."

"That is God's work you are doing, Sister."

"It is indeed, Father Muldoon. I have had girls coming to me twenty years after they have left this school, thanking me for saving their souls."

"Saving souls is what we all want to do, Sister. The dance is to save our children from all the licentiousness that goes on around them. We won't have any of this pop music, talking about love and Heaven knows what other filth. We'll have good Catholic music from the Scallions Showband. They're from my home, Carlow. Mass and communion every week, so I'm told – and they played for the bishop." He pulled out the cutting from the *Nationalist*. "Bishop Cullen is very strict on observance. He wouldn't allow any easy-osey Catholics to play in his church."

As Sister Maria Immaculata read the cutting, her expression softened a little.

"I have met Bishop Cullen and I hold him in very high regard. If I agree to this dance of yours, Father Muldoon, it will be on very strict conditions."

"Of course, Sister. I think I will be every bit as strict as you."

"To start with, I must insist on proper dress. Boys must be in suits and ties. I don't want to see any of these things called jeans, or shirts undone to the waist. And it goes without saying, that the girls will be in skirts that come down well below the knee."

"I agree with you there, Sister. Proper dress is most important."

"Then, chaperones must be there to ensure that there is clear distance at all times between couples when dancing."

"Chaperones are most important too, Sister."

"Finally there must be no lewd or lascivious songs, particularly those about things that you and I would not bring ourselves to mention."

"You can rest assured there, Sister. Only decent and patriotic Catholic songs will be sung. I will make sure of that."

"Very well then, Father Muldoon. I will agree to your proposal. You will keep me informed at all times."

"Of course, Sister."

***

Fifty pounds! Who had that sort of money to spare? There was only one that Father Muldoon could think of – Frankie Fahey, the bookmaker. Hadn't he trouser pockets that reached down to his ankles to hold all his takings? It was time Frankie Fahey did a little charitable work. He picked up the phone.

"How are you, Father? What can I do for you?"

"I'm well enough, Frankie, and how's yourself and your good wife."

"Philomena is in the pink, Father, after her operation, thanks be to God. She's taking a party of the Legion of Mary on another pilgrimage to Fatima. She likes to do a pilgrimage every year. She's been all over the continent with them."

"You have a saint there, Frankie, no question."

"She does it for the love of God and out of the goodness of her heart, Father. She never thinks of any reward in Heaven."

"That's the spirit of sanctity right enough, Frankie. And the Knights of Saint Columba, are they keeping you busy?"

"They are indeed, Father. As Supreme Grand Knight I have to organise a lot of meetings and functions to make sure we raise money for all our charities."

"It's grand work you do, Frankie. Where would the St Vincent de Paul Society be without the Knights of Saint Columba?"

"Thanks for saying so, Father. We like to think we do our bit for the poor and needy of this world."

"I'm sure you do, Frankie. The Knights of Saint Columba are known to help all who come to them and that's why I'm giving you a call. We are having a dance at the school with our boys and the girls from Saint Brigid's."

"Oh that's grand, Father, grand. It's always grand to see young people get together."

"It is, Frankie, and the Scallions Showband from Carlow will be there to play for them."

"Oh, the Scallions Showband – that's grand, too. I've heard good things about them. They are very well thought of, I believe."

"They are, Frankie, and they think well of themselves too. It will cost us £50 to have them and the school doesn't have £50 to spare, so we are looking for a kind soul to help us out. No soul, I said to myself, is kinder when it comes to helping out than Frankie Fahey, Supreme Grand Knight of the Knights of Saint Columba that he is."

There were a few seconds before the reply.

"I would like to help, Father, but we do have our other charities."

"You do grand work with the Knights, Frankie. I was only saying so the other day to Superintendent O'Driscoll. He has a very high opinion of your work, too. He was telling me that he always keeps an eye out when you are having one of your dinners, to make sure your cars are not bothered by any busybody bluebottle wanting to know if you've had a dram or two when you leave."

There were another few seconds of silence.

"You have a very persuasive way with you, Father. On behalf of the Knights of Saint Columba, I would be pleased to pay for the Scallions Showband to play at your dance. After all, some of those boys may want to join the Knights one day."

"God bless you, Frankie. You're sure of a reward in Heaven."

***

Father Muldoon looked over the senior sixth form of Blessed Edmund Campion.

"Boys, I have some good news for you. Soon you will be leaving this school and going out into the world. In due course, many of you will be getting married and settling down to raise a family. As you know, the Church urges all Catholics to marry within the faith and in his decree, *Ne Temere,* Saint Pius X warned against mixed marriages to Protestants and the difficulties and temptations that can occur. So we must make sure that good Catholic boys can meet good Catholic girls and show how much better such companionship can be with a shared faith. And so, I have arranged with Sister Maria Immaculata, the headmistress of St Brigid's Academy, that the girls of their sixth form will be invited to a dance to be held in this school on the twentieth of next month."

It took a second or two for this bombshell to sink in, before Father Muldoon found himself looking at a sea of grins and hearing intakes of breath and a few very muffled cheers. Gratified, he continued.

"Now there must, of course, be music at a dance. I have often warned you against the iniquities of so called pop music, so we shall have none of that. Instead I have invited one of Ireland's finest bands, the Scallions Showband, to play for you. I am sure you will find them much more enjoyable than the rubbish many of you listen to."

Grins became puzzled expressions. Eventually, Hearne felt he needed to speak.

"What sort of music do the Scallions Showband play, Father?"

"They play good, clean music, Hearne. What would you expect?"

Expectations were beginning to sink.

"Could you give us an idea of the songs they play, Father?" asked Dempsey.

"All the good old songs, Dempsey. You must know them – 'Danny Boy', 'The Rose of Tralee', 'She Moved Through the Fair', 'The Star of the County Down' – and then they know all the patriotic songs about Ireland's fight for liberty. They put those Beatles in the shade. What is that they sing? 'She loves you, Yeah, Yeah Yeah.' The Devil will be rubbing his hands every time he hears those words. He knows where all that lovey-dovey nonsense leads."

"So will they be playing songs like 'Off to Dublin in the Green', Father?," asked Clancy.

"It wouldn't surprise me, Clancy. That's a grand song. I've sung it myself many times."

He started to sing the refrain.

And we're all off to Dublin in the green, in the green
Where the helmets glisten in the sun
Where the bayonets flash and the rifles crash
To the rattle of a Thompson gun

"Isn't that a grand song, Clancy?"

"Isn't it about killing, Father?"

"Not at all, Clancy. It's about the fight for liberty. Being a soldier and fighting for your country is a manly thing to do, is it not?"

"So singing about fighting is better than singing about loving, Father?"

"Singing about that sort of fighting is better than singing about that sort of loving, Clancy. I'm surprised you even have to ask. Now there is one other thing I have to tell you all. You are expected to be a credit to the school and to your parents, so you will wear a suit and tie for the occasion. If you do not yet possess a suit, I suggest you acquire one very soon. You will certainly have need of it in the future. You will get nowhere in this world if you are not properly dressed."

***

Father Muldoon stood on the stage and clapped his hands. Along one side of the hall was a line of boys, in suits that varied in the way they fitted their wearers. Clancy wore his new Marks and Spencer outfit with a mixture of distaste and embarrassment. "St Michael – it's your patron saint," said his mother. "You can't beat St Michael for quality." He didn't bother to reply. Opposite them on the other side was a line of girls in dresses of subdued hues that reached from mid calf to near ankle. By each wall sat a nun, looking impassively on.

"Girls and Sisters from Saint Brigid's Academy, it is a great pleasure to welcome you all to Blessed Edmund Campion School and to this dance. This is a chance for Catholic boys and girls to get to know one another, so let us begin with a short prayer to Saint Vitus, the patron saint of dancing, who I'm sure will be looking on and helping things go well."

Father Muldoon raised his eyes and held his hands together.

"Dear holy Saint Vitus, look with favour on the boys and girls gathered here and help them to enjoy the dancing in a spirit of reverence and chastity."

There were muttered Amens from the nuns and a few of the others. Father Muldoon clapped his hands again.

"You have all drawn a number out of the boxes. Now please go and find the boy or girl who has the same number as you. They will be your partner for the evening."

The combination of expectation and dread in the hall was palpable, as eyes sought their opposite numbers. Clancy could not suppress a giggle as Hearne found himself matched with a gangly girl half a head taller. Then he, and the rest of the Campion boys, were consumed by jealousy as Dempsey, of all boys, was joined by the prettiest girl in the room, a willowy blonde with a dazzling smile and an alluring figure that even her loose fitting dress could not conceal.

Clancy looked along the line and felt a surge of relief as he spotted his opposite number, a slim, pertly pretty girl in a calf-length green dress with hair in an auburn bob. She had already seen him and was approaching.

"Hello, I'm Frances, Frances Malone."

He held out his hand.

"Michael Clancy. How do you do?"

She touched his hand lightly.

"Are you always so formal, Michael?"

He felt himself beginning to blush.

"No, well maybe. I thought it was the polite thing to say."

She smiled.

"Polite, too. Do you have any redeeming features?"

He found himself laughing.

"Some, I hope."

She looked around at the other couples, who had begun, hesitantly, to talk to each other.

"I see we are doomed to enjoy each other's company. Shall we begin with the boring bits? What subjects are you doing for A-levels?"

"Sciences – physics, chemistry and maths. How about you?"

"English, art and French. Does that make us incompatible?"

"Oh, I don't know. They say opposites attract."

She gave him a quizzical look.

"Who are they that say such silly things?"

"Well it's true in science – negative and positive electricity, north and south pole magnets, that sort of thing."

"Hmm. I like to think I'm positive. Are you saying you're negative?"

He shook his head.

"No, that's not what I meant."

"Let's change the subject. Are you hoping to go to university?"

"Yes, Sussex."

"There's a coincidence. So am I."

Just then there was a loud feedback buzz from the stage and they turned to see half a dozen men in beige suits, rather obviously bought when they were younger and slimmer, bound onto the stage brandishing their instruments – guitars, trumpet, saxophone and drums. One, without instrument, came forward and grabbed a microphone.

"Hello, boys and girls from Blessed Edmund Campion School and St Brigid's Academy. I'm Carlo and this is the Scallions Showband from the County Carlow in the Emerald Isle. How are you all, this evening?"

The response from the audience was distinctly muted, but Carlo appeared undaunted.

"Grand, grand. To kick off the evening, we're going with a great number from the late, great, Jim Reeves, 'Welcome to My Home'."

Expressions on the dance floor ranged from surprise to disbelief as Carlo began to croon, canoodling the microphone.

> Welcome to my home
> Won't you step inside?
> You and I will stay there
> No more need to roam

Some of the couples decided that they might as well make the best of things and began, hesitantly, to move, more or less in time to the music and more or less in step with each other.

Clancy thought that Hearne would soon get a crick in his neck looking up to his partner. Plump, ungainly Dempsey, on the other hand, seemed to be getting on famously with his blond goddess, much to the envy, not to say bewilderment, of his classmates. Worsley, typically, tried a couple of jive moves, but was reeled back rapidly when his partner saw black looks from the sitting nuns.

"I can't stand country and western," said Frances, "can you?"

"No," replied Michael.

"It's boring, sentimental and reactionary. Who do you like – Beatles, Stones?"

"Yes, though I tend to go for rather harder-edged stuff – Cream, Hendrix."

"They're not bad. Have you heard of Karlheinz Stockhausen?"

"No. Who does he play with?"

She smiled.

"He's not a rock musician, but that's for another time."

The door is always open
As you will always find
We will make a home there
For now and evermore

"I suppose we had better dance," she said. "Anything to take our minds off this racket."

Clancy hesitated.

"I've never actually danced before."

"There's nothing to it. You take one arm like this and the other like this and just move. We have to keep our distance though, otherwise the Marys will notice."

"Who?"

"The nuns here. We call them the Marys."

"Why?"

"That's their names – Sister Mary of the Nativity, Sister Mary of the Resurrection and Sister Mary of the Assumption. They all come from the same place in Ireland."

They joined hands as instructed and began to move. Clancy found it surprisingly easy and then, to his further surprise, began to enjoy it. Frances was quick and light on her feet and guided him, so they almost glided across the floor as Carlo and the Scallions went through their repertoire of country and western staples like 'King of the Road', 'Okie from Muskogee', 'North to Alaska' and 'The Green, Green Grass of Home', interspersed with Irish classics, 'Fields of Athenry' and 'Danny Boy'. Then it was time for the interval.

Sister Maria Immaculata had forbidden any notion of alcohol being served. Instead they had to make do with lemonade or tea in cups, accompanied by egg and cress and fishpaste sandwiches, with their crusts cut off, small savouries, that for some reason were called *canapés*, iced cupcakes and sponge slices.

Interval over, they went back on the dance floor and the Scallions performed more ballads. Then Carlo made an announcement.

"Boys and girls, I have a special request from someone you all know well – Father Muldoon. Are you there, Father? Ah, yes, I see you there at the back." Father Muldoon nodded in acknowledgement as Carlo continued, "Father Muldoon tells me it's his favourite song, a song that sure to stir all your hearts – 'Boolavogue'. Take it away, boys!"

The band played a rather mournful intro as Carlo began to sing.

At Boolavogue as the sun was setting o'er the bright May meadows of Shelmalier
A rebel band set the heather blazing and brought the neighbours from far and near
Then Father Murphy from old Kilcormac spurred up the rock with a warning cry

"Arm, arm," he cried, "For I've come to lead you, for Ireland's freedom we'll fight or die.

Frances looked puzzled.

"What's this all about?"

"It's an Irish rebel song," said Clancy. "Have you never heard it?"

"No, why should I have?"

"Are your parents not Irish?"

"No. I think one of my great grandmothers was."

Look out for hirelings, King George of England, search every kingdom where breathes a slave
For Father Murphy of County Wexford sweeps o'er the land like a mighty wave.

"Was this Father Murphy any relation to your Father Muldoon?"

Clancy chuckled.

"In spirit, maybe."

Twas at Slieve Coilte our pikes were reeking with the crimson blood of the beaten yeos
At Tubberneery and Ballyellis full many a Hessian lay in his gore
Oh, Father Murphy, had aid come over, the Green Flag floated from shore to shore.

"He's a bit of a bruiser, Father Murphy, isn't he? I think I've heard enough. Shall we go outside?"

"Do you think the Marys will let you?"

"Don't worry, they will."

She led him to the door, where one of the nuns sat.

"I'm feeling a bit queasy, Sister. I need some fresh air and to go to the lavatory." Frances gave her a meaningful look. "Michael Clancy here has offered to go with me to make sure no boys go in when I'm there."

The nun looked suspicious, but then nodded.

"Don't be too long, Frances Malone."

As they went out, Clancy asked which Mary that was.

"Resurrection, the worst."

"How did you manage to persuade her?"

"Oh, you know, Michael. Time of the month."

Clancy felt himself blush as he took her down a corridor and out of a door that opened onto a path by the playing fields. They stood, breathing in the night air.

"Perhaps we will meet again at Sussex." said Clancy.

"I expect we will," said Frances, "although I will be busy the first couple of weeks, because I intend to lose my virginity then."

It was several seconds before Clancy could think of a reply.

"Why there?"

"You mean why not here?" she said, a note of scorn in her voice. "You must be joking. Who with? Besides, my parents are very nosey, always asking what I'm doing."

Clancy's expression was part smile, part smirk, which she had no trouble in interpreting.

"Not with you, though, Michael. You're sweet, but I don't think you're my type and you're too young. I want to do it with someone a little more mature. My friend's sister goes to Sussex and she says to get it over with in the first couple of weeks with a third-year or a postgrad. After that I will have affairs, probably with a lecturer or two. My friend's sister says they're all at it with their students."

Clancy pondered the notion that he might have to wait a year or two before willing maidens offered themselves to him for defloresence. He hoped that some would be less discriminating than Frances Malone.

"Will you go to mass when you are at university?"

"Of course not. Why would I?"

"What about when you come back for the vacations? Will you go then?"

"I expect so. Anything for domestic peace. I still love my parents, even if I don't believe what they do."

"Communion, too?"

"Yes. It's only like eating a biscuit, Michael. You don't believe it's the body and blood of someone, do you? Transubstantiation is complete rubbish, isn't it?"

Clancy could not suppress a sense of shock, even though he knew intellectually that she was right. She saw it in his face and laughed.

"You do believe it, don't you?"

He shook his head several times.

"No, no, I don't really, it's just that..."

She cut him short.

"What is it the Jesuits say, Michael? 'Give me a child till he is seven and I will show you the man.' That was Ignatius Loyola himself, no less, the Jesuit number one. By the time that child leaves school, the damage has been done."

"So you think we're damaged, you as well as me?"

"I hope not irreparably, but you have to admit it can leave some scars if you take it too seriously."

"Which you don't?"

"Of course not. The more I think about it, the more absurd the Catholic Church is – a giant edifice run by a bunch of hoary old celibates. They say believe in the one true God and then they tell us there are three of them – Father, Son and Holy Ghost. What on earth, or rather in Heaven, is a Holy Ghost? You know he's often called the Paraclete. Paraclete in Greek means 'helper'."

Clancy burst out laughing.

"So now we have God the Father, God the Son and God help us."

Frances had to laugh too.

"It reminds me of the Rolling Stones' song, 'Mother's Little Helper', the little pill that helps get her through the day. The Holy Ghost seems to be the little helper that the other two run to when there's a bit of dirty work to be done. No doubt it gets them through their busy day, too. The Apostle's Creed says, Jesus 'was conceived of the Holy Ghost, born of the Virgin Mary'. Really? What was a god doing impregnating unsuspecting virgins? There's a touch of the Greek myth about it, isn't there? Zeus was always impregnating virgins, whether they liked it or not."

Clancy chuckled.

"I hadn't thought of it like that, but now you mention it ..."

Frances was now in full flow.

"Can you imagine the talk over the breakfast table? Mary says to Joseph, 'I've something to tell you, darling. I'm up the duff by the Holy Ghost.' Joseph would not have been best pleased."

"Put like that, I see what you mean."

"Exactly, Michael. He's the 'now you see him, now you don't', God. He didn't even break the good – or bad – news to Mary himself. He got the Archangel Gabriel to do it instead. For some reason the gospels don't record what the Archangel thought about it. I expect he was cringing with embarrassment."

Clancy burst out laughing again at the idea of an embarrassed Archangel.

"Do you think everything about the Church is absurd? What about all the art that it inspired, the pictures and sculptures and the cathedrals?"

She tossed her head, scornfully.

"That's all gone. Dead. Where are the Leonardos and the Michelangelos of today? Want another Sistine Chapel? You'll have to go whistle. The Catholic Church is just a husk, Michael. It doesn't inspire any more. It's just a bunch of old men going through the motions, but they instil just enough fear to keep the whole thing going. You might not want to believe it, but you have a secret fear that all the Catholic stuff might be true and your immortal soul will be damned."

That was too near the mark for Clancy to admit.

"And you're not worried about your soul?"

"I don't have a soul, Michael, and neither do you. This is all we are."

Clancy knew that was true and he hoped to believe it soon. He found himself fascinated, almost enraptured, by Frances' freedom of thought, her ability to jettison, effortlessly, all the baggage of her upbringing. Was this, he wondered, what falling in love was like?

"Maybe we had better go back," she said. "Resurrection might be getting suspicious."

As they went in, the dance was coming to its end. Clancy saw Carlo singing with his hand on his breast and then recognised a familiar tune.

Frances looked puzzled.

"What's that song and what language are they singing in?"

"It's the 'Soldier's Song'. It's in Irish," said Clancy.

"What soldier?"

"It's the Irish national anthem."

Frances was even more puzzled.

"Why are they singing the Irish national anthem?"

"I don't know. Maybe they've forgotten that they're not in Ireland."

She shrugged.

"Well, at least it's a better tune than 'God Save the Queen'."

Clancy nodded. Did he feel English or Irish or both? He wasn't sure, or even that he cared, but he had to agree with her. No tune was quite as bad as 'God Save the Queen'.

Apologetics pro vita sua

"We've had five years of boring old RE lessons and now this," said Hearne, throwing the rather tattered book across the table. They were sitting in the sixth form common room after lunch. "Does Fahey really think that one quick read and we would all be marching forth, ready to batter legions of Protestants, atheists and agnostics into intellectual submission? It almost makes you nostalgic for the Catechism. "

"Yeah. Give me a lesson on the sixth and ninth commandments any day." said Worsley.

"You were always complaining that we never got to the good bits." said Dempsey.

"Yeah, but you could think of them, couldn't you?"

"The Catechism as wanking fodder. That's got be a new one," said Docherty, laughing.

Clancy picked up the dark brown, cloth-bound tome, its title, in gold letters, just visible, *The Principles of Christian Apologetics. An Exposition of the Intellectual Basis of the Christian Religion*. He flipped through the contents pages.

"It was published in 1919! Welcome to the swinging sixties – and turgid doesn't come into it. 'Errors opposed to theism', 'A General View of the Nature and Attributes of God', 'The Nature of Man' and on and on and on. Life's too short to be doing with all that stuff. Can't see anything about the sixth and ninth either."

"Why is it called Apologetics?" said Docherty, "The one thing the Catholic Church doesn't do is apologise."

The others looked back at him and shook their heads.

"Fahey thinks that Vatican II will somehow revive the Church. Some hope. Mass in English is even more boring than mass in Latin," said Clancy.

"Do you still go?" said Worsley, surprised.

"If I can't get out of it. I go for my Mum. What was it that French Protestant said when they offered him the throne of France – 'Paris is worth a mass.'"

"Bit pompous, don't you think?" said Hearne "Although I suppose a Mum is worth a mass. Anyway, let's go and see what Fahey has to say for himself."

Father Fahey leaned back in his chair as he surveyed the faces of the entire Campion sixth form, arts, science and classics, and felt a small sense of satisfaction. He had finally persuaded the Canon of the need to treat sixth formers as the adults they would soon become and not to try to ram the tenets of the Catholic religion down their throats and instead show them something of its intellectual foundations. It had been something of a struggle. Father Muldoon in particular had expressed scepticism, bordering on derision. "If they don't know what it means to be a Catholic by now, no book will change their mind." Father Fahey disagreed. Instead he would lead them ineluctably to the conclusion that Catholicism was intellectually coherent in a way than no other religion, let alone atheism or agnosticism, could be.

"Boys, although this is, strictly speaking, a religious education lesson, it will be very different from those you have had before. I want to treat the lesson as a discussion. If you have a question or want to challenge something I say, please don't hesitate to speak and if you want to discuss any other subject, feel free to do so.

"When you leave school, especially if you go to university, you will encounter arguments against the Church, against the existence of God and about differing views on morality that you may find difficult to refute. The Church has a whole body of knowledge to counter and defeat those arguments. It is called Apologetics. What is apologetics? Apologetics is quite literally the defence of the faith; the Greek word apologia means defence like that which a lawyer gives at a trial. In yours, as in every generation, people face the challenges, questions, and concerns of the gospel message of the Christian faith. Apologetics will give you the tools to answer those challenges.

"I have managed to get hold of some copies of *The Principles of Christian Apologetic* by Father Walshe. Unfortunately there are not enough to go round so you will have to share. As you can see, it is a very substantial work, covering many topics, but we will only have time for a few in these lessons. We will start with what I think is one of the most important topics – arguments for the existence of God. This is a subject that has preoccupied religions and philosophers throughout the ages. As far as the Church is concerned, it was settled definitively by Saint Thomas Aquinas, who was a Dominican priest and lived in the 13th century. He is sometimes known by another name. Can anyone tell me what that is?"

Gallagher's hand shot up.

"Yes, Gallagher?"

"The Angelic Doctor, Father."

"Correct, Gallagher. Saint Thomas Aquinas is one of the Doctors of the Church, a title given to those who have made a great theological contribution to Church doctrine, and he is known as the Angelic Doctor, because he led a pure and holy life."

Purity and holiness were the last things on their minds. The gloom that had descended on the class at the prospect of another religious education lesson became more pronounced as Father Fahey continued.

"Aquinas defined five ways by which the existence of God might be proved. The most important, in my view and the one most easily grasped is that from causality. The law of cause and effect is universal. Every effect must have a cause and so there must have been something that is the first cause of everything and that is God."

There was a long period of silence before Dempsey finally piped up.

"Why does it have to be God at the end, Father? Couldn't it be anything, like, say, the Wizard of Oz?"

"What?" said the priest in disbelief.

"Well, you might follow the yellow brick road, or all these causalities, and at the end you find a little old man with a beard who says 'Surprise' and then hops off in a balloon."

"I don't think you are taking this seriously, Dempsey."

"Why does there have to be a first cause, Father?" said Digby, "Couldn't things just go on forever? There was an article in *New Scientist* last week about something called the Steady State Theory of the Universe that suggests that the Universe has always existed and will never come to an end, so there wouldn't have been a first cause, would there?."

"Anyway, Father," interjected Clancy, "the whole idea of causality is out of date."

The priest's eyes widened in surprise.

"What do you mean, Clancy?"

"Quantum mechanics, Father. John von Neumann, who is a very famous mathematical physicist, has proved that reality is just statistical now. Cause and effect are history."

Father Fahey's eyes narrowed. He had no idea who John von Neumann was and suspected that Clancy's grasp of quantum mechanics was a hazy as his own. He had left all that stuff to the physicists. Chemistry was his abiding interest. The dance of molecules in a test tube, the almost infinite, yet predictable, variety of their intertwinings were what fascinated him. He decided to play for time.

"I don't think it's quite as simple as that, but you raise an interesting point, Clancy. Perhaps we could discuss it in another lesson."

Another boy spoke up.

"Yes, Edmunds?"

"The book says that one of the arguments is from perfection. Everything on earth is imperfect but there are better things and then even better things and finally God is the most perfect thing that could exist. Couldn't you argue that the other way?"

Father Fahey was baffled.

"What other way?"

"Well," replied Edmunds, "there are plenty of bad things in the world, like Hitler or cancer or earthquakes."

"And Crystal Palace," interrupted Dempsey, amid laughter.

The priest was rapidly losing track of the argument. He had no idea how Croydon's only football club could appear in the panoply of evil.

"Crystal Palace, Dempsey?"

"Yes, Father. They're not just bad, they're terrible. They even lost to Grimsby last week."

More laughter, accompanied by jeers. Edmunds, determined, ploughed on.

"There's a bad thing, and then there's an even worse thing and so on and finally you get to the worst thing there could ever be. Why isn't that God?"

Father Fahey was lost for words. The concept of God as the quintessence of evil was not one he had ever encountered. He decided to dissemble with the "everything around us is beautiful" line.

"I don't think that holds water, Edmunds. Why would God create this world full of beauty if He was evil?"

"Maybe to fool us, to lull us into a false sense of security." said Hearne.

The priest shook his head. This wasn't going to be as easy as he had thought. Perhaps Apologetics was too dry and academic a subject for young minds. He needed to find some other, more relevant topics.

***

As he sat in his room, Father Finbar Fahey frowned as he read the letter from the *Irish Journal of Ecumenical Studies*, its response to his paper on the two Patricks. It was not just the queries it raised, some of which he regarded as plainly erroneous, others as simply footling, but its tone. It was not the scholarly, objective response he might have expected. Rather, it was a mixture of the dismissive and the supercilious. He began to suspect that the editor of the journal had felt a tap on the shoulder on behalf of a certain archbishop who had very fixed views on all aspects of Irish history and Catholic observance and whose attitude towards the second Vatican Council and all things ecumenical was known to be less than whole-heartedly supportive. Nothing directly contradicting the paper would be said on the archbishop's part. Instead, the editor would be pointed to a scholar of impeccable reputation who could be relied upon to cast doubt on its conclusions. From the points raised in the letter, Father Fahey was almost certain that that scholar was Dr (and Very Reverend) Dermot Cleary SJ, a leading figure in the theology department of University College Dublin.

The response had the characteristic Jesuit hallmarks – an air of intellectual superiority, coupled with condescension and doctrinal intransigence. Father Fahey felt himself almost admiring the way Dr Cleary could interpret the facts as evidence for a single Patrick and not two. If Patrick had arrived in Ireland in 431, how was it that some of those who had worked with him were still alive, decades into the sixth century? Early marriages and an adjustment of dates would do the trick. The evidence of

Christians in Ireland before St Patrick? Dr Cleary simply dismissed the notion as unproven, with remarks about the need to respect historical tradition.

Respecting historical tradition was one thing; being held prisoner by it was another. Finbar Fahey was forever finding himself wrestling with the contradictions of his faith. Pontius Pilate had a point when he asked of Jesus, "What is truth?" What better bolstered that faith – the real historical truth about Patrick, or the cosy, sentimental myths? Part of him looked genially on the faithful praying before garish statues and mementoes of long-dead saints and lapping up tales of their impossible miracles. Another part was appalled at what he saw as hardly better than superstition.

***

"In our last lesson the question was raised whether there was some incompatibility between science and religion."

Father Fahey surveyed the faces looking back at him to see if that had stimulated any interest. It didn't seem so, so he continued.

"Many people claim that science has somehow superseded religion and that the real truth about the world can only come from science. I disagree and I want to tell you about someone who was both a renowned scientist and a Catholic priest. He was Pierre Teilhard de Chardin, a Jesuit. He published many science papers in geology and palaeontology. He was particularly well known for his studies of Pekin Man, which some of you might know is thought to be one of the earliest ancestors of mankind. Teilhard believed in evolution – which, at the time, a great many in the Church and outside it did not – but he saw it as a process leading towards an end and that end was Christ. His great book, *The Phenomenon of Man*, united science and religion with its vision of the cosmos unfolding and the evolution of matter leading to consciousness and ultimately to man and the convergence with Christ, at what Teilhard called the Omega point. "

After a lengthy silence, a hand was raised.

"Yes, Gallagher?"

"I believe the works of Teilhard de Chardin have been condemned by the Church, Father."

For a moment, Father Fahey was surprised that Gallagher knew anything about Teilhard and then remembered that he was always looking to sniff out any hint of unorthodoxy.

"I'm not sure condemnation is the right word, Gallagher. There were some doctrinal questions raised. The Church always takes its time with these questions, but comes to the right answer in the end. Look at what happened with Galileo."

"That took a few hundred years, Father." said Clancy.

"Better late than never, Clancy"

"Was Teilhard a modernist?" asked Gallagher, still suspicious.

"In some sense, I suppose you might say that."

"Ah," said Gallagher, more than a hint of triumph in his voice, "Saint Pius X condemned modernism. I believe he called it the synthesis of every heresy."

Father Fahey thought Gallagher was becoming the synthesis of every annoyance, but knew he had to be emollient in replying.

"Saint Pius X was a great and holy pope, but theology was never his strong point, as he was the first to admit. I believe he once condemned the Tango."

"Was that an infallible judgement?" asked Clancy as the laughter died down.

A smiling Father Fahey shook his head.

"I hardly think so."

"Are you sure, Father?" said Hearne. "I thought the Pope gives *ex cathedra* judgements on faith and morals. The Tango can be, let's say, a pretty lascivious dance. It might have a big impact on the faith and morals of the dancers."

A wry grin appeared on the priest's face as he thought about an answer.

***

In his darker – or perhaps clearer – moments Father Fahey wondered what was the point of a school like Edmund Campion. Parents sent their sons to the school and the school duly educated them in the hope that they would be good Catholics for the rest of their lives, yet he knew that was the vainest of hopes. Most of the boys would lapse almost as soon as they left; only a few would return later in their lives. Worse, the cleverer, the more questioning, the boy, the more likely he would reject the Church. He knew that only a handful of the sixth form would ever go to mass again once they had left, yet it was never mentioned at the school. He had tried to raise the subject both with the Canon and Father Muldoon, but neither seemed to take any notice – the Canon because his thoughts were always elsewhere and Father Muldoon because, well, he was Father Muldoon. He was left to ponder whether they were all engaged in a Sisyphean task, forever pushing their pupils upwards towards the glorious temple on the mountain summit, only for them to escape and scamper gleefully downhill.

Why? It had, he was sure, something to do with the English air. He thought of life back in Ireland, of his mother – daily communicant, a pile of prayer books by her bed, Stations of the Cross every day in Lent and the rosary every night with her children. For her, and millions like her, the idea of rejecting Catholicism was inconceivable, an almost physical impossibility, as well as a one-way ticket to Hell. Yet Catholic schoolboys in England, brought up in the same atmosphere, in the same schools with the same instruction, seemed able to cast off their religion like an old overcoat, with hardly a moment's thought.

Of course all the distractions of modern life for the young – music, girls, TV, clothes, as well as the normal adolescent urge to rebel – played a part, but he was convinced there was something deeper. He had come to understand that, for the English, religion was not something embedded in the very fabric of life, but an accessory, like a nice handbag or a smart tie, to be worn lightly, with little thought to its meaning. The Church of England, with a theology so elastic that all but the deepest-dyed atheist could be a member, had all those magnificent churches and cathedrals, but hardly a congregation to fill them. It was now reduced to mere initials – the C of E – its bloody and turbulent history almost forgotten.

For the English, all history seemed to be no more than a half-remembered backdrop to things, largely a motley collection of monarchs – Henry VIII, Richard the Lionheart, Good Queen Bess, William the Conqueror and their like – with little idea of chronology or what they did, together with a succession of glorious victories and no mention of defeats. In the de Valera dominated Ireland that he knew, it had been very different. History was ever present, a litany of woes and wrongs, to be wallowed in and railed against in song and word and deed. The thought that gnawed ever deeper, until it became almost dread, was that the English might be right and that forgetting might be better than remembering.

***

"So it's Vatican roulette or nothing, is it Father?"

Father Fahey's sigh was not heard above the laughter provoked by Docherty's question. His hopes for the second Vatican Council were diminishing by the day. He could only summon a half-hearted response.

"I think Pope Paul takes the view that he is bound by the edicts of his predecessors and that artificial contraception is against natural law."

"What I don't understand," responded Clancy, "is why the Church thinks it's 'natural' for a woman to take her temperature every day and only," he hesitated for a second, "only do it with her husband when her temperature goes up – or is it down?"

The priest shrugged and spread his hands, to more laughter.

"So why is that more natural than taking a pill every day?" continued Clancy.

"And then doing it when you fancy," added Worsley, amid guffaws.

Even Gallagher, the custodian of the orthodox, who had followed every twist and turn of the Council, was sceptical.

"The Pontifical Commission on Birth Control produced a report that was signed by 69 of its 72 members saying that artificial birth control was not intrinsically evil and that Catholic couples should be allowed to decide for themselves whether to use it. A minority report was produced, led by Cardinal Ottaviani, that went to the Pope and he used it to produce the encyclical *Humanae vitae*. There are a number of eminent theologians who disagree with its conclusions, Father."

"They're not the only ones," said Worsley, "No one's going to take any notice of a bunch of old celibates, are they?"

For a moment the priest thought he should reply on behalf of not quite so old celibates, then decided against and threw the question open.

"What does everyone think?"

"The Church is going to have to change its mind, like with Galileo," said O'Malley.

"That took hundreds of years, as we know." said Clancy.

"Same with torture." said Dempsey.

The entire class turned towards him.

"What do you mean, torture, Dempsey?" said Father Fahey.

"I'm reading this book, Father. It's called *Torture Through The Ages*. It's brilliant. It tells you all about things like the Iron Maiden. It said the Pope allowed the Spanish Inquisition to torture heretics, but it's not allowed now."

"We can all thank God for that." said the priest.

"What about slavery, Father," asked Hearne, "Didn't the Church once allow that?"

"I hardly think so, Hearne"

"I think you might be wrong, Father. I've been looking it up. The Church usually thought that making Christians slaves was wrong but it was another matter for non-Christians, especially in South America. The Church has condoned slavery in the past. For example, in 1488, Pope Innocent VIII accepted the gift of 100 slaves from Ferdinand II of Aragon, and distributed those slaves to his cardinals and the Roman nobility.

"A lot of regrettable things happened in those times, Hearne, but I'm sure that the Church always held that slavery was intrinsically wrong."

"I don't think that's quite so certain, Father," said Gallagher, "If you remember, in his epistle to Philemon, Saint Paul says he is sending the runaway slave, Onesimus, back to his master, Philemon, although he does say he should be well treated."

The priest couldn't remember anything about Saint Paul's epistle to Philemon. He wasn't even sure that he had ever heard of it.

"And if the Church can change its mind on torture and slavery, maybe it can do the same on things like contraception and divorce," said Hearne.

"And what about abortion?" said Clancy, "It's legal here now."

"I think the Church will draw a line there, Clancy."

"It didn't always, Father," said Galagher, keen as always to be helpful. "In the early Church, ensoulment was considered to take place about forty days after conception, so it was permissible to abort before then because the foetus didn't have a soul."

Clancy grinned.

"They'll come round to it – in a few hundred years."

***

That evening, Father Fahey found himself musing on Eamonn de Valera's most famous speech, which began, "The ideal Ireland that we would have, the Ireland that we dreamed of, would be the home of a people who valued material wealth only as a basis for right living, of a people who, satisfied with frugal comfort, devoted their leisure to the things of the spirit," and then went on to describe a rural idyll of cosy homesteads, happy maidens, athletic youth and serene old age, ending, "The home, in short, of a people living the life that God desires that men should live."

He shook his head. Always be careful what you wish for. It might come true. Frugal comfort was certainly what Ireland had had all these years. Were the Irish satisfied with it? Not from the emigration figures. For over a century, a tide of Irish humanity had poured from its shores in a never-ending stream, abandoning their cosy homesteads to work in the country from which they had supposedly just escaped – in the hospitals, on the building sites and in the factories of England. The most troubling aspect for Father Fahey was how far the Church was responsible for the plight of its people. Did it confuse frugality – or to give it its proper name, poverty – with spirituality? Did it confuse the form of religion – all those holy pictures and statues, the reverence for saints bordering on idolatry, ritual incantation masquerading as prayer, a rigid adherence to doctrine and much else – with a true spirituality? Did the Church, with its teaching that this world was a mere prelude to the next, encourage those who wanted a better life to leave and discourage those who stayed from bettering themselves? Had it come to believe that the only true Ireland was a Catholic Ireland and the only true Irishman was a Catholic Irishman?

The Irish who came to England were escaping poverty, but were they also escaping the burden of history? From a viewpoint in London or Manchester, the preoccupations of those left behind might begin to seem less important, dwelling on them seem petty, almost self-indulgent. As Humphrey Bogart's Rick put it in another of his favourite films, *Casablanca*, Ireland's obsessions "don't amount to a hill of beans in this crazy world".

Were their descendants, the boys in the school, simply breaking the last ties of ancestry and throwing off the last of what they saw as shackles? Might they be happier, perhaps even better, for doing so? What then would God think of a Church that decried happiness? Had the Church – and he could hardly believe he could ask the question – made a grave error? If to be Irish was to be Catholic, then to be English was … what?

Increasingly, a sense of futility assailed him. Were all his efforts pointless? In those moments he feared that the two Saint Patricks would never find acceptance and all Campion schoolboys would be lost to the Church. Was faith all he had left to rely on? A faith that defied all evidence and left him only with hope and, in hoping, to reconcile belief with reality. Sometimes he feared it was not enough. In those moments, he could only turn to the words of Aquinas: "To one who has faith, no explanation is necessary. To one without faith, no explanation is possible."

The next morning, as he stepped out of the sacristy to say mass, he found he could go no further. He turned round, dismissed the altar server, saying he felt ill, and went back into the sacristy, shutting the door after him. He sat down with his hands over his face, feeling the tears coursing down his cheeks.

The Debate

Sister Maria Immaculata regarded Father Wendell with evident approval. So cultured, so refined, so much less given to the peccadilloes and doubtful habits of some other clergy of her acquaintance.

"So, Father Wendell, you are proposing that there should be a debate involving girls from this school and boys from your own?"

They were sitting in Sister Maria Immaculata's wood-panelled office, its walls adorned with the obligatory crucifix and portraits of the Pope and the Sacred Heart. Father Wendell's eyes were distracted, drawn to a gold-framed painting of the Annunciation. With its airborne angel, it reminded him irresistibly of the Titian Annunciation he had seen in Venice. He was surprised at how good it was, clearly by a talented follower of Titian, possibly even from his studio. Who would have thought to find it in a Croydon convent? Sister Maria Immaculata's voice intruded into his musing.

"Father Wendell?"

"Ah, yes, quite, Sister, the debate. These boys and girls are about to go out into the world, many of them to universities, where they are bound to meet opinions and arguments contrary to the ideas of the Church. It is our duty to make sure that they are equipped to counter these false notions. That needs, as I'm sure you will agree, both knowledge and the ability to express themselves clearly and well. Debating, in my view, is an ideal way to develop those skills."

Sister Maria Immaculata nodded.

"I am inclined to agree with those sentiments, Father Wendell, but I think you will find that the girls of St Brigid's are more than capable of holding their own in any debate and expressing themselves with clarity."

Father Wendell did not doubt it. He had more than once been on the receiving end of convent schoolgirls and their opinions.

"Do you really think a debate with the boys of your school will be of any help to them?" she continued.

"I do, Sister. Now that some of them have met at the recent dance, I think a debate between our two schools will be a different experience for both. It always helps to practice one's skills. Practice, as they say, makes perfect."

Sister Maria Immaculata pondered before replying.

"Very well, then. Do you have a subject in mind for this debate?"

"I do, Sister: The age of chivalry is not dead."

Sister Maria Immaculata looked puzzled.

"Could you explain to me why you have chosen that particular topic, Father? I thought you might have chosen something more directly concerned with the Church, such as some of the topics discussed in the Second Vatican Council, or perhaps the importance of prayer in modern life."

"Those are, of course, important questions, Sister, and eminently suitable for debate, but I think that my suggestion is perhaps more suitable for debate by young people, because it raises many questions of interest to the young mind, including those that you mention, of faith, morals and the role of the Church in the modern world."

It was several seconds before Sister Maria Immaculata replied.

"Yes, I can see your point now, Father. Which side do you agree with?"

"I think it is finely balanced, Sister, with good arguments on both sides. It will, after all, be a debate. It will enable the boys and girls to stretch their minds. It gives them great and whoever comes up with best and most convincing arguments will win the debate. I shall, of course, remain neutral and listen."

***

Clancy stared at the blank sheet of paper in front of him and began to regret that he had volunteered to lead the debate. He now realised that he had been too taken with the idea of parading his wit and intellectual panache before the admiring gaze of the girls of Saint Brigid's, without giving any thought to what he would say. The more he stared, the less occurred to him. He shook his head several times and tried to force himself to think about the age of chivalry. What was it about? Knights on horseback, King Arthur, Lancelot, Guinevere, jousting, castles, dragons, damsels in distress, the Holy Grail, troubadours. He couldn't see how to begin to make the argument that it was not dead. Knights in armour were to be found only in books and films. Who was looking for the Holy Grail these days? Rescuing damsels in distress? Chance would be a fine thing.

Then, just as he was losing hope, inspiration came. Troubadours sang songs, didn't they? Songs about undying love and the trials and travails that came with it. Who was singing songs these days? Didn't they call this the swinging sixties? The airwaves were full of the songs of the many groups that had sprung, almost as if by magic, from the most unlikely places; the shops were full of their records. The songs were often about love and longing, of adoration from afar, of joy and despair, of searching and finding. Surely pop and rock groups were the modern troubadours, embodying in their own way, the essence of chivalry?

He pondered. Maybe "surely" was stretching the point, but he thought he could at least make an argument and besides, he didn't have any other ideas. So who could these modern troubadours be? First and foremost had to be the Beatles and the Rolling Stones. The Stones, however, might be a bit of a problem. Songs like 'Sympathy for the Devil', 'I Can't get No Satisfaction' and 'Let It Bleed', to say nothing of 'Let's Spend the Night Together', might be hard to fit into conventional ideas of chivalry. The Beatles' song book looked more promising: 'Lady Madonna', 'Eleanor Rigby', with its mention of the priest, Father McKenzie, 'Here, There and Everywhere' – a metaphor for God, maybe – and any number of songs with love in the title. The Beatles it would have to be. He started making a few notes.

***

The debate was to take place in the library on a Friday afternoon at the end of the school day. On the day, Clancy arrived early to have a last read through his notes. Gallagher, who would be opposing the motion, arrived shortly afterwards and nodded to him, rather curtly. Did he look confident? Clancy couldn't be sure. He looked out the window and saw the large coach bringing the St Brigid's girls drive through the school gates and then disappear from sight behind the chapel. Who, he wondered, would be joining him? He didn't have to wait long. He could hear a chorus of voices, at least an octave higher than the usual tones of late male adolescence, a full minute before any of the girls entered the library. Some he recognised from the dance. Then out of the gaggle one emerged and his heart skipped several beats. It was Frances Malone.

"Hello, Michael," she said cheerily as she sat in the chair beside him, extending a hand that he almost forgot to take. "So we meet again. I understand we're to be speaking on the same side."

Clancy felt himself beginning to blush, but there was nothing he could do about it.

"Oh, that's, er, great. Do you want to propose or second?"

"Oh, I think you should go first, Michael. I'm sure you'll slay them with your wit and wisdom and all I'll have to do is mop up afterwards."

He was sure she was being ironic, but couldn't have told from her expression.

"Just so we don't argue at cross purposes," she continued, "can I ask what sort of line you're taking. Don't tell me too much. Just the gist."

"In a word, troubadours."

"Troubadours?"

"Yes. What it means to be a troubadour in the modern world."

She grinned.

"So no knights in shining armour? No dragons? No damsels in distress?"

"No. I couldn't think of anything to say about them."

"Excellent. I think that will go nicely with what I want to say."

Clancy smiled, relieved.

"So what will you be saying?"

"I'll talk mainly about the ideas behind chivalry."

"What ideas?"

She gave him a wink.

"You'll have to wait to find out, Michael."

The library was beginning to fill. Father Wendell had invited some members of staff but Clancy only spotted a couple of masters from the English department, Mister Walker and Mister DeAth. Father Wendell took a seat in the front row, then through the door came Father Muldoon, who looked over the assembly, took a chair and sat against the back wall.

The chairs had been set out with an aisle running through the centre. The girls had obviously all been told to sit together on the right. A few stared straight ahead, but most gave coy, sideways glances at the boys across the aisle, who in turn gave rather less coy looks in their direction. Several girls tried to suppress giggles as Worsley and McDowell made gestures for them to cross over and sit beside them. Clancy noticed a dark shape among the blue of the girls' uniforms.

"Who's the nun?" he whispered to Frances.

"Sister Mary of the Rosary," she whispered back. "Don't worry, she's quite sweet. Besides she's deaf without her hearing aid."

"Why hasn't she got her hearing aid?"

"I think someone may have hidden it," said Frances, *sotto voce*, and gave another wink. "Who's on the other side?"

"Gallagher," replied Clancy. "He's a bit of a holy Joe. Always says he's going to a seminary but never gets there. What about your girl?"

"Fionnula Delaney, a nun in all but name. Let's give these two something to think about."

Hearne, chairman of the Edmund Campion Literary and Debating Society, sat behind a desk on a raised dais. He banged a gavel a couple of times, asking for silence. Clancy saw that the usual food stains had disappeared from Hearne's blazer – he must have had it cleaned for the occasion – and his tie sported a massive Windsor knot that entirely obscured his Adam's apple. He began in tones part stentorian, part smarm.

"Can I welcome everybody here, especially the girls of St Brigid's Academy, for what I am sure will be a most interesting and stimulating debate on the subject 'The Age of Chivalry is not Dead'."

Hearne looked around and saw Father Wendell nod slightly, then saw Father Muldoon looking impassively back at him.

"And, of course," he added, "we must not forget that this debate will, I am sure, be conducted in the Catholic ethos of courtesy, faith and charity that so exemplifies both our schools."

Clancy groaned inwardly and glanced at Frances, who raised her eyebrows momentarily. "Andy, you idiot," he said to himself. "You don't need to say stuff like that."

"Now," continued Hearne, banging the gavel again, "I call upon Mister Michael Clancy to propose the motion."

Clancy rose, slowly, deliberately, to his feet. He looked around at the boys' faces looking back at him, trying to decide whether they wanted to listen to the debate or didn't care and were only there to ogle the girls. He reckoned it was about three-quarters for the girls. He gave his notes a little shuffle and began.

"What do we mean by the age of chivalry? For many it conjures up visions of knights in armour, of jousting in front of nobility and royalty, of crusades, of righting wrongs, perhaps even of slaying dragons and rescuing damsels in distress and searching for the Holy Grail. Now all that, I concede, has gone. After all, how many knights in armour have you seen on the streets of Croydon lately, to say nothing of dragons. Dragons are particularly thin on the ground nowadays."

He paused for the hoped-for laughs from his rhetorical flourish. A few female titters did come. He went on.

"However, one aspect of chivalry does live on and in my view it is as strong as ever – that of the troubadour. What is a troubadour? Let me give you a definition that I found in a dictionary: 'A troubadour is one of a class of lyric poets and poet-musicians often of knightly rank who flourished from the 11th to the end of the 13th century chiefly in the south of France and the north of Italy and whose major theme was courtly love.' Notice the words: 'whose *major theme was courtly love*'. Does that remind you of anything?"

The faces looking back at him suggested it didn't.

"Let me put it another way: *All you need is love.*"

This time there were chuckles of recognition. Worsley gave a cheer and McDowell a thumbs-up sign.

"My contention is that the tradition of the troubadour is alive and well and it can be found in pop songs, particularly those of the Beatles. In them and others like them, the age of chivalry lives on."

That provoked laughter, some clapping and cheers and a few mutters of disagreement. Clancy saw that Father Wendell could not suppress a rather quizzical smile, while Father Muldoon's expression did not change. The laughter spurred him on and he decided to push the argument well beyond any logical conclusion and claim that the Beatles songs had meanings that his audience, and probably the Beatles themselves, had not realised were there.

"Let's look at the lyrics of some Beatles songs. Some of the very earliest, like 'I Saw Her Standing There', were about falling for someone from a distance – he couldn't dance with another when he saw her – like a knight and a lady of the court. And like in the medieval tradition, that love is all consuming, as in 'And I love her', where the singer gives all his love, that's all he does.

"The troubadours sang too of love lost, like 'Yesterday, love was such an easy game to play', and of its spiritual nature, free from money-grubbing like 'Can't Buy Me Love', and you can find any number of other Beatles songs that would fit into the same tradition."

The audience seemed to be warming to his theme, but Clancy knew he was stretching things. He had another card to play. If in doubt, spread some religion about.

"The troubadours sang in a much more religious age, but there are Catholic references in several Beatles songs. In 'Eleanor Rigby', Father McKenzie writes 'the words of a sermon that no one will hear'. That's dedication for you. Following his vocation, whatever the hardship. There are some tough parishes in Liverpool, so I'm told."

More laughs. Clancy thought he even saw the hint of a change in Father Muldoon's expression. "And in 'Lady Madonna', of course, there is an explicit reference to Our Lady, though transported to the modern day, with children at her feet and money not being heaven sent. With Our Lady, quite a lot *was* heaven sent, but even when there is no explicit religious references, there are plenty of implicit ones."

He looked up, expecting approval of this sop to the more pious of the audience, but only saw puzzled stares. Nothing for it but to press on.

"There is too, in some Beatles songs, a recognition that life is not all about pleasure and immediate gratification. It must be seen in the round, the sum of all experiences. In 'In My Life', the singer looks back over his life and loves, the dead and the living, and says that in his life he has loved them all.

"So I hope you get the picture. In my view the songsters of today are the true heirs to the troubadour tradition. Their songs of love and yearning, of spiritual awareness and final acceptance of life as it is, are the very essence of chivalry. Chivalry never died. It lives on today, and so I ask you to support the motion."

Clancy felt pleased as a decent smattering of applause followed. He looked towards Frances, who smiled and whispered, "Nice one, Michael. I bet they didn't expect that."

Hearne banged the gavel again.

"Thank you Mr Clancy. I now call upon Mr Vincent Gallagher to oppose the motion."

Gallagher rose with a disbelieving shake of his head.

"While I give Mr Clancy full marks for ingenuity I can't give him any for his grasp of history. Troubadours are still with us? Really? I doubt if any of those songs or those who sing them will be remembered a decade from now. Let us forget all about them and turn to the motion.

"In my view, chivalry died with the Reformation. Protestantism, with its emphasis on individual salvation, independent of mediation by ordained clergy, is a conscious repudiation of the hierarchy and order that characterises Catholicism and underpinned every aspect of chivalry. The French historian Léon Gautier described what he called the ten commandments of chivalry. I won't list them all, but the most important were:

- Thou shalt believe all that the Church teaches and thou shalt observe all its directions.
- Thou shalt defend the Church.
- Thou shalt make war against the infidel without cessation and without mercy.
- Thou shalt perform scrupulously thy feudal duties, if they be not contrary to the laws of God.

"You can see from these how intimately the Church and chivalry were connected. With the split in Christendom, there was no longer a universal view on how best to serve God and how society should be ordered. By the time of Elizabeth I, chivalry was dead, never to be revived, despite, according to Mr Clancy, the best efforts of the Beatles."

Gallagher then launched into latter-day Counter-Reformation mode, turning to what he thought should take the place of chivalry in this modern world – more vocations, lashings of Vatican II and more than a dash of the Church militant. Protestants and their fellow-travellers, atheists and agnostics, would be sent reeling. He finished to enthusiastic applause from about half the audience, including, Clancy noticed, from Father Muldoon and rather more sedately from Father Wendell.

Hearne banged the gavel and thanked Gallagher.

"I now call upon Miss Frances Malone to second the motion."

Clancy leaned back in his chair to get a better view of Frances as she rose. Even clad in the dowdy, dusty blue of the St Brigid's uniform, her figure won out, the skirt distinctly above the knee, doubtless to the disapproval of the nuns, her auburn hair falling lightly onto her shoulders. He felt a rising tide of desire as she began to speak.

"Mr Gallagher describes chivalry in terms of its ten commandments. Like Moses before him, he is clearly a creature of the Old Testament. I think chivalry belongs in the New Testament, to the age in which we live. Why? Let us go back to its origins, which, as Mr Clancy has mentioned, are in the notion of courtly love. C S Lewis, who most of you will know was an Anglo-Catholic – not the real thing, of course, but close – wrote what I think is the best book on the subject, *The Allegory of Love*. In it, he said the poetry of the troubadours was new, different from all that had gone before. I quote directly: 'The sentiment was love, but love of a highly specialized sort, whose characteristics may be enumerated as Humility, Courtesy, Adultery and the Religion of Love.'"

Clancy's eyes widened. The audience reaction to the mention of adultery ranged from shock, through puzzled looks, to barely suppressed sniggers, as Frances continued.

"What did Lewis mean by these? Humility and courtesy I don't think need an explanation. On adultery, he is quite straightforward. He says, 'The poet normally addresses another man's wife, and the situation is so carelessly accepted that he seldom concerns himself much with her husband.' As for the religion of love, we have the well-known tale of Lancelot and Guinevere, where Lewis asserts that Lancelot, in obeying Guinevere's wishes, is 'carnally rewarded', but is also 'treating Guinevere with saintly, if not divine, honours'."

Clancy saw Worsley whisper something to McDowell and smirk when he heard the answer. He suspected he had asked what "carnally rewarded" meant.

"Mr Gallagher is fond of commandments, but, as Lewis points out, courtly love had its own injunctions. They were listed in a book called *De Arte Honeste Amandi* ,'The Art of Loving Virtuously', written in the twelfth century by Andreas

Capellanus, Andrew the Chaplain, presumably an ordained priest. He lists over thirty maxims by which courtly love is to be conducted. The first is, 'Marriage is no real excuse for not having a lover' and another is, 'Nothing forbids one woman being loved by two men or one man by two women.' I think you will find, let us say, many echoes of those sentiments today."

That brought a burst of laughter from the audience, some of it tinged with embarrassment. For a moment Clancy thought Worsley was going to give a wolf-whistle as he raised his fingers to his face, but it was only to brush something off his nose. Frances went on.

"I readily concede that very few women are treated, like Guinevere, with divine honours these days, but adultery is another matter. If, by some mischance, you were to pick up a copy of one of the more popular Sunday newspapers, you would find news of any number of erring vicars, licentious lords and cheating husbands – not to mention straying politicians. The Profumo affair involved half the British establishment and brought adultery to every breakfast table and living room in the land."

Again there was a burst of laughter. Clancy felt himself growing in awe of Frances' self-confidence and daring.

"So adultery, which C S Lewis, a devout Christian, remember, says was at the core of poetry in the age of chivalry, is alive and well in this modern age. Some might argue that it never went away, just as Mr Clancy has said the troubadours have never gone away. So in conclusion, with the survival of the courtly traditions of troubadour and adultery, who could now say that the age of chivalry is dead? I urge you to vote for the motion."

There was a second or two of silence, as if the audience could not quite believe what they had heard, before they applauded, some enthusiastically, others rather less so. Clancy noticed to his surprise that Sister Mary of the Rosary was among the most enthusiastic, while Father Wendell was again more measured and Father Muldoon gave only a couple of desultory claps.

Hearne then introduced the final speaker, Fionnula Delaney, a plump girl with round spectacles, who, as Frances had said, had the indefinable air of novice nun about her. His eyes began to glaze over as she spouted code words of Catholicism – apostolic, faith, charismatic renewal, ecumenical, chastity, pope, magisterium and more – sprinkling them seemingly at random, with little or no relevance to chivalry. Naturally she received the greatest and most sustained applause when she finished, with Sister Mary of the Rosary particularly animated.

Hearne then banged his gavel, thanked the speakers and announced that he would now take the vote.

"We will first have a show of hands. Will all those in favour of the motion, please raise their hands."

Clancy saw that about half the audience raised their hands.

"Now all those against the motion."

It looked close.

"Are there any abstentions?"

A smattering of hands rose.

"I can't tell from the show of hands," said Hearne. "We will have to take a count. Will all those in favour raise their hands again."

Hearne counted them off, then did the same for those against and abstentions.

"For the motion 37, against 34, abstentions 10. I declare the motion carried."

As the count was announced, Clancy noticed Father Muldoon get up from his chair and leave, his face still expressionless. The debate over, the audience streamed out of the library. Frances leaned over to Clancy and whispered.

"I knew adultery would do it, Michael. It's a winner every time."

Clancy laughed and then decided to seize the moment.

"Would you like to meet for a coffee sometime?"

Frances smiled. She seemed hardly surprised.

"OK. How about Saturday in the Wimpy Bar in Surrey Street, about three?"

The Wimpy Bar

Raindrops streamed down the Wimpy Bar window as Clancy glanced at his watch. The hands were coming up to three. He knew she would be late, but that didn't make him less anxious as he scrutinised every figure hurrying along outside. It was almost a quarter past by the time she arrived.

"Hello, Michael. Sorry I'm late."

He knew she wasn't sorry. He knew that her being late was another mind game, but he didn't care. It was enough that she was there. She slipped off a short, white plastic mac with black trim and draped it over her chair. She was wearing a tight fitting, light blue top and patterned mini-skirt. Clancy gazed at her, speechless, almost paralysed by desire. She gave him a look that told him that she knew what he was thinking. Again, he didn't care. Eventually he thought of something to say and passed her the garish plastic menu, its red-toned pictures a match for the red and white, plastic- and Formica-clad interior of the cafe.

"Would you like a burger, or maybe a bender?"

She smiled, but hardly glanced at it.

"No thank you, Michael. I'm really not hungry. Shall we just have a coffee?"

The waitress brought over the milky, insipid coffees in glass cups and saucers.

"Only three months to go before you leave school, Michael. How will you fare in this big, wide world without all those priests telling you what to do?"

Clancy ignored the jibe. He was beginning to recognise Frances' tactic of gaining first advantage in conversation.

"Oh, I guess about as well as you without all those nuns telling you what to do."

She smiled.

"*Touché*, Michael, well, almost. I've rejected all that nonsense. Are you sure you really have, yet?"

The last thing Clancy wanted to talk about was religion. He had become almost obsessed with their last conversation and the idea of her losing her virginity to some anonymous student. Why not with him? They could both open their innings in one glorious orgasm. True, she had laughed at the idea at the school dance, but he thought he had a way to change her mind, or at least, to make her regret that she hadn't changed it. She had a penchant for things literary and intellectual, so what better way to win her than with a poem? What poem? That could be a problem. The only poem he could remember anything of was *The Charge of the Light Brigade* – hardly suitable. He had consulted Docherty, who was doing A-level English. Docherty had pulled out a book of English poetry and turned to a page. Clancy read and knew it was exactly what he was looking for.

Clancy fixed Frances with what he thought was a meaningful gaze.

"Why discuss religion? There are much better things to talk about."

"Are there? What might they be?"

Clancy thought he saw a slight fluttering of the eyelashes.

"I think you know?"

"Do I?"

He was sure her eyelashes fluttered. He recognised the signals – the coquettish turn of the head, the pout of the half-opened lips. She was flirting with him. Time to play the literary gambit.

"Had we but world enough and time, this coyness lady were no crime."

Frances collapsed in laughter.

"Are you trying to say I'm your coy mistress, Michael?"

Clancy felt his face reddening even as he tried to affect nonchalance.

"Are you saying you're not?"

She laughed again.

"Hardly. I've never been called coy before. So you've been reading Marvell. Makes a change from all those dull physics books, I suppose. How far did you get? Just the first line or did you learn any more of it?"

"All of it."

"Very good, Michael, but I bet the lines you liked best were:

> *The graves a fine and private place,*
> *But none, I fear, do there embrace.*

Clancy gave a wry smile.

"Well, they're rather good lines."

"They are indeed. Enough to make a girl pop her cherry, do you think?"

Clancy felt his face reddening again.

"That wasn't quite what I meant."

"Of course it was, Michael. Now who's being coy? So you want to seduce me by bringing your friend Andrew Marvell along. At least you chose *To His Coy Mistress*, probably the smartest poem in the English language. Let's see if it works, shall we. How does it go?"

> *We would sit down, and think which way*
> *To walk, and pass our long love's day.*

"And here we are, passing our long love's day in that most romantic of settings, a Wimpy Bar in Croydon. So let's go on:

> *An hundred years should go to praise*
> *Thine eyes, and on thy forehead gaze;*

"Absolutely entrancing. How could a girl resist? She will be swooning with desire. So now we get down to the nitty gritty:

> *Two hundred to adore each breast*
> *But thirty thousand to the rest;*

"That puts things in perspective, doesn't it, Michael? No beating about the bush. You'll spend a little time on the tits, but we all know what you really want."

It was a little time before Clancy could think of a reply.

"It's just a poem. You don't need to take it literally. Haven't you heard of poetic licence?"

Frances laughed again.

"Of course. Poets have always given themselves a licence to take anything they want, including women. So how does Marvell go about it? It's the old *carpe diem* trick."

"What?"

"*Carpe diem*, Michael – seize the day:

But at my back I always hear
Time's wingèd chariot hurrying near;

"How old are you, Michael, eighteen? You're a bit young to be hearing winged chariots, don't you think? But let that go. So, as Marvell says, unless we seize the day, those deserts of vast eternity will lie all before us and we will find ourselves lying in our marbled vaults :

then worms shall try
That long-preserved virginity,
And your quaint honour turn to dust,
And into ashes all my lust;

"I'll let you into a little secret, Michael. The worms are too late. My quaint honour has already gone."

Clancy felt utterly deflated. For a moment he could hardly breathe.

"I thought you were going to do it at Sussex?"

"I didn't want to wait. It was in the last holidays. My parents were away for a week and this friend of my best friend's sister was down from Cambridge. He's good looking, witty and a Marxist.

He's doing a PhD in anthropology with South Sea islanders. They have some very interesting practices. He told me all about them."

Clancy was assailed by a swarm of emotions. Lust as he thought of Frances in orgasm, jealousy that someone else was first, frustration that he could not compete with a Marxist PhD student with a knowledge of South Sea Island sexual practices and humiliation at the way she had laughed at his attempt at a literary wooing. He had to change the subject.

"Are you a Marxist?"

"Of course, Michael. What other coherent alternative to our screwed up capitalist world is there?"

He couldn't answer directly. He had been growing disillusioned with Harold Wilson's government and his leftist inclinations were hardening, but he had only very fuzzy ideas about Marxism. He had gone on a couple of anti-Vietnam war marches and had encountered the myriad grouplets that attended them, with names that seemed to be arbitrarily culled from a list that included, socialist, revolutionary, communist, workers, international and movement, all proclaiming the inevitability of a workers' revolution at some indefinite point in the future and all claiming to be the true believers in the gospel according to Karl Marx. He asked the only question that came to mind.

"I suppose you think religion is the opium of the people?"

She nodded, a little condescendingly he thought.

"Did you know the full quote is 'Religion is the sigh of the oppressed creature, the heart of a heartless world, and the soul of soulless conditions. It is the opium of the people'? I doubt if anyone has ever put it better."

Clancy found himself neither shocked nor even surprised. Frances clearly wanted to jettison all the conventions of her upbringing. This was just another one.

"So is Marxism your antidote to religion?"

"One of them."

"One of them?"
"Yes. The other is sex."
Clancy winced. Was she laughing at him again?
"Sex?"
"Of course. Don't you feel it every time you have a wank?"
This time he could not stop the shock showing on his face.
She smiled.
"Give me your hand."
She took his hand, raised it, so both their elbows were on the table, and entwined her fingers with his. Every bit of him tingled and he felt himself becoming hard. He squeezed her hand. There was a distinct squeeze back. Their heads moved closer and her light green eyes seemed to sparkle, even in the dull light of the afternoon.
"You do wank, Michael, don't you? Of course you do. So do I."
He was shocked again at a girl talking so openly and casually. She smiled even more.
"Didn't you think girls did it? Well, I'll let you into another little secret. We do, all the time. Don't you find that every time you have a wank, you think a little less about God and a little more about all the other things you could do in your life. Why do you think the Church has such a thing about sex? They talk about it as if it's the worst sin in the world – worse than theft or murder – because they know that it's the quickest way to lose one of their captives. I like the way my best friend's sister puts it. She says, 'Every fuck is another step out of the clutches of those bloodsuckers.' I think I'll follow in her footsteps."
This time shock was followed by an erotic frisson. He had never heard a girl say fuck before – a convent girl at that. He was astonished how arousing that word dropping from those lips could be. He stared back at her, trying to think of something smart to say. Nothing smart came.
"I think I will, too."
She squeezed his hand a little more.

"Michael, you have a doe-eyed appeal, with your dark hair and blue eyes. Some girls will find that very attractive. I promise to introduce you to some, if we get to Sussex."

She looked at her watch, let go of his hand and drank the last of her coffee.

"I'm afraid I have to go. I have to meet my mother. She wants me to help her choose new curtains for the living room."

She took his hand again and gave him a peck on the cheek.

"Goodbye, Michael. Thanks for the coffee."

As he watched her leave he realised that he was hopelessly smitten and understood, too, that the emphasis was on the hopeless. That was it, he thought. He had experienced the height of emotion, the apogee of passion. Was Frances Malone beyond reach? Unattainable? He was sure that he would never again feel quite the same as he did on that wet afternoon in a Wimpy Bar in Croydon.

Leaving

"Was that your last day at school, Michael?"

Clancy wondered why his father seemed puzzled.

"Yes, Dad. That was my last exam - physics. No need to go back to school after that."

The puzzled expression remained on his father's face.

"Don't you have to go in to say goodbye?

Now it was Clancy's turn to be puzzled.

"No. Why would I? I think we're all glad to leave."

His father shook his head.

"In Ireland in my day, leaving school was a big thing, Michael. The whole school had to be there with the Head Brother and all the other Christian Brothers. The names of all the boys leaving and what they would be doing were read out. Half of them had no job, of course, and were going straight to England."

"So what did they say you were going to do, Dad?"

His father smiled.

"My name was read out first. I had pride of place. I had a scholarship to the university. There were only two in the county that year."

Clancy looked at his father, surprised, almost startled.

"You never told me that before, Dad. Did you go?"

His father's smile turned a shade rueful.

"No. They said I had to study agriculture. I had no interest in being a farmer. I wanted to do civil engineering, but they wouldn't let me, so I told them what they could do with their scholarship. They weren't best pleased. The parish priest came round to our house to say I was a stupid and ungrateful boy. My Da sent him away with a flea in his ear, but then the Mammy laid into him for talking back to a priest. She wouldn't let us hear the end of it for weeks."

"That's terrible, Dad. Weren't you angry about it?"

His father shrugged.

"That was they way things were in those days. Michael. There was nothing you could do about it. You just had to accept it. No point in being bitter."

Clancy was sure he would have been bitter. His father had spent over twenty years in the Inland Revenue, taking the train every day to London Bridge. He never talked about his work, but Clancy was sure it must be something tedious and mind-numbing. How different would his life have been if he had become a civil engineer? He might have gone on to construct motorways, to build skyscrapers or plan whole towns. He felt a pang of anger at the waste.

"Don't you regret it though, Dad? You could have built things."

"To be honest, son, there's plenty of things I like doing, like shooting and fishing. There's enough Micks in the building trades without me adding my little bit. Now, are you doing anything to celebrate leaving school?"

"I'm going out with some of my mates tonight."

He didn't add they were going on a pub crawl, but his father didn't need telling. He took two pound notes from his wallet.

"I suppose you'll be having a few jars. Here, you and your friends can have one on me."

"Wow, thanks Dad."

Clancy had every reason to be grateful. He had only 3/6d to his name that day, enough for little more than a pint, and had been about to ask his father for a loan. Two pounds would do very nicely. If they stuck to public bars on their crawl, the beer shouldn't be more than half a crown a pint.

"Leaving school is worth a few jars, son. You have your whole life ahead of you. Don't let it go to waste and don't let that university tell you what to do."

***

Clancy, Hearne, Dempsey, Docherty and Worsley convened after the exams in the Croydon Wimpy Bar and the conversation turned to their options after leaving.

"Have we all decided then?" said Clancy.

"I'm definitely going to read Greats at Wadham," said Hearne, rather pompously.

"What's Greats?" said Dempsey.

"Greats, you ignorant buffoon," replied Hearne," is the study of the Classical world – Latin, Greek and Ancient History."

"What's great about that?" said Dempsey, "I had more than enough of Latin by the fifth form. I can't think of anything worse than another three years of it."

"And I suppose you are scaling the intellectual heights somewhere else," said Hearne, sniffily.

Dempsey nodded.

"Yes. I'm going to do a diploma at the National College for Heating, Ventilating, Refrigeration and Fan Engineering."

For a moment the others were stunned into silence.

"You're going to be a plumber?" said Hearne.

"No, you wanker," replied Dempsey, visibly insulted. "I'm going to be an engineer. Don't you know that all buildings need heating and ventilating? While you're spouting Latin verses and tossing yourself off in that Wadham of yours, I'll be studying something useful."

"So where is this National College then?" asked Docherty.

"It's at Borough Polytechnic."

"Where's that?"

"Near the Elephant and Castle."

"Ah, the dreaming spires of the Elephant and Castle," said Hearne, as the others chuckled.

"Don't knock it. Could come in useful if we need our boilers mended," said Clancy, to more chuckles. "I've got an offer from Sussex to do Physics – two Bs and a C. Should be OK. "

"Why do you want to go there?" asked Docherty.

"It's a new university. I don't want to go to boring old places like Oxford or Cambridge. They're all public schoolboys and no women. Sussex is fifty-fifty, men and women."

"Really?"

"Yeah, really. My Mum was reading about it the *Daily Express*. It said that 90 per cent of the girls at Sussex weren't virgins. When she told my Dad about it, he just said, 'He's going to have a good time then.'"

"Jesus," said Docherty, "if I'd known that, I'd have put Sussex on my list."

"Have you made up your mind yet?"

"Yeah. The LSE want three Bs to do Economics. I think I've just done it."

Their eyes turned to Worsley.

"I'm looking at some offers. Haven't decided yet."

"Oxford and Cambridge must be on tenterhooks," said Hearne.

"You wait," replied Worsley. "I'll get somewhere good. Now let's forget about all this university stuff. Let's plan our pub crawl."

That met with unanimous approval from the others.

"I suggest we start at the Tudor Rose," continued Worsley, "and go up the High Street on the left-hand side and then back down again on the right, ending up at the Jolly Ploughman? That's six pubs and with a pint in each we'll be nicely primed."

"Good idea," said Hearne.

"Primed for what?" asked the ever-literal Dempsey.

Worsley gave his leering grin.

"Primed for a bit of what you fancy. I've heard that some of the St Brigid's girls are going to be in the Ploughman tonight.

You know what convent girls just let out of school are like. They'll all be lashed and I bet they'll be gagging for it."

The others looked at him with varying degrees of scepticism.

"How do you know?" said Clancy.

"I went out with Anna Burns last week. She told me about it."

Scepticism did not abate.

"Did you get anything?" asked Docherty.

Worsley tried to smile boastfully.

"Yeah. I got a bit of tit. I reckon I'll get a lot more next time."

That provoked derision.

"You liar," said Hearne. "I heard she was as tight as a chicken's arse. What colour was her bra?"

There was more than a hint of hesitation in the answer.

"White."

"White?" said Docherty, "Didn't she put on her black lacy one for you?"

"She's going to put it on for me next time."

"I bet you never saw it," said Clancy, "but let's not bother about that now. Are you sure they are going to be in the Ploughman tonight?"

"I'm sure. That's what Anna said."

"Who's going to be there?" said Hearne.

"Margot Shannon, for one. I know you fancy her."

"Well … I'm not sure I said that," said Hearne, beginning to blush.

"Yes you did. I bet you'd give her one if you had the chance. And," added Worsley, turning to Dempsey, "that blonde bit that you were with at the dance, she's going to be there."

"Deidre Baxter?" said Dempsey, grinning.

"Yeah, but you've got no chance. I hear she's been out with a bloke that has a Jag E-type. My brother says E-types are the biggest knicker-droppers in the business. You only have to drive up the road before they're off."

Dempsey's grin disappeared.

"How does your brother know anything about Jag E-types?" said Docherty.

"A bloke at his work has got one. He showed my brother his knicker collection. He keeps them as souvenirs."

That brought more derisive laughter.

"And wanks all over them, I bet," said Docherty. "Anyone can buy knickers at Marks and Spencers. I bet that's where he got them."

"What about Frances Malone?" asked Clancy.

Worsley nodded. "I'm pretty sure Anna said she would be there as well."

Clancy felt a tightening of organs from the throat to the scrotum. That familiar feeling – part anticipation, part apprehension, part desire. This could be a chance to make up for his tongue-tied appearance at the Wimpy Bar. Maybe after a few drinks, Frances' combination of quick wit and self-confidence would give way to desire, perhaps even to lust. Or maybe, after a few drinks, his wit and self-confidence would match hers and she would succumb to what she had called his doe-eyed charm.

"Let's do it," he said.

***

They met that evening in the public bar of the Tudor Rose, a large, incongruously mock-Tudor edifice, built in the inter-war years mainly to serve two nearby housing estates. They sat on two benches round a wooden table. "Anyone want a fag?" said Worsley, as he took out a gold packet of Benson and Hedges and offered them round. Only Dempsey took one, and spluttered as Worsley lit it for him. The others all knew he only took it for show.

"They're just an expensive way to kill yourself," said Clancy, "Haven't you been reading all the stuff about fags giving you cancer?"

"That's all bollocks," replied Worsley. "My Nan's smoked sixty a day since she was fourteen and she's over seventy now and still going strong. It's just a load of killjoys saying that. They want to stop people enjoying themselves."

Clancy shrugged and surveyed the bar, its floor liberally scattered with sawdust, its seating a mixture of hard wooden benches and fraying leather sofas, tufts of horsehair sprouting from their arms. Posters of old music-hall favourites lined the walls – Miss Vesta Tilley who sang 'Burlington Bertie'and Marie Lloyd with her 'A Little of What You Fancy Does You Good'. None of the clientele was their age. Most were middle-aged or elderly men. At one end of the room, a darts match was in progress, with much cheering, jeering and laughter from the spectators as darts hit the board.

"I suggest we all put a quid in for the drinks to start with," said Worsley, who had been instructed by his brother on the etiquette of pub crawls. That was agreed and Clancy was sent to order the round.

He stood at the bar trying to attract the attention of the barmaid, a buxom woman with a towering head of reddish-brown, permed hair, who seemed not to notice him. "Two brown ales and a light and bitter, please, Doris," said a customer. "A mild and bitter and a velvet stout, when you're ready, Doris," said another. A voice next to him said, "Are you still waiting?" The voice belonged to a man in a dark-blue uniform. "Yes," he replied. The man nodded and then said in a louder voice, "There's a young gentlemen been waiting to be served here, Doris."

Doris came over and looked at Clancy suspiciously.

"I thought he was with someone. Are you sure you're old enough to be in here on your own, sonny?"

"Yes," replied Clancy, feeling indignant. "I'm eighteen. I've just finished my exams. We're celebrating."

That brought a cackle of laughter from Doris.

"You don't need no exams to come in here, darling, unless we have to examine your wallet to see if you've got any money. And you can celebrate any time you like in here. What do you want?"

"Five pints of bitter."

"Coming up," said Doris and started pulling.

The man in blue turned to an older man standing next to him.

"You hear that, Reg? They done exams. We didn't have no exams in our day, did we?"

"No," said Reg.

He turned back to Clancy.

"We was sent off to the wars instead. My name's Bill, by the way. I was with Monty in the last one and Reg was in the first show. Having an exam don't do you much good when there's a bullet with your name on it winging your way."

"No, I don't suppose it does," agreed Clancy.

"Reg was in the trenches. Where was it you said you was, Reg?"

"Wipers," said Reg.

"Reg was at Wipers," said Bill. "Where exactly is Wipers, Reg?"

"How should I know?" came the reply.

"You said you was there, Reg."

"Yes I was *there*, but we was just told that we was at Wipers. You don't start asking where Wipers is when Jerry is coming at you with a bayonet. That's where I got this," he added, pointing to a deep scar on his right cheek. "I was hoping it was a Blighty one, but they just sewed me up and sent me straight back."

"What's a Blighty one?" asked Clancy.

"That's when you get wounded, not bad enough to kill you," said Bill, "but you have to be sent home to Blighty, so they can patch you up, and with a bit of luck you won't have to go back."

Clancy was silent for a few moments.

"What did you do after the war, Reg?"

"Shovelled shit," said Reg.

"Pardon?" said Clancy, not sure he had heard correctly.

"Reg worked for forty years at the shitworks, out past Redhill," said Bill. "You're retired now, aren't you, Reg?"

"Yes."

"What about you, Bill? What do you do now?"

"I'm a bus conductor," said Bill. "It's not a bad job. I'm on the 190s at the moment. They go out past Old Coulsdon, so you get a chance for a chat with the passengers. But in the end, I suppose I wouldn't mind a Blighty one."

"What do you mean?"

"Something to take me out of all of this, where I would be looked after and where I could think about what I wanted to do – though God knows what that would be."

As Clancy brought the glasses to the table he saw Worsley returning from the toilets.

"Any luck?" asked Hearne.

"No. It was out of order."

"What was?" said Clancy.

"The Johnny machine. There was a big notice on it," replied Worsley.

"He thinks he's going to get lucky tonight," said Docherty.

"You never know," said Worsley. "Be prepared. I used to be in the scouts. That was our motto."

The second pub was the Red Lion. The public bar, even seedier than the one at the Tudor Rose, was almost empty – a couple of old men, sitting well apart from each other, staring morosely at their drinks, and two young men playing bar billiards in one corner.

"Anyone fancy going to see Cream next week?" said Docherty, as Worsley went off to get the drinks.

"Where are they on?" said Clancy.

"The Marquee. Probably the last time we'll see them there. They're getting too big. I hear they're off to New York soon."

"Too big for Croydon, too big for Soho. Where will it all end? I reckon rock is beginning to eat itself," said Clancy, "Yeah, I'll go if you're going."

Worsley came back carrying a tray of glasses with a look of disgust on his face.

"They only have Watney's Red Barrel. If I'd known, I wouldn't have come in."

The others looked puzzled. Hearne picked up a glass and took a sip.

"Tastes like beer. What's wrong with it?"

Worsley looked even more disgusted.

"What's wrong with it? It's pure piss, that's what."

Clancy tried it. Piss might be a bit strong, but it did have a slightly rancid smell and it tasted rather more insipid than the few other beers he had drunk. Worsley was still in castigatory mode.

"My brother told me a joke that's been going round about it. Why is Watney's Red Barrel like making love in a punt?"

The others shook their heads.

"Because they're both fucking close to water."

Clancy spluttered into his beer, as the others chortled.

"Drink up," said Worsley. "We don't want to stay here much longer. I'm going to see if they've got a Johnny machine."

He came back less than a minute later.

"Nothing there. Looks like they had one from the state of the wall. I bet they took it out because no one who comes in here can ever get a shag."

"Like you?" said Clancy. The others guffawed.

"Hah, hah," said Worsley, "You just wait. I am definitely feeling lucky tonight."

The White Hart, Croydon's oldest pub, had found itself sandwiched between two massive construction sites, office buildings, whose steel skeletons, Clancy thought, must have reached at least twenty storeys and looked like they were going still higher. Croydon was beginning to resemble a mini-Manhattan. On the door, a notice stated that dirty workwear and boots were not allowed entrance.

"Doesn't say anything about dirty minds," said Worsley, laughing, as he pushed the door open. They entered a cavernous public bar filled with long tables at which the drinkers sat. All were male and most seemed not to be talking, although there was a low hum of conversation, interspersed with the clinking of glasses. They looked around and Clancy pointed to the one unoccupied table, next to the gents.

"Looks like we'll have to sit there."

It was Hearne's turn to collect the drinks. At the bar he stared, fascinated, at two Guinness taps, side by side, which seemed to be permanently on, the creamy liquid pouring into the glasses, dextrously manipulated by a barman. Most were filled, but some were removed when only half full and sent sliding down the bar. A voice interrupted his reverie.

"Do you want to order, or are you just standing there?"

Hearne saw the voice belonged to another barman.

"Oh, yes. Five pints of bitter please."

The barman seemed surprised.

"You want beer?"

It was Hearne's turn to be surprised. This was a pub, wasn't it?

"If it's not too much trouble. What beers do you have?"

The barman's lips pursed.

"The only one we got in the barrel right now is Bass. Will that do?"

Hearne was just about to answer when he heard a loud shout and turned to see a man at one of the tables standing, fists raised, waving and yelling incoherently. After a few seconds, a much larger man, sitting next to him, reached up, without rising from his seat, and pulled him down. The shouting and waving stopped. Nothing was said by either.

"What was that all about?" Hearne asked the barman.

"It's just Irish navvies, ain't it," said the barman. "They're all on big money from the sites next door and they come in here to drink it away. Most of them are on Guinness, but some are on Black Velvet. That's the real killer. They get fighting drunk."

"What's Black Velvet?"

"Guinness and cider. Rots your guts. God knows why they do it."

As the others waited, the conversation had turned to music.

"Looks like all the big boys have given up on live gigs," said Docherty. "Beatles, Stones, Dylan, I bet we never see them again."

"Nah, they'll be back," said Worsley. "For a start, I heard Dylan is coming next year."

"How do you know?" said Docherty. "No wait, don't tell me, your brother told you."

"As a matter of fact, he did," said Worsley, unabashed.

"We can forget that, then, though I can't say I'm devastated. I think Dylan has gone a bit off since he went electric," said Clancy

"You're in the Judas camp, then?" said Docherty.

Clancy hesitated.

"Not really. I like some of the electric stuff. 'Like a Rolling Stone' is really witty, but I find *Blonde on Blond*e a bit turgid and *John Wesley Harding* is just country and western pap. I think his best album is *Bringing It All Back Home*."

Docherty looked affronted. He had become something of a Dylan obsessive.

"You're wrong about *Blonde on Blonde*. It's a masterpiece. So you're Mister Tambourine Man, are you, dancing beneath the diamond sky with one hand waving free?"

"I like 'Mister Tambourine Man', of course, but I think the best track is 'She Belongs to Me'," replied Clancy,

"'She's an artist, she don't look back.' Who might that be, I wonder?" said Docherty, knowingly, "You will start out standing and end up on your knees."

Clancy gave a wry smile at Dylan's words, always dancing at the edge of meaning. Could Frances Malone take the dark out of the night-time and paint the day-time black? Could he ever be sure?

Hearne returned with the drinks and initiated the others into the iniquities of Black Velvet.

"That's the Irish for you," said Worsley.

"What do you mean?" said Clancy, beginning to feel indignant.

"You know what they say about Irish men?"

"No. What do they say about Irish men?"

"They say an Irish man is the only man that would climb over the bodies of ten nude women to get to a pint of Guinness."

In spite of himself, Clancy found himself laughing along with the others.

"I'm off to the bog to see if this place has any Johnnies," said Worsley.

He wasn't gone long.

"Any luck this time?" asked Docherty.

"It was empty. Sold out. This place can't even keep a Johnny machine filled up."

More laughter.

"Well, that proves you were wrong about Irish men," said Clancy.

"How come?"

"If Johnnies are sold out then some of these Micks must be getting it."

Worsley pulled a face and then grinned.

"I reckon I'm going to try a Black Velvet in the next one. I heard it puts lead in your pencil."

"Do you really think it does?" said Docherty.

"I bet it helps."

They looked at each other. The drink was beginning to have an effect. It sounded like a good idea.

It wasn't such a good idea. Visits to the next two pubs passed in something of a blur for them all, as the effects of Black Velvet proved to be more emetic than priapic. As they sat in the second, the Royal Oak, Docherty took a swig of Black Velvet and then Clancy saw his expression change to one of startled fear as he put his hand over his mouth and rushed towards the toilets. It was catching. "Oh shit," said Dempsey and gulped before rushing likewise to the toilets, hand over mouth, while Hearne and Clancy stood up and walked as quickly as dignity would allow to the nearby gents and spewed into the only two available bowls. After exhausting the contents of their stomachs, they splashed their faces for a minute or two until gradually some sort of equilibrium returned and they walked back to their table, trying not to look sheepish. Worsley pointed to Clancy.

"You've got a bit of sick on your jacket."

Clancy had to make another sortie to the gents to wipe off the offending emission. When he returned he joined the others, staring whey-faced at the glasses on the table. The room began to sway and he closed his eyes, only for things to start spinning faster in his head and his stomach beginning to spasm. He opened his eyes and the room was still spinning. Closing them again only made things worse – or did it? Should he go back to the gents or would it be better to stay sitting, in case he spewed before he got there? He could see the others, all except Worsley, were in the same state.

"Can someone stop this room going round and round," said Docherty.

"Urgh!," groaned Hearne, holding his head. "Urgh!"

"Stop saying that," said Dempsey. "You'll make me sick again. My stomach's going up and down like a yoyo."

"Let's go to the Ploughman," said Worsley, "The girls should be there by now. They'll be gagging for it."

The Jolly Ploughman

"They won't be in the public bar, you idiot," said Worsley, as Dempsey was about go into to the unprepossessing entrance of the Jolly Ploughman, "Don't you know anything about convent girls? They'll be in the saloon. The door's round there."

They went round the side of the pub and into the saloon bar. Their eyes scanned the room with its oak-panelled walls and hunting prints and saw only couples and a few elderly men. No one there was under fifty. Dempsey moaned, holding his stomach, and then set off towards the toilets.

"So where are they?" asked Docherty.

"Gagging for it somewhere else, I bet," said Hearne.

Worsley's expression was a mixture of surprise and indignation.

"Anna Burns told me that they would definitely be here."

"She probably didn't want your hands on her tits again," said Clancy, as the others jeered.

"She wasn't lying. She has the hots for me. Let's ask the barman."

They went over to the bar and Worsley beckoned to the barman.

"Has a group of girls been in here tonight?"

"Who's asking?" said the barman, suspiciously.

"We're friends of theirs. We're supposed to meet them tonight."

The barman nodded, then smiled.

"As it happens, we did have some young ladies in earlier. Lookers they were, too. You should have seen the skirts on them – or rather, you could hardly see them. They were that short."

There was a collective groan.

"Do you know where they've gone?" said Docherty.

"They said they were going to a party."

"Where?" said Worsley.

"How would I know? I wasn't invited. It sounded a good do, though. They were definitely up for it after a few drinks. I bet some young bucks get lucky tonight."

"Are you sure they didn't say where the party was?"

"They only said it was in a big house. Purley, maybe? I dunno."

"Shit," said Worsley.

"Shit," agreed Clancy. Now his lust really had turned to ashes.

"Shit," responded Hearne and Docherty in unison.

They looked at each other despondently, still feeling the effects of the Black Velvets and wondering what to do next.

"Might as well be hair of the dog," said Worsley. "Get another beer down you and you'll feel better."

They ordered more beers. Consolation? It didn't really matter. The girls had gone. As they were being served, Dempsey returned from the toilet.

"I've just had a look in the Snug bar. Guess who's in there? Muldoon and Fahey."

It took a second or two for this news to sink in.

"What, together?" asked Hearne.

"Yes."

"I thought they couldn't stand each other."

"It's all change now," said Clancy. "Vatican Two, the sexual revolution and all that. They can't afford petty squabbles. The Church is circling the wagons."

"Should we go in and say hello?" asked Dempsey.

"Why?" said Worsley.

"Well, it might be a nice gesture. We'll probably never see them again."

They looked at each other and shrugged.

"Why not?" said Clancy, "Lead on, McDempsey."

Father Muldoon looked up as they approached. Clancy was surprised to see that he seemed pleased to see them.

"Hello, boys. What brings you here?"

"We're celebrating the end of A-levels, Father," replied Clancy.

"Ah, that's well worth celebrating, isn't it, Father?" he said, turning to his companion.

Father Fahey smiled and nodded.

"And I suppose you'll all be hoping that the results will let you go to university."

"Yes, Father" said Hearne.

"Oh, I wouldn't worry too much about that. I've heard great things about you boys from your teachers."

They heard him with varying degrees of astonishment and disbelief. None of them had ever seen Muldoon in an affable mood.

"Now boys," he continued, "I have something to show you. Last Easter I went to visit the shrine of Saint Catherine Labouré in Paris. Have any of you heard of her?"

They all looked blank.

"A wonderful saint. Her devotion to Our Lady is second to none. That's a lesson for you boys. No prayer to Our Blessed Mother goes unanswered. Saint Catherine Labouré was a nun in France over a hundred years ago. You can still see her there in her tomb. Not a whiff of corruption on her body after all these years. Our Lady appeared to her three times and told her to strike a special medal that would assist all who held one to lead a good and holy life. It's called a Miraculous Medal."

He reached into his jacket pocket and brought out a silver medallion that he laid on the table.

"This is a Miraculous Medal from the very tomb of Saint Catherine herself. You can see on one side Our Lady crushing the serpent Satan under her foot. On the other, the twelve stars represent the Church. Many are the stories of Catholics who had felt the urge to stray, but were saved because they had in their possession a Miraculous Medal. Now I'm sure you would all like one, but I only have this one, so which of you do you think it would most help?"

Clancy felt a mounting anxiety, hoping that he would not be the chosen one, and could sense that the others felt the same. Father Muldoon lifted the medal from the table and proffered it.

"Mister Worsley, I think the medal will stand you in very good stead in life."

Clancy tried to stifle a sigh of relief as Worsley began to stammer.

"Th, th, th … ank you, Father, but I don't feel I deserve it."

Clancy saw the two priests look at each other and smile, before Father Muldoon answered.

"No need to be so coy, Mister Worsley. I've seen plenty of your reports. We'll say no more about them, now you're on your way out into the big, wide world. The Miraculous Medal will keep you on the straight and narrow."

Worsley mumbled thanks again, unable to think of anything more to say. Father Muldoon, his mood turning even more affable, beamed.

"Now, since you are here boys, celebrating, perhaps you would like to celebrate a bit more and offer Father Fahey and myself a drink?"

Hearne was the first to react.

"Of course, Father, what would you like?"

"Whisky, and make sure it's Teacher's or Bell's, not any of that other rubbish that they have behind the bar. Now boys," he continued as Hearne went off, "I expect you will all have found out where the Catholic chaplaincy at your university is. Make sure you talk to the chaplain. He will keep you safe from all the temptations that I hear are all too common in universities these days."

Before any of them could think of a suitable reply, Hearne returned with the drinks. Father Muldoon raised and lowered his spectacles and peered into his glass suspiciously.

"What's that in there?"

"Whisky, Father," replied Hearne, mystified.

The priest turned the glass in his hand, adjusting his spectacles again.

"There's something there, right enough, but I couldn't tell you what it was. Go and ask Dave behind the bar. He'll put you right. And take Father Fahey's glass with you too."

Hearne returned to the bar, still mystified.

"Father Muldoon says it's not whisky in there."

Barman Dave chuckled.

"You should have said it was for the Fathers. They always drink doubles. You're lucky," he added, glancing at a clock, whose hands showed five to ten. "It's trebles after ten."

Hearne brought the glasses back and Father Muldoon beamed again. He held up his glass.

"Here's to you, boys. May your futures be bright."

The boys nodded in acknowledgement as he took a couple of sips, closing his eyes, evidently savouring the drink. He opened his eyes and looked at them.

"Off you go then, boys, and leave Father Fahey and myself in peace."

They went back to the saloon bar and stared at their drinks. Dempsey gave a moan and held his stomach again. Clancy, Hearne and Docherty were not feeling a lot better.

"Hair of the dog, boys," said Worsley, raising his glass and glugging. "That's what my brother always says you need after a skinful."

"Does your brother always talk crap?" said Docherty.

For a moment, Worsley looked affronted, then he laughed.

"Quite often. Anyway, I know they've got a Johnny machine in this place. I'm going to get some."

"Why?" said Clancy. "The girls have gone we know not where and you had no chance with them anyway."

Worsley winked.

"Be prepared. Always been my motto and sod the boy scouts. You never know when you might get lucky."

He went off to scornful looks in the direction of the gents. He returned a few minutes later, smiling.

"You did get lucky, then?" said Hearne.

"Certainly did," said Worsley, "but you'll never guess how. I put a half-crown in and it went straight through and out the bottom. I tried it a few times but it wouldn't take it. Then I thought that the medal that Muldoon gave me is about the same size as a half-crown, so I tried it – and guess what? In it went and stayed in! *Hey presto.*"

He held up the little packet for the others to see.

"That's what I call a miracle," said Clancy, as they all burst out laughing. "That's got to be a first. A saint in a Johnny dispenser – and a nun to boot. What about her vow of chastity? What would the Pope say?"

"Actually, it's Our Lady on the medal," said Hearne

"Oh yeah, of course. So what would Jesus say?"

"Come out, Mother, for God's sake," said Worsley, as the others fell about laughing.

"Do you think Muldoon has any more?" asked Docherty.

"I think he'd be a bit suspicious if we asked him," said Hearne.

"Maybe we could go to Paris and get some," said Dempsey.

The others looked at him and shook their heads.

"It's a long way to go for a cheap Johnny," said Worsley.

"There's a shop near Westminster Cathedral," said Clancy, "that sells Catholic things like rosaries and holy pictures and statues that glow in the dark. I bet they have Miraculous Medals. If they're less than two and six then we're in the money."

"Yeah, but when we've all got our packet, what are the chances?" said Docherty.

There was silence.

"How long do they last?" asked Hearne.

They all looked at Worsley.

"How would I know?"

"I've been told that they shrivel up after about three years." said Clancy.

Worsley waved his hand dismissively.

"What are you worried about then? Who thinks it's going to take them more than three years to get their leg over?"

***

"Do you ever ask yourself, Father," said Father Fahey, as they sat in the snug bar of the Jolly Ploughman with their whiskies, "whether it would have been better for all the Irish here to have stayed in Ireland?"

He watched Father Muldoon take a couple of sips of whisky before replying.

"I often ask myself that, Father. Ireland is a good and holy country and its children are the firmest in their faith of any country in the world, but I have to admit that Ireland is no country for jobs. The first duty of any man is to his family and if he cannot earn enough for them to eat, then he has to go to look for work somewhere else. I say far better that they come here than go to the ends of the Earth, like to America or Australia. The Irish built this country. They came with no money in their pockets and slaved away with their shovels to help make England the country that it is now. Precious little thanks did they get for it. Look around you, Father, and you'll hardly see a building or a road or a bridge that wasn't made by Irishmen. McAlpine's Fusiliers they've been called. Do you know the song?"

As down the glen came McAlpine's men
With their shovels slung behind them

They sweated blood and they washed down mud
With pints and quarts of beer
And now we're on the road again
With McAlpine's fusiliers

McAlpine's God was a well-filled hod
Your shoulders cut to bits and seared
And woe to he who to looks for tea
With McAlpine's fusiliers

Father Fahey was surprised that his companion had a pleasant baritone voice and, as always, he felt a touch of envy at the older priest's certainty about everything and a pang of despair at his own inability to be certain of anything. He had always thought of science, with its insistence on only believing its predictions when they had been tested, as a touchstone of truth. Everything in science was provisional; nothing was definitive. For Father Muldoon, it seemed, everything was definitive, nothing was provisional.

"Well sung, Father, but don't you think too many Irish men and women deluded themselves about what they would find over here? I have another song for you."

Oh, Mary, this London's a wonderful sight
With people here working by day and by night
They don't sow potatoes nor barley nor wheat
But there's gangs of them diggin'
For gold in the street
At least when I asked them
That's what I was told

So I just took a hand
At this diggin' for gold
But for all that I've found there
I might as well be
Where the Mountains of Mourne
Sweep down to the sea

Father Muldoon shook his head scornfully.

"That's a Down man for you, Father. They often say that a Kerryman is not the brightest button in the box, but, believe me, any Kerryman is a genius compared to a man from the County Down. Down men will believe anything they're told. You wouldn't find a man from Carlow so easily fooled. Any Carlow man would say he wanted five pounds even to look at a dig and twenty-five pounds a week if any digging was required. You have to get up very early in the morning to pull the wool over the eyes of a man from the County Carlow."

Just then, Dave the barman come over with two glasses.

"You're in fine voice tonight, Fathers. Singing about the old country, are you?"

"We are indeed, Dave," replied Father Muldoon. "Irish songs are the best. The English have nothing to match them."

"I'll take your word for it. Here's something to match the Irish in spirit – Scotch. On the house. It's the guv'nors birthday. He said to give all our regulars one from him."

"That's grand, Dave. Our compliments to him. Would he be a Catholic, by any chance?"

"What? The guv'nor? I've no idea."

"What about yourself?"

"No. I don't go to church. I'm C of E."

"No matter, Dave. I'm sure there's a place in Heaven to be found for a man that gives out whisky gratis." He took a couple of coins out of his pocket, "Here, have one for yourself."

"Thanks, Father," said Dave and returned to the bar.

Father Muldoon took another sip of whisky.

"There is one thing you can say for sure, Father. Irishmen never forget where they came from. There's a song for that too."

He began to sing, the voice rising and falling with the melody.

I wish I was in Carrickfergus
Only for nights in Ballygrant
I would swim over the deepest ocean
The deepest ocean, my love to find

Father Fahey felt a lump rising in his throat. 'Carrickfergus' had been a particular favourite of his father. He and his brother Martin had often accompanied his father singing it at home. He brushed away the trace of a tear.

"A lovely song and a beautiful melody, Father, but in the end isn't it full of sadness?" He began to sing.

But the sea is wide and I cannot swim over
And neither have I wings to fly
If I could find me a handsome boatman
To ferry me over, my love and I.

My childhood days bring back sweet reflections
The happy times I spent so long ago
My boyhood friends and kind relations
Have all passed on now like melting snow

Father Muldoon made a sound that could have been a snort.

"Of course it's sad, Father. All the best Irish songs are sad, the one's that aren't about fighting the English anyway. Isn't there more than enough to be sad about in Ireland? The English only have songs that go *hey nonny no* and the like. Nothing to them at all. You want a song that tugs at the heart and brings a tear to your eye. You get that aplenty from an Irish song."

Father Fahey found himself with more than enough reasons to agree.

"The Irish have the English beaten for sad songs, Father, I'll admit it's no contest. But isn't there something else about 'Carrickfergus'? Something more than just sad? The way it ends?"

But I'll sing no more now till I get a drink
For I'm drunk today and I'm seldom sober
A handsome rover from town to town
Ah but I'm sick now my days are numbered
Come all ye young men and lay me down

Father Muldoon seemed surprised.

"Your man dying of drink. What could be sadder than that? There's more than one Irishman over here that has gone the same way."

"Wasn't that the point of the song, Father? Those here lose touch with home, because the ones they knew have gone away or died, and they turn to drink."

"Drink is a curse everywhere, Father. The Devil is always up to his usual tricks when a man takes to drink. Maybe a few more fall by the wayside in England. The Devil will always claim his own, but they would be far fewer, in my opinion, if the English bishops had the gumption, like the Irish bishops, to support the Pioneers, the Pioneer Total Abstinence Association of the Sacred Heart, as they are properly called. I can't remember the last time I saw a Pioneer pin in England. English bishops wouldn't dare say boo to a Protestant brewer."

"A teetotal life is not for everyone, Father. You and I, after all, are sat here drinking. Might it not be hypocritical for us to advocate it for others?"

"Not at all, Father. Drink is a gift from God. Didn't Jesus himself turn water into wine at the marriage feast at Cana? If it's good enough for Our Lord, it's good enough for God's anointed, like ourselves. The working man is different. The working man is a child, a child of God, but a child nevertheless. As with all children, he can have too much of a good thing and never knows when to stop. Some can take their drink, but too many let it go to their heads. It's our duty as priests to get them to stop drinking, at the peril of their immortal soul."

"I agree with you there, Father, but how exactly can it be done? In my experience it's very difficult to get an alcoholic to stop drinking."

"No drunkard will ever wean himself off drink by himself, Father. He needs help, help from Our Lady and the blessed saints, especially from patron saints. The first step should always be a prayer to the patron saint of drunkards."

For a moment Father Fahey found himself almost lost for words.

"I'm sorry to say that I didn't know there was a patron saint of drunkards, Father. Who might he be?"

"You could be forgiven, Father. Far too few have heard of him. He's not yet a saint, but he soon will be, so I'm told. The Archbishop of Dublin and the Vatican are very keen on his canonisation. He was a working man and a Dublin man to boot. His name was Matt Talbot."

Father Fahey's brow furrowed. In the great panoply of Irish saints and divines the name Matt Talbot rang only the faintest of bells.

"Matt Talbot? Didn't I hear something about him being found in chains, Father?"

"You did indeed, Father, Matt Talbot came from a long line of drunkards and by the time he was thirteen he could be found drunk as any man in Dublin. But he saw the light. He stopped drinking and gave every moment of his waking life to prayer and good works. He slept on a plank for a bed and another bit of timber for a pillow. He had mass every day and several times on Sunday and spent every evening on his knees. One day he dropped dead on a Dublin street and when they got him to hospital and took off his clothes they found that every bit of his body was bound in chains. He did it for penance, for mortification of the flesh, like many a blessed saint before him. When the doctors and nurses saw it they were astonished. They knew they were looking at a very holy man. The word got out and now Matt Talbot is destined for the communion of saints."

Father Fahey tried hard to suppress his scepticism. His reading of psychology, particularly Freud, had led him to conclude that there was rather more to mortification of the flesh than simple holiness.

"Do you really think that the intervention of Matt Talbot can save a man from drink, Father?"

"I do, Father. A word to Matt Talbot has saved many a sot in Ireland and when he becomes a saint there will be many more saved all over the world."

Once again Father Fahey found himself up against a certainty to which he had no answer. He changed tack.

"Do you think we are doing our duty to the sons of those who came, Father? How many of the boys at the school do you think will still be Catholics once they leave?"

Father Muldoon took another sip from his glass.

"No one who was a Catholic ever really leaves the Church, Father. They may never go to mass, their last confession might be decades ago, they may have broken every one of God's commandments, but deep in that erring breast you will find a beating Catholic heart. When it come to the end, when they know they'll have to meet their maker, you'll find them calling for their Mammy and asking for a priest. They won't want to be banging on the Pearly Gates as the Devil is coming to take them away. They will remember who they are and where they came from, just as the Irish here never forget where they came from.

"The best of them came here, Father, even though they never make a song and dance about it. Oh, the Irish make a lot of noise in America, but Irish Americans are all mouth and trousers, parading their paddywackery for a few votes or a few dollars. Half of them are hardly Irish at all. They can't hold a candle to the ones that came here. Many here still hearken back to the old country. They thought they would save enough from all the money they earned to have a little nest egg, so that they could go back home and perhaps build themselves a little house and retire."

He drained the last of the whisky from his glass.

"But, you know something, Father? They never go back. No, they never go back."

Postscript

Following the retirement of the Canon in 1969, **Father Aloysius Patrick Jean-Marie Vianney Muldoon** became headmaster of Blessed Edmund Campion School. It was renamed Saint Edmund Campion School in 1970 when Pope Paul VI canonised the forty English martyrs. He retired in 1986 and died from a heart attack in 1997, returning from the Cheltenham Festival. His last bet had been on the winner of the Gold Cup, Mr Mulligan, ridden by AP McCoy, at odds of twenty to one.

Father Richard Mowbray Fitzhoward Arundell became chaplain and sole remaining priest at the school, after the fall in vocations for the priesthood meant that all other priests had been sent out to parishes. He remained in post at the school until his death in 2002.

Father Finbar Dermot Fahey left the priesthood in 1972 and subsequently married Fidelma Kelly, formerly Sister Teresa Benedicta of the Discalced Carmelite order of nuns. They set up and ran a home for destitute Irish immigrants until his death in 2008 from pneumonia.

Father Michael Edward Brompton was sent in 1972 from the school to a parish in South London. He revitalised the parish, setting up a school and a new parish hall, as well as giving talks on ancient history and conducting regular tours to the British Museum. He died from cancer in 2010, much mourned by parishioners, who commissioned a bust in his memory that is now on display in the parish church.

Father Anthony Xavier Wendell left the school in 1976 to teach in schools in southern Africa. He returned to Britain in 1988 to start a hospice for sufferers from Aids. He died in 1994 following complications from an Aids-related condition.

Francis James (Frankie) Fahey ran a successful off-course turf accountancy business until his retirement in 1994. His son, also called Francis, continued the business and was an early entrant into online betting. He sold the business in 2012 for a considerable sum to a large betting corporation.

Superintendent Thomas Proinsias O'Driscoll retired from the Metropolitan Police in 1978 and became an advisor, *pro bono,* on security matters to the Archdiocese of Southwark and a number of Catholic charities and organisations. He commissioned a statue to Saint Plodraigh that was installed in his parish church. As far as is known, it is the only one of its kind in either Britain or Ireland.

Michael Clancy studied for a degree in physics at Sussex University and later became a journalist.

Printed in Great Britain
by Amazon

42305952R00159